DRACO

Book I of the Inquisition War

THE BLACK CREATURE which had been Meh'Lindi unlatched the door and darted into a wide corridor, misty with smoke. Several armed hybrids roamed, seeming lost. Was Meh'Lindi thinking any of the alien thoughts of a genestealer? Understanding how it would react? Perhaps even radiating some protective aroma of brood empathy around herself? She bore down on the hybrids and, with her claws, she killed them almost before they realized.

A cloaked man who accompanied them gaped. His mouth opened in mute protest at this perversion of the proper order of affairs. Meh'Lindi ripped his head off...

A WARHAMMER 40,000 NOVEL

Book I of the Inquisition War

DRACO

Ian Watson

A BLACK LIBRARY PUBLICATION

First published in 1990 by GW Books Ltd.

This edition published in 2002
by The Black Library,
An imprint of Games Workshop Ltd.,
Willow Road, Lenton,
Nottingham, NG7 2WS, UK

First US edition, September 2002

10 9 8 7 6 5 4 3 2 1

Distributed by Simon & Schuster
1230 Avenue of the Americas
New York, NY 10020

Cover illustration by Clint Langley

ISBN 0-7434-4318-7

Set in ITC Giovanni

Printed and bound in Great Britain by
Cox & Wyman Ltd, Cardiff Rd, Reading, Berkshire RG1 8EX, UK

See the Black Library on the Internet at
www.blacklibrary.co.uk

Find out more about Games Workshop
and the world of Warhammer 40,000 at
www.games-workshop.com

My lord high inquisitor,

I have now examined this particular archive, as you requested of me. I can state that the text does truly date from a time around twelve hundred years before the present day. However, in the absence of a true physical copy of the work, dating a record that exists only as a data file upon our cogitator with any real precision is beyond the abilities of even my most skilled tech-priests.

As to its content, there is little to tell. I have been unable to acquire any evidence of the existence of an inquisitor of our Ordo by the name of Jaq Draco. Indeed, my researches have led me to believe that none of the Ordos have any record of such a personage. However, I have not been permitted access to their most hidden archives, and I cannot therefore offer a definitive answer as to his non-existence.

Of his outlandish companions, I have more mixed feelings. The work itself states that the Callidus temple acknowledges the presence upon its roll of infamy a such-named assassin. Yet in all my years I have never heard of such a request for information producing such an unequivocable result – that the secretive leaders of the assassins' shrines openly would even acknowledge any such query from those outside their order is frankly unbelievable. The Navigator... well, well we know of old the scorn with which our 'brothers' in the Navis Nobilite regard outside enquiries. As to the abhuman, the thread is cut. The accursed hive fleet of the tyranid put paid to that line too long ago. I cannot believe, however, that even a renegade inquisitor, if that is what this Draco really was, would tolerate the presence of such a disgusting mutation.

Lord, I understand full well that my role is to examine the facts as they are presented, to report upon the technical aspects of this archive alone. But I must confess to you now: I am sorely troubled. I have been serving you in my capacity as master librarian for two centuries now, but never have you asked me to report upon such a tangled morass of bare half-truths and inferences. If even a fragment of what this memoir purports to reveal is truthful, it implies a conspiracy of the most mind-warping complexity.

Yet where is the evidence? Without it, this work can be nothing but a blasphemous heresy, a traitorous farrago of the most evil kind. This work would be better destroyed than be recorded in any form, lest it one day be revealed, to cause who knows what damage to the minds of scholars less sceptical than ourselves. I implore you, lord, let me erase this heresy.

May the Golden Throne watch over you,

R.

Ordo Malleus Archive Decimus–Alpha
Record 77561022/a/jj/fwr/1182/i
Added 3721022.M39
Reclassified 1441022.M40
Clearance level: Vermilion.

WARNING!

What follows is the so-called Liber Secretorum, or Book of Secrets of Jaq Draco, the renegade inquisitor.

This is a book which may have been deliberately designed as a weapon to sabotage faith and duty. The primary purpose of the Liber may be to sow distrust and discord among the Hidden Masters of our order so as to undermine the Ordo Malleus from within. The intention might also be to cast doubt upon the motives of our immortal God-Emperor himself, praise His name. We do not know.

Anyone authorised to scan this Liber Secretorum is privy to the darkest of conspiracies. Anyone not thus authorised faces the penalty of mindscrubbing or death. In either event, you are warned.

PROLOGUE

BELIEVE ME. I intend to tell the truth as I experienced it.

What does the name of *inquisitor* mean? Many people would answer: destroyer of mutants, hammer of heretics, scourge of aliens, witch-hunter, torturer. Yet really the answer is: a seeker after truth, however terrible the truth may be.

As a member of the Ordo Malleus I am already a secret inquisitor. Yet the truth I must disclose involves the revelation of even deeper, more sinister secrets than those known to members of our covert order.

My story includes a journey to the Eye of Terror itself. Not to mention an incursion into the Emperor's own throne room in the heart of his heavily guarded palace on Earth, something that you may consider almost impossible; yet I have achieved it.

Ah yes, I won through – only to find that the Emperor may keep secrets even from himself, in his fragmented mind; which you may not believe, either. But such is the case. So I swear.

My story involves a sleeping menace which you yourself may harbour. And you, and you, unknowing!

In a galaxy where more than a million worlds harbour human beings – or variations upon human beings – and where this multitude is but the tip of the iceberg of worlds, and where that vast iceberg itself floats in a deeper sea of Chaos, there must be many secrets. Likewise: guardians of secrets, betrayers of secrets, discoverers of secrets. The whole universe is a skein of secrets, many of which are dire and hideous. Possession of a secret is no blessing, no hidden jewel. Rather, it is akin to a poison toad lurking inside a gem-encrusted box.

Yet now I must open that box for your inspection. I must betray my secret, or as much as I know of it.

Believe me.

I! Me! It sounds odd for a hidden inquisitor to reveal his identity in this fashion. Aside from the obvious considerations of security, who can doubt what a powerful instrument a name can be? Why else will a daemon use almost any trick to avoid vomiting its true name forth from its own treacherous lips? For instance, whosoever knows the name of Thlyy'gzul'zhaell can bind and summon that vile entity... until such time as Thlyy'gzul'zhaell gains the upper claw; whereupon woe betide the foolish summoner. Naturally, a malicious daemon will readily reveal a rival daemon's name...

Though no daemon I, I feel in my bones that it might prove inauspicious to utter my own name overmuch *in my own voice*, lest somehow I may be summoned and bound – by hostile human forces. Therefore, *I* shall become *he*. I, Jaq Draco, will tell the story of Jaq Draco as witnessed by a fly upon the wall, committing Jaq Draco's experiences to this data-cube in the hope that the Masters of the Malleus or of the Inquisition itself may authenticate the truth of what I report and determine to take action.

In that event, you (whoever you are, wherever, whenever) may be scanning these words as part of a briefing, poised on the brink of a deadly mission.

I hail you – fellow inquisitor, Space Marine commander, whomever.

Firstly I should briefly introduce Jaq Draco's travelling companions, without whom he would surely have failed. They were three: Meh'Lindi the assassin, Vitali Googol the Navigator, and Grimm. (Little Grimm the squat; do not despise this plucky, ingenious abhuman. Do not mock his youthful foibles.) When Draco landed on the planet Stalinvast accompanied by these three, the inquisitor was in the guise of a rogue trader, an incognito that he often used. Googol was his pilot; Grimm, his engineer. Seemingly, Meh'Lindi was the trader's mistress, though in truth... a secret inquisitor needs a secret assassin, does he not?

One of the nastier poison toads of the universe was about to launch itself out of its box, under the energetic prodding of a much more public inquisitor by the name of Harq Obispal. Draco would keep vigilant watch in case any toadspawn remained behind uncleansed. He was likewise keeping watch on Obispal, a surveillance of which Obispal should ideally have remained unaware, though doubtless he might have relished the scrutiny, since Obispal was a performer...

ONE

SOME HIVE WORLDS consist of shell upon shell of plasteel braced by great pillars, as if the planet has grown a metal skin and then another skin and yet another, each successive skin being home to billions of busy human maggots, fleas, lice.

Other hive worlds are poisoned wildernesses punctuated by rearing plasteel termite mounds, vertical cities that punch through the clouds.

The cities of Stalinvast were more like coral reefs looming above a sea of hostile jungle. Kefalov bulged like some fossil brain adorned with innumerable ridges. Dendrov branched every which way, a forest of tangled stags' horns. Mysov was a mass of organ pipes, from which sprouted the fungi that were suburbs. Other cities were stacks of fans or dinner plates.

A thousand such cities, soaring, bulging, branching from the surface of Stalinvast and almost all involved in the manufacture of weapons for the Imperium. Stalinvast was a rich, important world. Its thronged reefs were proudly

stained rose-red, scarlet, purple, pink. Between the cities
the blue-green jungle was riven with great scars where
plasma cannon and barrage bombs had been tested.
Warrior robots, juggernauts, and great armoured vehicles
used the jungles as a proving ground.

The capital, Vasilariov, partook of most of the styles of
coral architecture. Fifty kilometres long by forty wide by
five high, currently Vasilariov was being scarred by some of
its own weapons as Harq Obispal raged through the hive
like an angry bear. Doing good work, oh yes.

IN THE EMERALD Suite of the Empire Hotel, a plate jutting
high above raw jungle at the southern edge of Vasilariov,
Meh'Lindi said, 'I think I shall go into town to practise.'

'Against the rebel hybrids?' asked Grimm. 'Huh! Count
me out.'

Which meant, as they all knew, that Grimm didn't
intend to miss any of the action.

'Dressed like that, Meh'Lindi?' Googol drawled archly.

The Navigator's large eyes assessed her gown of iridescent Sirian silk tied at the waist with a casual scarlet sash,
her silverfur stole, her curly-toed slippers.

True, even costumed thus as a trader's mistress she
would be armed – with a garrotte or two, some tiny digital
weapons for slipping on to her fingers, phials of the chemicals she used.

Reclining on a couch, Googol appraised Meh'Lindi's figure as she began to twitch subtly. The assassin was running
through some muscle exercises, using her enhanced body
sense to tense and untense. She was artful steel expanding
and contracting, tempering itself. Googol's own pose suggested languor. The spindly Navigator yawned.

Yet he was watching Meh'Lindi. As was Grimm; as was
Jaq himself.

Meh'Lindi was taller than most men, long-limbed and
sleek. Her height served to distract attention from the
power in her calves and biceps. Her face, framed by curly,
cropped raven hair, was curiously flat and anonymous –

almost forgettable. Its smooth ivory planes suggested beauty without exactly expressing it, as if awaiting a stimulus to burst into life. Her eyes were golden.

Meh'Lindi. She had been taken as a child from a wild jungle world of carnivores, flesh-sucking plants and hunter-warriors who had lost most of the arts of civilisation save for those of cunning, combat and survival. Borne away to commence a decade of training in the temple on Callidus, she had stubbornly insisted longer than most recruits on maintaining her identity. In her outlandish, simple dialect she had declared, 'Me, Lindi! Me, Lindi!' Soon enough the seven-year-old girl had killed an older pupil who mocked her. She became known as 'Meh'Lindi' thereafter among her instructors. They let her keep that part of herself, though much else changed. Now she smiled down faintly at the jungle below the crystal windows of the suite as if remembering home – though this day the really deadly jungle was within the city, not without.

Googol and Grimm both fed on her smile. As did Jaq. As did Jaq himself.

The inquisitor knew that he should only think of Meh'Lindi as a wonderful, living weapon. He sincerely hoped that the Navigator would never be foolish enough to try to charm Meh'Lindi into his bed. Meh'Lindi could crush him to straw like a constrictor. She could crack his hairless head like an egg. Googol's ever-hidden warp-eye would pop out from beneath the black bandana tied around his brow.

As for the red-bearded squat who only stood waist-high to Meh'Lindi... dapper in his quilted red flak jacket, green coveralls and forage cap, his was obviously a comically hopeless passion.

'Meh'Lindi...'

'Yes, inquisitor?' She inclined her head. Was she conceivably teasing him?

'Don't use that title while we're on a mission!' He hoped that his tone sounded severe. 'You must address me as Jaq.'

Ha, the power to order this remarkable and disturbing woman to address him intimately.

'Well, Jaq?'

'Yes is the answer. By all means go and practise within reason. Don't pull any stunts that draw lurid attention to yourself.'

'Vasilariov's in chaos. No one will notice me. I'll be helping the Imperium a little, won't I?'

'That isn't my purpose at present.'

Googol flapped a hand languidly. 'The whole of Stalinvast may be in chaos in the ordinary sense, but Chaos as such has nothing to do with it. Genestealers aren't creatures of Chaos even if they do hang out in hulks in the warp until they can find a world to prey on.'

Jaq frowned at the Navigator. To be sure, his companions needed to know enough about him and his goals to perform effectively, but Malleus policy on the subject of Chaos and its minions was one of censorship. Chaos – the flipside of the universe, domain of the warp – spawned many vilenesses of the ilk of Thlyy'gzul'zhaell which sought to twist reality askew. Innumerable such specimens? The Ordo Malleus attempted to numerate them! Yet *not* to broadcast knowledge of those. Oh no, quite the contrary. Even the natural menace of genestealers was daunting enough to require utmost circumspection.

'Huh,' said Grimm, 'nobody knows the stealers' true origin, so far as I'm aware. Unless you do, Jaq.'

Before Jaq could respond, Meh'Lindi kicked off her slippers. She discarded her stole. She loosed her sash, sending it snaking with a flick of her wrist so that Grimm jumped back a pace. Without ceremony she dropped her silk gown, standing naked but for her briefs and her tattoos, which were all black. A hairy spider embraced her waist. A fanged serpent writhed up her right leg as if to attack the spider. Beetles walked across her breasts. Most of her tattoos concealed long-healed scars, embellishing those cicatrices eerily.

Her hand now cradled a tiny canister; what a conjuror she could be. That would have been clipped somewhere inside the scarlet sash.

Poising acrobatically upon one leg then the other, Meh'Lindi proceeded to spray her body from toe to neck with black synthetic skin. Contorting herself elegantly, yet always remaining perfectly balanced, she missed no cleft or crease or dimple. At what stage did her briefs tear loose? Jaq hardly saw. He sensed her excitement and his own excitement; knew that those were two different species of excitement.

Hastily he redirected his attention towards the circular screen that he had hung on the wall in place of an oil painting of some horned, scaly jungle monster.

His psychic sense of presence buzzed as he recontacted his spy-flies. The screen lit with a hundred crowded little images, a mosaic of miniature scenes. Now that screen was the faceted eye of a fly, though the view from each facet was unique.

The mosaic occupied much of his consciousness so that he was only dimly aware – out of the corner of his eye, and mind's eye – of Meh'Lindi, a flexible ebon statue of herself, yet still with an ivory face. Now she was inserting the throat and ear plugs with which she would hear and communicate and breathe.

Jaq summoned a facet into full prominence. It swelled. Around it, like a thronged ring of moonlets each with its own scenery, all the other facets squeezed.

A skirmish in a hovertank plant...

Arrows of light cross-hatched a grey cavern housing half-completed vehicles. Hybrids armed with lasguns were pressing hard against a picket line of planetary guardsmen. Those guards were a loyal, uninfiltrated unit and they were losing. What brutish caricatures of human beings the hybrids were, with their jutting, swollen, bone-ridged heads, their glaring eyes, their jagged bared teeth. In place of a human hand, several hybrids sported the terrible, strong claw of the purestrain genestealer. When those hybrids overran the guards they might simply tear the last survivors apart.

Yet this wasn't the whole picture, oh no, not by any means. Jaq shrank that grim facet and expanded another...

Many hundreds of rebels swarmed across the roof of a rose-red plate-district, heading for a tree of administrative towers.

Mingling with hybrids, indeed outnumbering them, were rebels who looked truly human. Some of these would be the firstborn spawn of hybrids, human in looks yet able to procreate a purestrain genestealer. Others would be subsequent offspring, genuine human beings who still heeded the hypnotic brood-bond.

A series of explosions tore at the stem of the plate district where it was attached to the rest of the city. The entire plate sagged and snapped free. Briefly, the whole huge structure sailed on the air, then fell. Rebels slid and scrabbled for hand holds, claw holds, as the district plummeted towards the fringe of the jungle two kilometres below.

On impact – a tree-flattening impact – dust arose. The dust was rebel bodies. Even the plasteel of the plate cracked open. A well-aimed plasma beam from above ignited fuel storage tanks. Within and without, flame engulfed the fallen plate-district. The dust burned; as did any populace who lived in that plate, supposing they had survived the plunge of their factory-homes.

Many hundreds more rebels were dead now. Really the rebellion was entering its final, frantic, suicidal phase.

'Some people believe the genestealers were *designed* – as a living weapon,' Googol was informing Grimm. 'A fine joke, dreamed up by some vicious alien!'

'Huh.'

'Well, why not? Do you think they evolved that way? Genestealers can't breed on their own. How could they have come into existence in the first place without malicious midwives? They're compelled to infest other races and multiply like a cancer within.'

In his travels throughout the galaxy, doubtless Googol would have heard many rumours, despite best official efforts to suppress scaremongering talk.

'Perhaps,' suggested Grimm, 'a Chaos storm warped them from whatever they were before? Seems the pure-strains can't pilot a ship, can't fire a gun, can't fix a fuse. Otherwise, they'd be all over the place under their own steam. What a clumsy weapon! Huh!'

'Yet what an excellent dark joke against life and family and love.'

The stout abhuman muttered some oath in his own out-landish dialect.

'Now, now, Grimbo,' reproved the Navigator, 'we all speak Imperial Gothic here–'

Another, darker oath in the same patois.

'–like civilised beings.'

'Well, kindly don't call me Grimbo, then. Me name's Grimm.'

'Grimm in name though not grim in nature necessarily. You're but a sprout of a squat.'

'Huh. You're hardly antique yourself, despite appear-ances.'

Those wrinkles on the Navigator's face; and his mourn-ful tunic...

Meh'Lindi's hair was slicked down tight. When she sprayed her face, her visage became more of a blank than ever, a black mask with the merest hint of features. The syn-skin would protect her against poison gas or flame or the flash of explosions; it would boost her already-honed nervous system and her already-notable vigour.

By the time she wound the scarlet sash around her waist once more, miniaturised digital weapons hooded her fin-gers like so many baroque thimbles. The needler, laser and flamer were precious, alien, jokaero devices.

Jaq summoned another facet...

In a transit-tube station two different units of planetary defence troopers were fighting each other furiously at close quarters. Rainbow light sprayed and arced as the vibrating edges of power axes met the energy fields of power swords. One of these units must have been entirely genestealer brood in human guise. But which was which? Those who wore the black basilisk insignia, or the blue deathbats?

Reinforcements were arriving on foot through the tunnel. Flamers sprayed at the fracas, and at last rebels could be distinguished from loyalists, just as it became obvious that the new arrivals on the scene – pink salamanders – were also loyalists. For the black basilisks screamed and writhed and quit fighting as soon as superheated chemicals clung burning to them. Deathbats – those of the brood – rushed frenziedly, even as they blazed, to attack the wielders of the flame guns. Precision laser fire sliced through the berserkers, killing human torch after human torch until the last had fallen.

Presently, perhaps tardily, foam engulfed the platforms to douse the clingfire – blinding this particular spy-fly, though by now Jaq had registered the loyalists' hard-won gain...

Another facet: a ribbed hall of towering, icon-stencilled machine tools, littered with corpses, many of them as grotesque in death as they had been in life...

Jaq's hundred roving spy-flies and the screen-eye were another jokaero invention, perhaps unique, which the Ordo Malleus had captured. Those simian, orange-furred jokaero were forever improvising ingenious equipment, not necessarily in the same way twice, though with an accent on miniaturisation.

Debate still waxed hot as to whether the orange ape aliens were genuinely intelligent or merely made weapons as instinctively as spiders make web. Grimm, a born technologist himself – as were all of his kind, it seemed – had pointed out that this eye-screen required psychic input from the operator. So some Jokaero must have psyches. At least.

Most planets seemed to harbour biological flies. Swamp-flies, dung-flies, offal-flies, sand-flies, flies that liked to sip from the eyeballs of crocodiles, corpse-flies, rotting-vegetation-flies, pseudo-flies that fed on magnetic fields. Who would notice a little fly buzzing around nimbly? Who would mark that fly watching you, transmitting what it saw and heard back to the eye-screen from anywhere within a compass of twenty kilometres? Who would expect that the fly and its fellows were tiny vibrating crystalline machines?

'I go!' announced Meh'Lindi.

If she chose, she could speak as gracefully as a courtier, as deviously as a diplomat. In the face of imminent deadly action, she sometimes reverted to a more basic style of utterance, recalling her original primitive tribal society. Lithely and silently, swift as a razorwing, she departed the Emerald Suite.

With a piercing thought and a twist of will, Jaq detached one of several spy-flies hovering in the otherwise deserted corridor outside, detailed it to follow her.

He magnified that viewpoint, allowing it a quarter of the eye-screen. Meh'Lindi paused momentarily, glanced back in the direction of the spy-fly, and winked. Then she padded quickly away, pursued.

'Huh, so I'll be off too.' Grimm jammed his cap down hard, patted his holstered laspistol, checked his 'bunch of grapes' – his grenades – and scampered after her. Unlike when Meh'Lindi exited, this time the suite door banged shut.

'Noisy tyke,' commented Googol, uncoiling from the couch. 'Surprised he doesn't favour a boltgun. *Clatter-clatter-clatter.*'

'You know very well,' said Jaq, 'that he slammed the door to signal he was following her.'

Googol laughed giddily. 'He needs to run around to keep his legs short. And Meh'Lindi, to keep hers long.'

'She'll be back, Vitali, never fear. As will Grimm.'

'Grimm racing off to protect her... as soon set a mouse to escort a cat! It's really pathetic the way he dotes on her then pretends to bluff it all off with a *huh*. I suppose in the absence of any dumpy squat females Meh'Lindi must seem like a goddess to the little chap.'

And, thought Jaq, likewise to you? And even – somewhat – to me? 'A deadly goddess,' he said, 'who always has other things on her mind. As I have. So hush.'

The Navigator prowled to and fro. He picked up a crystal decanter of amber liqueur, set it down. He pricked his thumb against the corkscrew horn of a baby teratosaur skull mounted on one wall, its brow inset with a green jewel. He stirred a courtesy bowl of dream-dust, untouched within its force-membrane by any of them hitherto, then went and cleaned his hands under the vibrostat.

Nervous for Meh'Lindi's safety? What was Meh'Lindi's whole purpose, what was her very life, but to go into perilous places, always to emerge alive? What was her daily rationale but to keep herself tuned to a pitch, taut as a bowstring? Yet in those golden eyes of hers was a lively intelligence and even wit. Of course, her sense of wit could be alarming.

Jaq riffled through facets, summoning scene after scene into prominence in swift succession until he came to the spy-fly that was tracking...

Harq Obispal.

TWO

BRANDISHING A BOLTGUN in one hand and a power sword in the other, the burly inquisitor strode along a broad boulevard, glaring to right and left.

Obispal's ginger beard forked three ways as if hairy tentacles sprouted from his chin. His eyebrows were bushes of rusty wire. His belted black robe was appliquéd with glaring white death's heads. His swamp-hunter boots could have been a pachyderm's great feet lopped off and hollowed out. Weapons and other devices hung within his blood-red, high-collared cloak; and a communicator dangled from one earlobe.

The inquisitor was advancing in the vanguard of a squad of armoured Imperial Guardsmen. Guardsmen from the local garrison, rather than Space Marines from off-world. Obispal believed in the force of will, in his own ruthless aura; and indeed, except for the evidence of lurid, puckered scar tissue across one cheek, he might have seemed invulnerable.

Presumably he didn't rate the Stalinvast operation as requiring really major surgery – even though thirty hive cities had been devastated to date and several totally destroyed. Casualties? Twenty million civilians and combatants? Out of a thousand cities, housing billions...

Wistfully, Jaq quoted to himself the words of an ancient leader of the middle kingdom on bygone Terra: 'In the land of a thousand million people, what does the death of one million of these count in the cause of purity?'

Still, suppressing such a plague wasn't the same as purging it totally. Only one fertile genestealer needed to remain alive in hiding to undo all the good work within a few decades. Highly trained Space Marines would have been utterly thorough, and would never yield to the malaise of combat, that battle-weary yearning to be done with a ghastly campaign, to rate it a *probably* total triumph, a *practically* unqualified success.

Wrecked ground cars and tanks smouldered along the boulevard under a leaden ceiling so high that utility tubes and power cables seemed to be but a delicate tracery.

Many glow-globes had been shot out or had failed, so shadows lurked like intangible behemoths. Baleful fumes drifted from slumped ducts; corrosives dripped. Gloomy tunnels led aside into blitzed factories.

Jaq allowed sound to invade his awareness.

Obispal was howling execrations that echoed, multiplying as if his voice was that of many men.

'Death to the alien scum that steal our humanity! Death to polluters! Death to the polluted! With joy may we burn and cleanse!'

The inquisitor's voice, as picked up by the spy-fly, almost drowned the crackle of gunfire. Obispal whirled his sword around so that his right arm resembled a circular saw. He threw the deadly, humming weapon into the air and caught it deftly by the shaft. He could have been leading a parade, twirling the baton.

Yes: a parade... of extermination.

Obispal had certainly taken his time over the cleansing, even protracting the process. Backed by his men and by the many planetary defence troopers who were unpolluted

and loyal to the governor, he had commenced his activities
around a ring of other cities than the capital, moving from
one to the next, destroying. His actions had triggered full-
scale rebellion by the hybrids and by the vaster genestealer
brood of true-seeming humans. For decades these latter
had been infiltrating the administration and even the
troopers.

If Obispal had started by cleansing the capital the genestealer broods might have dispersed, escaping through
transit tunnels or even overland through the jungle to
more distant cities. So his strategy made sense at the same
time as it seemed wantonly ruinous.

It was as if game birds had been flushed by beaters and
driven towards a central point, forced to attack the heart of
power and authority in a desperate bid to secure this for
themselves and seal the planet.

Bees flying into a bonfire.

Troopers fought troopers. Administrators murdered
their superiors and released stocks of weapons to the
rebels. For the first time the ordinary workers and man-
agers glimpsed the true faces of the hybrids who had
lurked in their midst, cloaked and hooded, or masked.

Jaq scanned another swarm of these hybrids, on the
rampage with guns and blades. Their stooping posture
was of a person melting down, slumping into the stance
of a vicious carnivore. Amidst the swarm, handsome if
eerie human beings orchestrated the pandemonium.

'One has always heard whispers,' remarked Googol, 'yet
to behold with one's own eyes is quite an experience.'

It was on the tip of Jaq's tongue to point out that the
Navigator was only beholding courtesy of the eye-screen.
He refrained, not wishing to goad Googol into some display of bravado which might rob Jaq of such an excellent
warp pilot.

'Whispers?' Jaq enquired instead. '*Loud* whispers? You
were giving Grimm the benefit of your theories about
genestealers. Do Navigators gossip much? Might *you*
gossip?'

'Navigators travel to many places, hear many things. Some true, some half-true, some concoctions. Stories alter in the telling, Jaq.' A half-pleading, half-impertinent tone had entered Googol's voice.

The Navigator was remembering that Jaq might be attired right now as one kind of person, whereas actually he was someone else entirely... and Googol needed to be reminded of this.

Masquerading as a rogue trader of reasonable success, Jaq wore a pleated frock coat with silver epaulettes and baggy crimson breeches tucked into short white calf boots. The coat was capacious, a home to guns, and the boots were home to knives. Quite in line with any ordinary trader.

Googol licked his upper lip nervously. 'A true story that crosses the galaxy becomes a lie, Jaq.'

'So, can a lie similarly become the truth?'

'That's too sophisticated for me, Jaq.'

It wasn't, of course. No one who had stared into the insanity of the warp, no one whose living was to do so, could be unsophisticated and survive. In a sense the warp was the ultimate lie, since it continually strove to betray those who traversed it. Yet at the same time the warp was the ultimate background to existence.

Vitali Googol actively cultivated an air of sophistication, aided in this by the premature age lines wrought in his visage due to long immersion in deep space and in the warp. These lent a world-weary cast to a face that might otherwise have been babyish.

Within, the Navigator was still young and vulnerable – liable to foolish enthusiasms such as his attraction to Meh'Lindi. Knowing this, Googol tried to be wry about his own feelings and eschewed any dandified garb such as Jaq now sported. Vitali wore a black tunic stitched with purple runes which were hardly visible. Black was the void. Black was sophisticated. (Black was the colour of Meh'Lindi in her war paint.)

Jaq tried to imagine how Googol viewed him. The trader costume suggested a certain piratical business acumen, though not without honour, and in the service of a deeper sensuality. Which was all a pretence. Jaq's sensual lips were definitely at odds with his sceptical ice-blue eyes. On the one hand, Jaq must seem capable of irony and flexible tolerance – perhaps only so as to spring a trap. On the other hand, he had to be as hard as granite inside, harder even than a brutally flamboyant exhibitionist such as Obispal – since Jaq was a guardian of those who guarded humanity, an investigator of the investigators.

Am I really hard enough, Jaq wondered? Or am I vulnerable too?

'Let Navigators gossip among themselves like fishwives,' he said sharply. 'The genestealers must remain a secret from our multitude of worlds, save for leaders who need to know, lest confusion spreads.'

'If people in general knew–'

'That, Vitali, is what inquisitors are for. To find out, and to root out. Confusion is the cousin to Chaos. Knowledge causes confusion. Ignorance can be the strongest shield of the innocent.' The ghost of a smile twitched Jaq's lips. Did Jaq Draco really believe these maxims?

Quarter-facet... Meh'Lindi had quit a transit capsule, had ridden an elevator down and was sprinting effortlessly along empty north-bound mobile pavements.

The south-bound pavements were crowded with refugees fleeing from the fighting. A river of people surged, fighting to gain the central express strip where that panic-stricken river raced fastest. Some citizens were injured, bleeding; others bore bundles of possessions. Often a would-be escapee, whose one foot was on the express path and whose other was still on the slower acceleration strip, was whirled aside in an eddy and sucked underfoot.

Drizzle fell from malfunctioning fire-control nozzles. Lightning crackled overhead as cables shorted.

Quarter-facet... Mounted on a stolen power-trike, Grimm roared up the north-bound speedstrip.

Meh'Lindi glanced once over her shoulder then ran on, taking huge strides.

The abhuman stood up on the foot rests, throttling back.

'You want a lift somewhere?' he bellowed.

Meh'Lindi merely increased her pace. Impulsively, the squat swung the trike to pull alongside, so that one wheel dragged on the slower strip. The manoeuvre failed. The trike skidded and tumbled, throwing Grimm over the handlebars. Tucking himself into a ball of boots and flak jacket, the squat bounced and rolled half a dozen times. Briefly, Meh'Lindi broke step.

However, Grimm was already picking himself up, swearing, dusting himself off, retrieving his cap.

Meh'Lindi jerked one hand – in salute, or as a warning to stay away from her? – then she surged ahead.

Casting a disgusted glance at the buckled trike and at the throng pouring past him, south-bound, Grimm trotted northwards after the assassin.

Jaq surprised Googol – and himself – by chuckling, sympathetically, almost affectionately.

Meh'Lindi was soon way out of sight of the squat around a wide bend. There she quit the throughway, to race along feeder lanes, dodging through refugees who shrank from the fleeting, faceless, coaly-skinned woman. The spy-fly zipped along in her wake, down narrower, abandoned, grim alleys. Noise of battle grew audible. Shocks jerked at the fabric of the city, rupturing ancient sewage pipes.

Quarter-facet... and Jaq uttered a malediction. 'There's one of the fathers of evil.'

A middle-aged man and woman were escorting a pure-strain genestealer through aisles lined with crates in some ill-lit and claustrophobic warehouse.

How commonplace the human couple looked in their workers' overalls. Apart from the laspistols both held, awkwardly if purposefully. And apart from the glazed, doting madness in their eyes.

For these two were emotionally fixated on that monster, bonded to it by sentiments which were the cruellest parody of love and of family attachment.

The puissant alien walked crouched over in a permanent posture of attack so that the horns along its spine projected highest. Its long cranium jutting forward, fangs dripping gluey saliva. Its upper set of arms ended in claws which could tear armour open; and its carapace was as tough as armour. Fibrous ligaments corded its limbs. A horny tube of a tongue flicked out: that tongue which could kiss its own gene material into a host.

Momentarily, Jaq flinched at the creature's hypnotic gaze, even seen through the medium of the screen, and although he was psychically immune.

'Father of evil,' he intoned as if in a travesty of prayer, 'and grandfather too...'

Yes indeed. The human mother who gave birth to a deformed, bestial hybrid would dote on it blindly, as protective as a tiger of her cub, and as cunning. Offspring of hybrids would seem less alien in appearance. By the fourth generation, save for the charismatic light in their eyes, the spawn would appear human.

Yet the firstborn of such a semblance would be purestrain stealer again. With appalling, instinctive inevitability the cycle would recommence.

By then a whole family coven numbering thousands of warped persons would be infesting society secretly, a brood keenly alert to each other's alien needs. Somewhere, in deepest luxurious hiding, the overgrown patriarch which first began the pollution of a world would relish empathetically all the doings of its kin...

Quarter-facet... A genestealer tore a planetary defence trooper's chest open before darting back into concealment...

FOR A WHILE, Jaq let all hundred spy-fly images be present at once in mosaic on the eye-screen. Extending his psychic sense of presence, he felt how the battle inside Vasilariov was congealing, slowing and centring desperately about fifteen kilometres north of the hotel. That was where the surviving purestrains and minions were concentrating.

Maybe the patriarch was already dead. That was where
Obispal was heading from one direction. And Meh'Lindi
from another.

Quarter-facet once more... A darkened, elevated observation booth overlooked what seemed to be a laboratory.
Under flickering emergency lighting, arcane apparatus
fumed and sparked, abandoned by its operators. The
strobing of the light froze monsters in mid-motion, gath-
ering for some assault.

Jaq willed the spy-fly to see in infra-red.

Inside the booth above that scene, black in syn-skin,
Meh'Lindi crouched. She had dogged the plasteel door
shut. The observation window was doubtless of armoured
glass. And she was crouching over. Hiding? Had she locked
herself in a place of comparative safety?

The assassin was stowing her jokaero weapons away
inside her sash. She sprayed solvent onto a tiny patch of
her arm then stuck a needle through the little gap in her
syn-skin, injecting herself. She hunched even lower, rabbit-
legged as if about to hop.

Presently, bumps arose from her spine. Her head began
to elongate. Her fingers were fusing into claws.

'What's happening to her?' cried Googol. 'Has she been
infected?'

Jaq shuddered. 'I must say she does believe in challeng-
ing herself!'

'What's happening to her, man?' Googol clutched Jaq's
arm, appalled, for Meh'Lindi was becoming a monster.

'She injected polymorphine.'

'Polymorphine... Sounds like a painkiller, doesn't it?'

'It isn't.'

Assassins were proofed against pain, but surely
Meh'Lindi must be aware of some agonies as her body
strained to adopt a new shape in obedience to her will.

Googol cackled hysterically. 'Assassins' drug, right? They
use it to assume a new appearance. To disguise themselves.
Masquerade as someone else. Someone *human*, Jaq! I've
heard of polymorphine. It can't possibly change

someone's body as much as that!' His finger jerked towards the screen. 'Nor as quickly, neither!'

'She's in propinquity to other stealers,' muttered Jaq. 'She's concentrating on their body forms, feeling them with her senses...'

'That can't account for it!'

'Well, the syn-skin helps speed the reaction. It's galvanising her whole metabolism, accelerating her vitality. It's designed to do that as well as protect her.'

'You're lying, Jaq!'

'Control yourself. There is another reason... But you have no right to know, do you understand?'

Googol flinched, and gnawed at the ball of his thumb as if to stifle anguish or panic. But still he persisted, anxiously. 'I've heard how assassins are trained to dislocate their own limbs and even break their own bones so that they can writhe like snakes through narrow tubes—'

'You have no right to ask whatever! *Quieta esto, nefanda curiositas, esto quieta!*' The resonant hieratic words acted as a slap in the face.

True enough, Jaq had known the secret essence of the matter ever since his application to the Officio Assassinorum was fulfilled – his request for an assassin with previous experience of a genestealer-infested world, and one who could pose as a sophisticated mistress.

Meh'Lindi had formerly undergone experimental surgery to implant extrudable, shape-remembering plastiflesh reinforced with carbon fibre and flexicartilage which could toughen hard as horn. Thus she could pose as a stealer hybrid, could behave as one; and afterwards could suck those implants back into herself, softening, shrinking, reabsorbing them.

Extra glands had been grafted into her to store and synthesise at speed the somatotrophin growth hormone that ordinarily promoted growth of long bones and protein synthesis in a child... and glands to reverse the process. Her artificial implants were a living organic part of her. By the

same token her body of flesh and blood and bone was
partly artifice and artefact.

This, coupled with the polymorphine and her own
apparently chameleonic talent – perhaps potentiated by
the syn-skin, though of this aspect Jaq was truly unsure –
enabled her to undergo a wilder, faster transformation
than fellow assassins: a radical transmutation of her body
into, at least, stealer semblance.

Jaq knew that she was an initiate of the Callidus Shrine
of the Assassins – speciality: cunning – and the experiment
in the Callidus medical laboratory perhaps marked a perilous, agonising zenith of dissimulation. This much had
been confided to him; and he had deemed it discreet to
pry no further, had been persuaded of the wisdom of dis-
cretion.

Presumably Meh'Lindi's previous mission had succeeded and the Director of the Callidus Temple was
inclined to field-test her again... Or maybe the mission had
failed but she had survived. Maybe the extreme and somewhat specialised experiment had been abandoned? Maybe
Meh'Lindi was the lone surviving product of it. Jaq knew
not to enquire too deeply into the secrets of the Officio
Assassinorum when such particulars were not within his
brief.

Jaq had known... intellectually. Yet even so, the rapidity
and utterness of her transformation shocked him.

'She's becoming a genestealer!' babbled Googol. 'Well,
isn't she? Isn't she? She can't possibly be attempting a perfect copy...'

Indeed she wasn't. Meh'Lindi did not develop the lower
set of arms nor the bony, sinuous tail. Too much to expect
a new pair of arms to grow out of her ribs, or her coccyx to
elongate so enormously. Nor could Jaq imagine that she
could attain the full strength of a purestrain stealer –
though her own strength was formidable, even when
unenhanced.

Yet in dark silhouette she seemed almost a genestealer.
She was at least the image of an injured stealer, blackened

and fused by fire, one which had lost some appendages, perhaps lasered off, perhaps in an explosion; a stealer which still remained very much alive and able to use its deadly main claws. Syn-skin still wrapped her, having stretched to accommodate her new shape. The syn-skin sealed her toothy snout shut. Her face, her jaw had been implanted too in the Callidus laboratory...

Injured stealer... or hybrid shape. One or the other... Hybrids comprised a whole gamut of deformities. If taken for a hybrid, could she really fool a stealer brood, or their patriarch, over a period of time? Maybe, thought Jaq, that was where the Callidus experiment had come unstuck... if indeed it had come unstuck.

'That's... the woman we share quarters with?' Googol's voice was filled with black wonder, with a fearful admiration, a certain desolation of the heart, and yes, a horror that nevertheless coursed thrillingly through his nerves. Jaq too felt deeply perturbed.

Already, Meh'Lindi's own skin seemed to be stiffening under that black second skin. It was forming a tough bony carapace as stimulated cells altered their nature, hardening to horn.

'Can any assassin ever have tried this trick before?' exclaimed the Navigator. 'Wrenching her organs, distorting herself so utterly? And tried it in the midst of a combat zone?'

'*Curiositas, esto quieta!*'

'She did say she needed exercise.' If Googol hoped to sound supercilious, he failed.

The black creature which had been Meh'Lindi unlatched the door and darted into a wide corridor, misty with smoke. Several armed hybrids roamed, seeming lost. Was Meh'Lindi thinking any of the alien thoughts of a genestealer? Understanding how it would react? Perhaps even radiating some protective aroma of brood empathy around herself? She bore down on the hybrids and, with her claws, she killed them almost before they realised.

A cloaked man who accompanied them gaped. His mouth opened in mute protest at this perversion of the proper order of affairs. Meh'Lindi ripped his head off.

No one seeing her on the move, rushing headlong through drear fuming tunnels, would really note the missing arms and absent tail, the sealed face, the scarlet sash. Or at least not note those betraying absences until far too late. She was keeping to the more furtive by-ways of the city and away from loyal troops.

Quarter-facet... Grimm arrived, puffing, at a narrow archway leading into a domed plaza. Three great avenues radiated away, choked with fighting, reeking with smoke. Explosions flared like novas inside a dust nebula. Shockwaves rippled downward from some higher level of the city which boomed with devastation. Walls and braced ceiling groaned. Drums of architecture were being beaten until they burst.

A smoky miasma masked glow-globes, reddening the scene as if here was the lurid sunset of the heart of this city before final night consumed and extinguished it. A massive detonation shook the plasteel heights. Had a munitions factory exploded? The roofs of the avenues sagged, pillars buckling. Abruptly the dome collapsed, shattering like an eggshell. Whole buildings, vehicles, and machinery came tumbling from above, wearing necklaces of fire.

Grimm scuttled away up a ramp, pursued by debris and clouds of dust.

Half-facet... Obispal spotted a lone purestrain genestealer lurking some way down a dismal arcade lined by shuttered clothing stores. The stealer loped slowly away as though injured, dodging from one steel column to the next.

Swinging his power sword and shouting to guardsmen, the inquisitor pounded after the fugitive alien. Was it sheer bravado on Obispal's part that he disdained to fire explosive bolts at that creature which itself could not manipulate a gun? Or was it blood lust? He intended to cut it apart personally with his power sword – sword against claw – and be seen to do so.

The arcade proved to be a cul-de-sac. Twisted steel blocked the far end. As the inquisitor realised this, he grinned hugely. Though only briefly.

Activated by some unseen hand, a disaster-shutter of woven steel crashed down behind him, cutting him off from his guardsmen.

Obispal whirled.

'Carve through with a power axe, and quickly!' he bellowed.

The genestealer was no longer fleeing but racing towards the inquisitor, claws outstretched. Swiftly, Obispal confronted it; and now bolts from his hand-tooled, burnished-steel gun hammered at the alien. Many of the explosive-tipped shells missed entirely. Some caromed off its carapace. One, however, detonated successfully, making instant *purée* within the creature's armoured head.

Yet already hatches in the ceiling were springing free. A dozen hybrids and another purestrain dropped down into the arcade. Still more hybrids followed. A whole rabid pack was rushing at Obispal, firing a medley of weapons inaccurately, hatred written on all their twisted faces.

Las-fire, gouts of flame, and ordinary bullets ripped and charred his clothes but were deflected by the ornate armour he wore beneath. His head was unprotected. With a juggler's dexterity he switched the boltgun swishingly to full automatic. Ejected cartridges sprayed like grain at harvest time on some granary world. Firing the bolter with one hand he waved the sizzling power sword frantically in front of his face as if fanning wasps away. The explosive clatter in the arcade was ear-splitting. Obispal's cloak caught fire.

As Obispal backed against the front of a store the grille that sheathed it tore open from within. A genestealer claw reached and plucked the inquisitor through the gap.

THREE

BACK THROUGH THE gap flew his blazing cloak, still weighted with a few grenades. These exploded in the face of the mob. Obispal's power sword sailed out in an arc and danced across the floor, severing several feet. All of a sudden, the point of view shifted into the darkness beyond the torn grille, just as the purestrain leapt over the bodies of its kin to force entry.

Claws as mighty as its own batted the purestrain's claws aside and ravaged its head so that the purestrain shrieked and hung incapacitated, blocking the gap. In infra-red the scene was clear. It was the monster-Meh'Lindi who had jerked the inquisitor to safety. She had disabled the stealer which tried to follow. Now she was simply restraining Obispal, holding the disarmed man firmly at claw's length.

That high-pitched whine must be the sound of a power axe or two butter-slicing through the disaster shutter outside.

Obispal writhed. 'What?' he cried. 'Who? You aren't a genestealer. You aren't a hybrid. What are you?'

37

How clearly could Obispal see? Meh'Lindi didn't reply. How could she through that snout of teeth sealed with syn-skin, even if she wished to?

Outside, now: gunfire, screams, sizzling. The guards must be through the barrier.

'Aaaah–' Obispal sounded to be on the verge of deducing the truth.

'Watch out within!' came a call. Laser fire began to slice through the crippled purestrain. The claw released Obispal, thrusting him away. Meh'Lindi turned and raced off up a steel stairway. Obispal stamped his elephantine boots in furious pique before composing himself, locating his discarded boltgun and preparing to welcome his rescuers.

'Shade ungrateful, ain't he?' drawled Googol.

'He walked into a trap,' said Jaq. 'The whole universe is full of traps for the unwary. For a moment Obispal was unwary and he knows it. He knows that someone else knows, which is humiliating. At the eleventh hour, he underestimated the genestealers – as if they had only been his playthings. His campaign went so well up until now.'

'Ah yes, he did so well,' echoed Googol sardonically. He scrutinized the tiny facets of devastation aswirl around the eye-screen. 'Whole cities destroyed, millions slaughtered. So splendidly.'

'Stalinvast will very soon be cleansed, Vitali. There can be worse fates for a world.'

'Can there be?'

'*Exterminatus*,' Jaq whispered to himself.

'What?'

'Never mind. Vasilariov won't be totally ruined. The tide of battle won't even reach us here in the hotel.'

'That's consoling to know.'

'No more does the tide of Chaos threaten our Emperor.'

Meh'Lindi in stealer guise was racing at a crouch through dark ducts and service tunnels. She mounted ancient stairways that spiralled so high around shafts dribbling with condensation as to shrink into their own vanishing points.

She crossed gantries bridging delving chasms. She descended other stairways. She popped through hatchways into alleys and back into ducts again. Always she chose the most deserted routes. Only occasionally did she encounter fugitives from the slaughter who had wisely dodged into such hidey holes. These she brushed aside and raced by, to their evident great relief. Still, from the major avenues the rumble and squall of flight reached her constantly, a doleful drum-backing to her own claw-clicking progress.

At one intersection, she paused, senses alert.

Quarter-facet... Grimm trotted along a precarious overhead catwalk above a river of humanity, puffing, 'Huh, huh, huh.'

Below, the surge was growing ever denser as if that river had met a dam ahead. Moving pavements must have failed under the weight they bore, otherwise one side of the crowd would surely be pulled to the rear.

Bodies were conglomerating together, asphyxiating. Corpses were carried along, standing upright. The nimblest escapees hopped across the heads of the living and the dead, until a twisted ankle or a gasping angry hand brought them down. Then they sprawled afloat upon the waves of craniums, arms thrashing.

The very walls of the avenue seemed likely to burst. Upthrusts of men and women forced cones of tangled, crushed bodies higher than the rest of the mass. The flood of tormented flesh appeared to be one single myriad-headed entity which was now compressing itself insanely until eyes started, skin split, until blood vessels sprayed. If Grimm fell into that...

Already human trees were growing towards his catwalk as survivors clawed and clutched upward. Glow-strips flickered, as if to this stifling hell of pain and terror was soon to be added darkness.

'Why no knock-out gas?' Grimm shouted over the groans and shrieks, as though some responsible official might heed him. 'Does your governor want even more of his population culled?'

A hatch popped. A black claw seized Grimm. Lifting him clear off his feet, a horny black arm hugged him. The little man's head was pressed against a jutting jaw.

Grimm gibbered in his own tongue, obviously regretting his impetuous excursion to visit the war front.

Then Jaq and Googol heard him pray squeakingly in proper Imperial Gothic, as if thus he might be heard across the galaxy. 'Oh my ancestors! Oh let me not betray my race!' That prayer might as well have been couched in his own patois. In Imperial Gothic he should have been praying to the God-Emperor for help.

Googol guffawed. 'The poor tyke must think she's going to give him the genestealer kiss. Oh, *la belle dame sans merci*.'

'Don't utter sorcerous spells,' Jaq said sternly.

'I wasn't. That's a phrase from some antique poem. It suggests, well... a fatal woman. Meh'Lindi.'

'Very fatal,' agreed Jaq.

'Not towards our friend Grimm; though he doesn't realize.'

Meh'Lindi had darted back into a service tunnel and was decamping as fast as could be, cradling Grimm, who was wailing like a baby.

'She's taking him somewhere special and secret to deliver the fatal kiss,' decided Googol. 'That's what he'll be thinking. Forever after he'll have to stay celibate to avoid polluting his people.'

'Celibate? You're joking. The victims of stealers forget that they've been infected. The stealer that kisses mesmerizes too. So the victim simply yearns to mate?'

'With ordinary mortals, ha! And enthral those in the same enchantment.'

The hybrid babies that were born would likewise hypnotize their parents to perceive beauty where there was twisted ugliness.

'Alas,' sighed Googol, 'our flustered friend hasn't noticed certain discrepancies yet. He must really be wetting his britches.'

Hugging Grimm to her, Meh'Lindi scaled gloomy networks of girders bracing shafts, dived along murky tunnels.

'Even so,' murmured the Navigator, 'to languish in her arms...'

'Are you a *poet*, Vitali?' Jaq asked. 'I do believe you're blushing.'

'I compose a few things during slack times on journeys,' Googol admitted. 'A few verses about the void. Love. Death. I might scribble them down if I like them well enough.'

And you probably *do* like them well enough, thought Jaq.

'Beware,' he said, 'of romanticism.'

Meh'Lindi had reached a small neglected storeroom cluttered with dusty, cobwebbed tools. A glow-globe on stand-by provided a dim orange light.

Shouldering the door shut, Meh'Lindi set the squat down somewhat abruptly, though not ungently. Grimm stumbled away a few paces. Since there was nowhere else that he could go, he faced the seeming monster almost defiantly.

'Huh! You shan't. Huh, I'll kill myself.'

'How very bashful.'

Googol's tone suggested not only mockery but yearning, impossible desire.

The mock-stealer gestured at her snout, clad in syn-skin. With her claws, which were hardly designed for delicate manipulations, she displayed her sash, tapped the various items of equipment clipped inside the fabric.

At last the light of understanding dawned in the little man's eyes. Hesitantly he approached her, reached for a little canister. Meh'Lindi nodded her horse-like head. The solvent, yes.

Grimm sprayed her, and first her jaws snapped open, revealing dagger-fangs. She hissed at him. Was she trying to force that alien throat and ovipositor of a tongue to master human words? Still he sprayed, now almost without flinching – her chest, her arms, her back – until all the syn-skin had dissolved away. If anything, revealed, she looked even more evil.

'She needed his hands,' sneered Googol. 'That's the reason she snatched him. Soon as he injects her with the
antidote to polywhatnot, she'll leave him to find his own
way home.'

But Meh'Lindi neither gestured for the hypodermic nor
did she abandon Grimm. Picking the squat up again, she
tore the door open and resumed her journey through the
obscure, sombre entrails of Vasilariov. She could scale the
heights and shin down depths that the squat could never
have tackled on his own, or at least not so swiftly.

'Damn it, Grimm looks positively snug now. He's enjoy-
ing his ride in her arms, don't you think, Jaq? I suppose
he's just her voice in case she needs to identify herself!'

'Jealousy, Vitali, is a consequence of romanticism...'

THE DOOR TO the Emerald Suite flew open and in darted the
monster-Meh'Lindi. She set Grimm down. The squat
tugged his flak-jacket straight, brushed dirt off it, combed
his gingery beard with his fingers, flicked at his knotted
ponytail as if a fly had landed on it. For a moment he
smiled lavishly at Meh'Lindi, then thought better of it.

'Huh, huh, quite a caper.'

'We've been watching,' said Googol. 'A virtuoso exhibi-
tion, my dear!' He sketched a graceful bow in the direction
of the assassin.

'I did tell you not to pull any stunts,' Jaq reminded her.
'Now Obispal knows that there are other Imperial agents
on this world unbeknown to him. On the other hand, he's
still alive, which might salve his ego.'

Meh'Lindi advanced and knelt before Jaq. Was she beg-
ging his pardon? No, she was presenting her genestealer
semblance for his inspection.

He reached out his hand and stroked her horny, savage
face. Googol whistled agitatedly. Despite himself, Jaq felt
fascinated. He could touch – he could caress – Meh'Lindi
in this murderous alien guise like someone stroking a kit-
ten, as though he was absolved from the normal punctilios
of duty and common sense. In this form she was perhaps

more deadly than ever; yet for that very reason she refrained from causing harm, suppressing her reflexes.

He examined her carapace, her tough coiled-spring legs; and knew that he was examining Meh'Lindi intimately, yet at the same time he wasn't. He was hardly aware of his audience. Meh'Lindi hissed cacophonously.

'She needs to eat, boss,' said Grimm. 'For energy, before changing back.'

'Can you understand her?' Googol asked incredulously.

'Understand her? Understand? Huh! Who can plumb and penetrate such a person? Her mouth makes noises and I interpret. I have, after all,' and Grimm grinned raffishly, 'enjoyed rather longer in her company than either of you two. Just recently.'

'Shall I call room service for something special?' Googol enquired coolly. 'Such as a whole genuine roast sheep? Supposing that chefs and scullery lads are still alive, haven't fled, or aren't all pressed into service to boil up synthdiet for all those refugees. Our lady needs a banquet. Or would that be too flamboyant? Would we draw attention to ourselves?'

'As you know full well,' said Jaq, 'she can make free with our own food stocks.'

Which, presently, Meh'Lindi did, ravenously consuming fish, flesh and fowl from out of the stasis-boxes which they had brought to the suite from Jaq's ship, the *Tormentum Malorum*, which went by the alias of *Sapphire Eagle* while they were visiting Stalinvast. Rich planet though Stalinvast was, real food couldn't necessarily be guaranteed in a hive city, even in a wealthy hotel, not least in a time of strife.

Jaq noted how wistfully Grimm regarded what he rated as gourmet ambrosia disappearing into the monster's maw remorselessly.

Did Meh'Lindi relish exotic veals, smoked fillets of sunfish, sirloins of succulent grox? Or was she trained, and her body geared, to subsist on any available fodder whatever, algae, cockroaches, rats, who cares? Could she taste the difference?

Grimm could.

Which wasn't wholly surprising. The race of squats had evolved away from the human norm inside the caves and cramped, carved-out seams of bleak mining worlds which were barren save for minerals. Squats had become stocky, tough and self-reliant. During the millennia of genetic divergence, while warp storms cut their worlds off from the rest of the galaxy, they were forced to manufacture their own food and air. They knew famine – and still commemorated those hard times. Squats thrived in adversity. Often they preferred a harsh world to a sweeter one.

Yet they did like to eat, and handsomely, if they could.

Their artificial hydroponics gardens were famous for nutritious output; and after recontact by the Imperium they spent a fair tithe of their mineral wealth on importing exotic foods. If their staple diet still consisted of hydroponically grown vegetables, these were deliciously spiced and sauced – a far more piquant diet than the recycled synthfood that was the lot of the majority of most populations on crowded worlds. Given the slightest encouragement, a squat's appetite was – to judge by Grimm – that of a keen connoisseur.

Oh yes, Jaq noted the hungry glint in the squat's eyes. It wasn't greed. In his bluff, homespun way Grimm was courteous, even chivalric. It was plain to the little man that the assassin, who had exerted herself hugely, must eat first. Yet he too was also at least a little famished; and he did appreciate cuisine.

'Eat something yourself, Grimm,' invited Jaq. 'Go ahead: that's virtually an order.'

Gratefully, the little man chose from stasis the smoked drumstick of some bulky flightless avian.

He nodded appreciatively.

Plenty more such finger-licking, lip-licking food on board *Tormentum Malorum*. An inquisitor could commandeer whatsoever he wished and Jaq had provisioned his own ship exquisitely. For Jaq by no means equated iron duty with iron rations. That was a false and sanctimonious puritanism, such as had dogged the inquisitor's own youth.

To be sure, one could sympathise with the sentiments of some of those penitents who refused themselves pleasures because the Emperor, undying saviour of mankind, could experience no pleasure whatever, locked as he had been for millennia in his prosthetic throne...

Though Jaq, in his role as a rogue trader, pretended to patronise a mistress, the reality was that during his thirty-five years of life he had only bedded one woman – almost on an experimental basis so that he should at least be acquainted with the spasm of sex.

Those who yielded to passion forsook their self-control. Jaq similarly drew the line at wine, which could fuddle the senses and put a person in needless peril.

Thus his stocking of the ship's larder with delicacies was, to his mind, a far cry from self-indulgence. Rather, it was a way of rejecting unctuous, masochistic denial – which might narrow his perspectives.

Unlike Grimm, Googol hardly seemed ever to notice what he ate. How could a self-styled poet be so oblivious to taste? Ah, perhaps he who gazed so much into the warp existed on a more ethereal plane... except when a Meh'Lindi was around.

Grimm, however, had set the drumstick aside after a single bite.

'Something amiss?' asked the Navigator.

'I'm thinking about those trampled mobs, those shattered streets. Millions dead, and here I munch. Why didn't anyone use knockout gas on all those panicking refugees?'

'They were a sacrifice to purity,' murmured Jaq.

'More like a sacrifice plain and simple, an offering on a bloody altar, if you'll pardon me. Huh!'

'Do you really think so?' Jaq brooded. So many corpses; and then some more, to sugar the porridge of death.

Ruefully, Grimm took up the drumstick again and gnawed. Meh'Lindi seemed sated at last.

Emerging from his reverie, Jaq wondered whether he would be able to watch her changing back, whether he might witness the melting of the monster and the re-emergence of a perfect female human body. But Grimm nodded towards Meh'Lindi's bedroom enquiringly and she too nodded her horse-head. Discarding the bird bone, Grimm gathered up Meh'Lindi's silk gown, stole and slippers from where they still lay and headed for the bedroom door, followed by Meh'Lindi.

'I say,' protested Googol.

Grimm rounded on him. 'And *what* do you say, eh?'

The Navigator glanced appealingly at Jaq.

Jaq wondered at his own motives for wishing to view the mock-stealer changing back into a woman – teasing, ambivalent motives. An inquisitor must not be ambiguous. Alert to subtleties and paradoxes, oh yes. But not fickle. It was wiser not to tantalise oneself. He gestured for Grimm to proceed.

As the bedroom door closed, Googol adopted a peeved expression and pretended great interest in a fingernail.

Jaq concentrated on his spy-flies.

The havoc was all but over. Obispal was triumphantly mopping up. Soon only ruin, death and injury remained.

Presently, Jaq blanked the eye-screen and relaxed, though with a puzzled air.

When Meh'Lindi emerged from the bedroom, begowned and jewelled as Jaq's mistress once more, her face was a study in expressionless hauteur; though when Grimm trotted out after her, looking dazzled, fleetingly a hint of mischief twinkled in her eyes.

'Let us pray,' said Jaq. 'Let us thank our God-Emperor who watches over us – for the purification of this planet, for its redemption from alien evil...'

As he recited familiar words, Jaq puzzled why he had really been detailed to be present on Stalinvast during its purge. The proctor minor of his chamber, Baal Firenze, had assigned him this mission, presumably acting on the instructions of a Hidden Master.

'Watch whether anything remains uncleansed,' Baal Firenze had said.

What puzzled Jaq was that the genestealer rebellion, now so bloodily suppressed, was a *natural* threat. Stealers weren't Chaos spawn. Their imperatives were comparatively simple: to procreate and protect themselves and perpetuate the social order – preferably under their own control – so as to ensure a supply of human hosts.

Whereas Jaq was of the Malleus and a daemonhunter. His Ordo was primarily concerned with the forces of Chaos from the warp which could possess vulnerable individuals of psychic talent, twisting them into tools of insanity.

That was hardly the situation on Stalinvast. So why was he trouble-shooting a non-psychic threat?

Protect us from the foul ministrations of Khorne and Slaanesh, Nurgle and Tzeentch...

He spoke those words silently, only to himself. A common squat, a Navigator, even an assassin – should not even hear those arcane names of the Chaos powers.

His companions' heads remained bowed. The names would only have sounded to them like unfamiliar ritual incantations.

Or, he thought grimly, like eldritch poetry.

'Protect us from those who would twist our human heritage,' he recommenced.

Why Stalinvast, why?

True, his own Ordo also served as a secret watchdog over the Inquisition at large. Could Harq Obispal's furious, if successful, excesses be regarded as a symptom of potential possession by daemonic forces from the warp? Hardly, thought Jaq. Nor could Obispal exactly be viewed as incompetent, despite his last-moment slackening of judgement when he charged into that trap in the arcade.

A cynic might say that Obispal's activities were directly responsible for triggering the rebellion, and thus for all the deaths, including those of millions of bystanders. Yet could such a nest of vipers have been left to writhe and breed unstirred? Of course not. Though Obispal might have adopted a more subtle surgical strategy than hacking the body to pieces to extract the festering organ.

The squat's remark about a sacrifice upon the altar worried Jaq. The death-scream of millions could serve as a call to Chaos; could be part of a conjuration.

'And protect us from ourselves,' Jaq added, drawing a curious glance at last, from Grimm.

By now Jaq too felt starved.

He dined discriminatingly, from out of a stasis-box, on spiced foetal lambkin stuffed with truffles; and he sipped gloryberry juice.

FOUR

'Do you suppose any wild natives live in those jungles?' Meh'Lindi asked Jaq, exhibiting a hint of nostalgia.

Half-facet... an aerial view of the sprawling spaceport, an island of ferroconcrete within a sea of rampant vegetation...

'Human natives?' he asked incredulously.

'Descendants of runaways? Criminals? Disaffected workers who have formed their own tribes?'

'I suppose it's possible. Human beings will adapt to almost any vile conditions. And now, the ranks of these hypothetical runaways might be swelled?'

Most of the jokaero spy-flies were transmitting tiny facets of war's aftermath within the city, a grim mosaic. Vehicles smouldered amidst wreckage. Foetid flooded sumps bobbed with bodies. Corpse collectors were sorting fresh human meat for recycling. Rotten meat and all cadavers of genestealer kin were destined for furnaces. Troopers and vigilantes patrolled. Gangs looted; looters were executed. Tech-priests and servitors were bracing and splinting

Vasilariov's terrible urban wounds, the city's ripped skin, its splintered bones, injured organs, torn arteries. Acrid miasmas coiled from ventilation ducts and sewage flooded avenues.

On Vasilariov's many levels – some of which had slumped into chasms – surviving refugees trudged through debris or foul floodwater back to their shattered factory-homes. They crowded whatever elevators still worked or wearily scaled buckled stairways or girders. These refugees fell prey to marauding gangs, even to troopers, or to one another. It seemed as though rival nests of ants had been poured together willy-nilly.

Nevertheless, the stringent regimen that was normality for many – even in a lavish burg – was staggering back towards normal. The ants were trying to return to their separate nests, or what was left of them, if anything. Jaq had spied no absconders from the devastated city, the alternative to which was hardly inviting...

A plasteel wall circled that spaceport, which lay some fifteen kilometres from the southern edge of Vasilariov. Heavy defence lasers and plasma cannons studded the rim. Jaq presumed that periodically these would be switched on to prune the jungle back.

Armoured train-tubes on pylons linked the port with Vasilariov, from where other elevated tubes radiated towards other cities, high above the tangled savage vegetation.

The flora of this world was forever bubbling and festering, like a green soup on the boil. Vines in tree-tops strangled each other. Lianas writhed towards the light from bilious decaying depths. Lurid parasites swelled and bloomed and rotted.

'You aren't thinking of going out into the jungle to exercise for old times' sake?' Jaq enquired of Meh'Lindi. 'By any chance?'

'No, now is the real job. Right?'

'Hostile environment,' Grimm hastened to remind the assassin, to be on the safe side. 'Don't suppose anything intelligent lives out there. If the saurians don't get you, barrage bombs or juggernauts will.'

'I lived in such a jungle once,' said Meh'Lindi. 'Somewhere very like out there. Am I not intelligent?'

'Oh yes! But–'

'But what?'

'You have matured.'

At which, Googol tittered.

Some thirty great cargo shuttles sat in blast-bays, and other vessels too, including the *Tormentum Malorum*. Jaq summoned a different half-facet, the scene close to the customs house, which quite belied the spectacle of ruin within much of Vasilariov.

The planetary governor, Lord Voronov-Vaux, and his entourage were seeing the victorious Harq Obispal off with a fanfare.

Several hundred loyal planetary defence troopers stood to attention. A band in gold-braided uniforms blew long brass trumpets. Lesser lords and bodyguards thronged two reviewing stands. Servants circulated with wines and sweetmeats. Banners fluttered. Preachers chanted prayers to the Emperor. Privileged merchants patted their paunches. Near-naked performers danced and juggled. Chained jungle-beasts, doubly confined within force fields, fought each other with horns, fangs and claws, sliding in pools of vermilion blood. Ladies eyed one another's gowns and intricate, suspensor-lifted, rainbow-hued hairstyles. Beefy Obispal would have enjoyed a number of those ladies' favours since the fighting died away. He had, Jaq noted, obtained a new cloak trimmed with dazzling white ermine death's heads. A gift of gratitude. Voronov-Vaux himself wore a casque that covered his whole head, making him seem to be a human lizard with great red eyes.

Tiring of the distant ceremonies and speeches and festivities, so at odds with the gangrenous suffering inside the city – climax to so much other death on Stalinvast – Jaq opened a case keyed to the electronic tattoo on his palm and removed a small package of flayed, cured mutant skin.

Inside, his Tarot deck.

The Emperor's Tarot was supposed to partake of the very spirit of the Master of Mankind, forever on overwatch throughout the warp. Immobile in his throne on Earth, that godly paragon who was so old that his personal name had long been forgotten both beamed out a beacon and sensed the flow of Chaos, through which his starships must swim and out of which could congeal... abominations.

The Emperor trawled, the Emperor sifted unsleepingly.

These cards, rumoured to be of his design, and said to be blessed by virtue of that design – psychically imbued with his influence – also sieved.

They sieved the tides of fate. Of probability and improbability. Of strengthening influences and weakening influences. They were an X-ray of embryo events in the womb of the universe.

The seventy-eight wafers of liquid crystal formed a chart of the human Imperium, its champions and its foes. Each image pulsed animatedly, responsive to the currents of fortune, to the ebb and flow of events, to the forces of cleansing light and of dark malevolent corrupt insanity.

Jaq rifled through the pack to find the card he used to signify himself: the black-robed High Priest, enthroned, gesturing with a hammer.

His very own face frowned back at him doubtfully as if a homunculus was imprisoned in the card, a mute model of himself. This homunculus could not speak to him. It could not *foretell* the future. It could only show, in conjunction with other cards.

Placing the High Priest on a table, Jaq slipped into a routine of slow rhythmic breathing to attune his psychic sense. Almost of their own accord his hands shuffled the rest of the pack. He felt the cards vibrate.

'Thee I invoke, oh our Emperor,' he prayed, the formula glowing neon in his mind's eye, 'that thou wilt infuse these cards this hour; that thereby I may obtain true insight of things hidden, to thy glory and to the salvation of humanity-'

Shutting his eyes, he dealt a star of five cards.

Then he looked at what he had dealt.

The Emperor card was present, the Emperor card itself! In its position, it marked the outcome of the matter. Consequently, this was a divination of deep significance.

Yet that card lay reversed. The grim blind face, locked into the prosthetic throne, confronted Jaq upside-down.

This orientation could signify confusion amongst the Emperor's enemies. Equally it could signal obstructions and contradictions of a more frustrating sort.

And, of course, it might signify compassion as opposed to stern authority. Though how could *that* be the case?

The other cards were Harlequin, Inquisitor, Daemon and Hulk – one each from the suits of Discordia and Mandatio, and two major arcana trumps, both menacing.

The Hulk was a towering, ruined spacecraft adrift in black void, wreathed with... spewed-out gases?

The Daemon was curiously amorphous. Usually the Daemon in that card snarled with bared fangs and reached out with wicked claws. Now it showed no face at all. Its arms were many, a writhing knot of arms more like tentacles. Sniffing, Jaq detected a cloacal effluvium of sewers.

The Mandatio suite concerned wealth, stability, the burdens of government. The Knight of Mandatio was a cloaked inquisitor brandishing a power sword and his face was that of... Harq Obispal.

Jaq heard the crackling hum of the sword, smelled ozone. Right now the real Obispal was on the verge of departing from Stalinvast with a flourish of trumpets and hallelujahs. He would fly through the warp to any one of a million worlds. Why should Jaq encounter Obispal again in the near future? In all likelihood Jaq would presently run across some other inquisitor entirely. Obispal was simply uppermost in his mind because of that particular inquisitor being on the eye-screen. Thus the card conformed.

The truth might be that Obispal had left unfinished business behind on Stalinvast. Which would be unfortunate. It was exactly what Jaq was here to watch out for.

The Discordia suit comprised enemies and aliens and fiends. In this particular Discordia card pranced a tall, lithe, deadly Harlequin of the eldar race. A clownish mosaic of shifting hues attired the Harlequin. A rainbow coxcomb crested its head. Faintly Jaq heard a skirling of wild, unearthly music. However, this Harlequin didn't wear the customary mask. Nor was its bare face the ethereally lovely, angular visage of that alien species. This particular Harlequin's face was purely human.

A man's face. The chin was slightly hooked, the nose long and jutting, the eyes of piercing green. The Harlequin man pursed his lips and sucked in his cheeks not in a cadaverous but in a speculative, mischievous style which nevertheless bespoke some fatal intent.

As Jaq leaned over this Discordia card, deep in concentration, the image smirked.

Its lips moved.

'The hydra is kindled,' Jaq heard the false Harlequin whisper inside his head.

Jaq recoiled, gesturing a hex.

Cards could not speak, only show!

Cards could not talk to the divinator. Yet this one had whispered to Jaq. Could the Tarot cards become a channel for daemonic possession? Could a divinator be invaded? Surely not while the Emperor's spirit imbued his Tarot!

Yet the image had addressed Jaq as if some outside force had been able to intervene in his holy trance through the agency of that Discordia card, hacking into the pack.

To what purpose? To alert him? To mock him?

A 'hydra' was no known daemon of the warp. It was... yes, some legendary creature from the distant prehistory of Earth. A many-headed monster: yes, that was it. If you cut off one head of a hydra, two others promptly sprouted in its place. A hydra might be a deal more plaguesome to purge than even genestealers... Surely one or two stealers must remain even after Obispal's campaign? Didn't the man care about that possibility? Off he was going, in triumph, almost as soon as could be.

Jaq refused to be distracted. He peered at the tangled convulsions in the Daemon card. He could see no definable head, nothing which could be stricken off even with doleful consequences.

The card squirmed, flickering within itself as if aflame, although all the tongues of fire were cold. The longer he looked, the more the tentacles seemed to stretch out thinly into obscure distance as if there was no limit to their elasticity. New tentacles writhed and grew, variously greasy and glassy and jelly-like.

If this was the hydra of which the false Harlequin spoke, then *what was it?* Where was it? And why?

Jaq considered the disposition of the star of cards. Ought he to deal out a full corona pattern? A full corona might tell him far more than he needed to know – so much that he would end up by knowing nothing precise at all.

Meh'Lindi peered past him. Her fingernail stabbed swiftly at the Harlequin.

'Who's he? He looks rather... delicious.'

Wearing that eldar body, the mysterious figure was indeed configured like Meh'Lindi herself.

'Or is that just an eldar wearing a human mask?' she asked.

'No, it's a human all right – I'm sure of it. I believe he has just left me his calling card.'

Meh'Lindi knew all about calling cards. Many assassins would plant their own special card from the Adeptio suit in an intended victim's vicinity, to announce to that target his impending and unavoidable doom. The condemned person might be well advised to commit suicide rather than await whatever fate the assassin was designing.

'Mark his face well, Meh'Lindi.'

'I already have, Jaq.'

Such was her instinct, such was her duty. But above and beyond... did that enemy face perversely *appeal* to her?

What did the word 'delicious' mean to someone who
cared not a fig about cuisine? Something to rend, to consume, to digest in her stomach acids? Meh'Lindi had once
mentioned a legendary assassin who swallowed a rebel
governor's young son whole so that the child should seem
to vanish into thin air. That heroine of assassins had dis-
tended her jaws and throat and belly by means of
polymorphine, like a python. Disguised and obese, she
had waddled away.

'Huh! You're missing out on the carnival.'

Harq Obispal and entourage were stomping towards
their many-buttressed ship. Trumpets wailed, acrobats
somersaulted, torn beasts died; some bejewelled ladies
blew kisses, perhaps only so as to kindle the jealousy of
rival ladies or of their own lords.

'I don't suppose you've seen many such splendid sights,'
Googol teased. 'You, from your pokey little caverns.'

'Splendid?' queried the squat. 'Do you rate such a farrago
as splendour? You with your eyes forever trained on the
gloomy sludge of the warp?'

'Touché!' the Navigator applauded.

Troubled, Jaq gathered the star of cards back into the
deck, feeling them grow inert and passive as he did so. He
picked up the wafer of liquid crystal which represented
himself and stared at the High Priest's face, his own, wishing that his own image could confide in him in the same
way that the Harlequin had.

And in a sense it could. For as Jaq gazed he sank deeply
into himself and he dreamed back to his youth...

A time of hope, a time of horror. Jaq was born on Xerxes
Quintus, fifth planet of a harsh white sun. Xerxes Quintus
was a world of farmers, fisherfolk – and of mutants and
wild psykers.

The planet had only been recontacted a century earlier.
For thousands of years, Xerxes Quintus had gone its own
course, ignorant of the Imperium. Memories of star-travel
had mutated into bizarre myths. Human beings had begun
to mutate too, in body and in mind.

Eyeless men could see through psychic eyes. The dumb could talk without tongues. The mouthless could feed through their skins. More sinister changelings became channels for daemons which walked the land in those host bodies, twisting and melting their anatomy into devilish monstrosities with scales and horns, claws and feelers – until the possessed bodies finally fell apart, until the vestiges of corrupted mind were sucked away as spirit-meat for those parasites from outside of normality.

Quintus was paradise and hell at once. Paradise was the lush coastal farms and the fishing islands where normal human beings preserved their traditions and their shapes by expelling all those who were born changed or who changed subsequently. Or by killing them.

Always, as worms out of an apple, as maggots out of meat, mutants emerged and fled – if they could – into the hinterland. There, if fertile, those mutants mated to make more and even stranger mutants.

The coastal inhabitants did not worship a god who might safeguard them in their own true image. Instead, they reviled the Lord of Change. Every tenth day, in special temples of execration, they cursed ritually and shouted abuse, before turning their attentions back to their beloved bountiful sea and soil.

Theirs was a religion of damning exorcisms. Their language, hardly even a bastard grandchild of Imperial Gothic, was salted with oaths, the whole intention being to drive their meddling malicious deity and its minions as far away as possible. They even expressed affection obscenely, as if to purge their relationships of any possible betraying taint. Neighbours always raised a child so as to exonerate parents from the need to reject their own offspring.

Recontact brought an Imperial expedition which admired the farming and fisheries potential of Quintus. One day, this planet could become an agricultural export world. If so, the Imperium could convert the barren fourth world, Quartus, into a valuable mining planet, its population fed from Quintus.

The expedition also found the coastal population to be a potentially fertile field where the Imperial cult could take root. Was not the God-Emperor the great guardian against change? Missionaries and preachers strove to switch the focus of hatred from the Lord of Change to the products of change dwelling in the interior. Ideally, the Imperium ought to seek to supplant the blasphemous Quintan language with Imperial Gothic; though this was no doubt too major a task.

Both of Jaq's parents were adepts of genetics. The Imperium had assigned them for life to Quintus, to assist in its uplift. Even in rapport with his significator card, Jaq only dimly remembered his mother and father. He recalled smiles and fondling and sensed that his parents were happy to conceive him and care for him. Imperials both, they did not follow the local custom of farming him out to a neighbour. Indeed, they seemed to cherish him. Certainly – from what little he was later told – both parents were fervent in their work and their loyalty to the Imperium. How proud they might have been to see him now, risen so high above their status; how fulfilled. But they hadn't conceived him as a duty, merely to increase the number of Imperials on the planet. Nor with a curse, as was the local habit. Rather, in happiness.

Vain happiness.

Jaq was barely two years old when daemon-possessed psykers slaughtered both his parents during a scientific probe into the wilderness. Jaq was raised thereafter as an orphan in a mission school.

Ultimately the scrupulous, strait-laced upbringing had left him distrusting the strictures of rigid minds. Oh, he remembered honeyed, frail evenings walking in the walled grounds of the orphanage. The tulip trees, the bowers. He remembered games and infrequent feasts. He likewise remembered punishments, usually caused by asking awkward questions.

'Magister, if the Quintans curse their god, won't they also curse the God-Emperor?'

'Beware, boy!'

'The Quintans don't have the voc-voc-vocabulary to adore our Emperor, do they?'

'Draco, you will write out the *Codex Fidelitatis* forty times, then you at least will possess the correct vocabulary!'

In his heart, the boy Jaq vowed vengeance against daemons and against psykers who were conduits for daemons for stealing his parents from him and bestowing upon him the honour of being raised by missionaries.

He learned piety, dedication. He learned restraint. Some of that restraint was protective camouflage for passions which he both felt welling within himself and denied.

When he was twelve, his psychic sense blossomed and he realised that he himself was one of those whom he had learned to loathe, taught both by his personal tragedy and by the missionaries.

He would lie abed in the darkened dormitory, sensing a sloshing sea of human and mutant existence surrounding him. In that sea twists and clumps of phosphorescence marked the minds of other psykers. Many displayed the malign green of corruption, the verdigris of spiritual gangrene. Some swelled bloatedly, streaked with red, as power from the deeps infused them. From such, tendrils descended into the abyss.

Indeed, threads dangled down from all life, psychic and non-psychic alike. Filaments linked living beings with the seeds of themselves in the deep-down ooze. Up some of these tendrils the substance and energy of the ooze could travel parasitically. This material was hostile to life yet also greedy for life and jealous of life. This energy was hungry and destructive, bestowing power upon a person but invariably injuring that person by virtue of the power it bestowed.

The abyssal ooze wasn't exactly like mud at the bottom of an ocean. As he peered through his mind's eye it seemed rather that the deepest water changed into a different type of material which sank down and down forever, tossed by its own fierce storms, swayed by its own currents that were

swifter than any ocean's – until far off elsewhere there sur-
faced from this *immaterium* yet other seas of life, which
were other worlds.

Potent creatures swam in the dark sub-ocean in between
worlds. These creatures should be distrusted, not desired.
Yet oh so many sparks of phosphorescence yearned for the
potency of the denizens of that other realm, or else signalled obliviously to those creatures, blinking their little
lamps – to summon the equivalent of sharks, or krakens of
twisted intelligence.

One evening Jaq perceived a material vessel emerging
from the ultimate deep. The vessel was diving upward
towards his world. Jaq understood that this must be a
warp-ship, protected against the forces in that ocean.

By straining his vision he glimpsed far off a beacon of
white radiance by which that warp-ship strove to navigate.
His heart swelled with joy and gratitude to the Emperor on
Terra, whose mind was that lamp.

Already, like flowers turning towards the sun or like bees
seeking pollen, in the wastelands of his world and in the
ooze below – in that deep dark underocean of power and
Chaos – Jaq sensed attentions focusing upon him tenta-
tively; and he blanked his own white spark. He hid it.

A white spark, yes. Not curdled, nor stained by influences from below.

Few other sparks seemed white. Was that because those
couldn't blank themselves, as he had just done? They
attracted pollutants as a light attracts filthy bugs.

'Surely, magister, the rogue psykers could shine whitely
if they could learn how to shade themselves?'

'What heretical paradox is this, Draco? You will commit
to memory the *Codex Impuritatis!*'

And so, resentfully, he learned concepts that could stand
him in good stead. In a sense, unknowingly, he had
already entered the kindergarten of the Inquisition.

Imperial preachers were haranguing the coastal populace to destroy... people like Jaq himself, people who
would become polluted through no real fault of their own,

in many cases. Or so it seemed to Jaq. His missionary teachers sternly announced the message that deviation from normality was a sin against the Emperor.

Surely the real enemy must be those warped, fierce, cunning entities which feasted on vulnerable human beings who shone their lights unshaded.

If he, Jaq – being a child of genetically wholesome parents – had begun to shine this light too, might not something in the nature of the world of Xerxes Quintus itself be to blame?

'Perhaps, magister, the water or the white sunlight poisons people so that mutants are born?'

'Perhaps! Expand your thesis, Draco.'

'But the really grotesque and venomous distortions of the human form only occur after daemons–'

'Daemons, daemons? Do not dote on daemons! Do not even think of daemons. Daemons are forbidden effluvia of the human phantasy, turned sick and evil. This must be stamped out.'

'After daemons possess those souls who, as it were, shine a light.'

'A light? What light?'

'The psyker light... as it were. Maybe this arises naturally within a person, naturally and purely? Are there not astropaths and other psykers in the service of the Imperium? Could not all psykers shelter within its fold?'

'Faugh! Purify yourself, Draco.'

He was whipped. So as to purge him of wicked curiosity? Or so as to test him?

He brooded for weeks. Finally he nerved himself and confessed about his visions.

After the senior missionary had interrogated him, the man folded pleased hands across his belly. The gleam in the missionary's eye suggested that Jaq's account of how much he could perceive– 'Even to a glimpse of the Emperor's beacon?' – and of how he could hide his own spark of phosphorescence, meant that this lad was singularly blessed.

This in turn would bless the mission and its master. Smug devious bastard, thought Jaq, of that missionary.

A few months later a shuttle carried Jaq up to a great black ship circling in orbit. He left the sun Xerxes behind forever.

A DIFFERENT SHIP was departing from a different world. Lifting from the spaceport of Vasilariov, Harq Obispal's shark-shaped ship rapidly diminished to the size of a bug, of a sparkle of dust in the sky. Then it was gone, on its journey of several weeks through normal planetary space to that zone on the rim of the system far from the worlds and moons where it could dive into the warp.

On impulse, Jaq slipped the High Priest card into a pocket then slid the other Tarot cards back into their box and wrapped the box again in its sheath of skin.

The skin was a souvenir of an exorcism which had, in common with most trouncings of daemons, both succeeded – and failed. The daemon was defeated, but the daemon's living vessel had been destroyed, not redeemed.

How could the outcome be otherwise?

Yet Jaq feared that for all its power the Imperium was slowly succumbing to the attentions of aliens, of renegades, of daemons. Each Imperial victory seemed to involve the crushing of some part of the vital substance of the Imperium itself, of humanity itself.

How could it be otherwise? Fire must fight fire, must it not?

Thus that dappled skin, peeled from a mutant, both reminded him of how he had been orphaned and reproached him too.

'There, but for the grace of the Emperor,' he muttered, 'go I.'

'Where?' asked Grimm brightly.

Jaq was pleased that his companion had been perturbed by the trashing of Vasilariov and the evisceration of other cities, destroyed in order to save them. He valued the squat's presence and his occasional sallies of sarcasm – just as, in a way, he valued Googol's pose of disdain. Fanatics such as Obispal were invaluable; yet they were akin to bulls set loose in china shops. Certainly the Imperium embraced a million china shops and more; much crockery could be wasted. However, a sceptic could often see what rigid enthusiasts overlooked.

'Why, here,' Jaq told Grimm. 'Right here, wrapping up this little box. In different circumstances this might have been my skin.'

The little man stared at Jaq, bemused, then simply retorted, 'Huh.'

Perhaps the concept was indeed too complex.

FIVE

'THERE SHE IS!' cried Grimm.

Meh'Lindi was waiting inside an odour bar in the grotesque, extravagant concourse of the station where elevated trains left for Kefalov and hives beyond. The walls were a collage of tens of thousands of reptile skulls carved in gloomy green jade and malachite, as if this place was a saurian necropolis. Pillars were massive columns of vertebrae.

Of the nearby cities, Kefalov alone had remained unpolluted and unwrecked. Now, a week after Obispal's departure, traffic between the partly ravaged capital and Kefalov seemed to have returned almost to normal. Planetary defence troopers patrolled, scanning arrivals. Licensed hawkers were circulating, braying the merits of spiced sausages containing only real animal protein – so they claimed.

Perhaps truly. Bearing in mind the recent huge casualty statistics, their sausages probably contained minced human flesh. Suchlike suspicions did not deter prospective travellers from paying the high prices asked for such authentic delicacies; maybe even encouraged brisker sales. Such train travellers, of course, would have funds; most Vasilariovites never left their reef-hive during a lifetime...

Two burly bodyguards stood by Meh'Lindi, eyeing anyone who so much as glanced in her direction. The sleek, expressionless woman wore a silvery skintight jumpsuit which almost appeared to have been sprayed onto her limbs, not donned. A score of fleshy-hued silk scarves fluttered from strategic points, acting as veils. The guards were clad in tough green leather from some jungle beast and draped in weapons. They had no idea that the woman they escorted was far more lethal than ever they could hope to be. Jaq had hired these bodyguards to lend credence to Meh'Lindi's role as a mistress, of perverse tastes, a tourist of disaster through the savaged and demolished sectors where a degree of anarchy still ruled. She had been on the prowl for days, though it seemed highly unlikely, to say the least, that she would come across the Harlequin man by chance... As soon hope to catch a particular fish by jumping at random into an ocean. But that individual had chosen to draw himself to Jaq's attention once already, had he not?

An hour earlier in the Emerald Suite, Jaq's comm-unit had bleeped.

In jumblespeech Meh'Lindi had reported, 'I've just seen the Harlequin man. I'm following.'

Jaq promptly consulted the eye-screen. Several spy-flies were tailing Meh'Lindi.

She was on a balcony level of an arcade which must specialise in manufacturing small components, and was still doing so. Baggy women and runty, raggy children slaved alongside their menfolk in a veritable honeycomb of family workshops, tier upon tier of plasteel caves linked by ladders and gantries. Swarf from lathes lay thick on the floor below. Wading through this, apace: a man taller than any of the artisans.

He wore a pastel-hued cloak and cockaded purple hat quite out of keeping with his surroundings. He attracted whistles and jeers and minor missiles, such as nuts and bolts.

Meh'Lindi's rented, streetwise duo guaranteed her much more anonymity; as to her motives, they exhibited no interest whatever.

Jaq had willed a spy-fly to home on the man, whose face he recognized from the Tarot card. Thus, while Meh'Lindi padded in pursuit with her mute chaperones, Jaq was also tracking the Harlequin man. At the Kefalov station the dandified fellow had boarded the transjungle transport, while Meh'Lindi stayed. The accompanying spy-fly clung to the ceiling of the carriage, surveying the Harlequin man until the train carried the spy-fly beyond its transmitting range. Until then, its quarry sat twiddling his thumbs and not quite smirking.

Jaq knew that he must give chase; he was virtually being challenged to do so. The Harlequin man had invaded Jaq's Imperial Tarot with the slickness of a lashworm snatching some flesh from a passer-by, and now that damned individual was contemptuously trailing his cloak for Jaq to follow. This, Jaq did not care for one little bit. Yet to ignore such provocation would surely be a greater folly than heeding it. Leaving Googol to safeguard their equipment, he had hurried with Grimm to the station to meet up with Meh'Lindi.

THE BAR WAS heady with attar of jungle parasite-blooms and other alien aromas that tweaked at Jaq's senses, causing mild wobblings of perception and confusions of taste and smell. Some of the odours were hallucinogenic and patrons wore a glazed look.

Perhaps those individuals were still shell-shocked by the ravaging of their city – of which Jaq and the squat had seen, and smelled, evidence aplenty en route to this rendezvous. Equally, the customers of the odour bar might be adopting a glassy-eyed demeanour so as to avoid seeming to scrutinise Meh'Lindi in what might be construed as an impertinent fashion.

'Sir Draco!' one of the guards greeted Jaq.

The bodyguard eyed Grimm as though the squat was some pet monkey of this merchant and ought to be on a lead. The mood-shifting scents were allowing sentiments to slip out.

'Huh! You can scoot off now,' cried the little man. 'Scram and skedaddle.'

Darting Grimm a cautioning glance, Jaq paid off the hired guards in local voronovs, plus a retainer so that they would continue on call if need be.

As soon as the two men had departed, in the direction of a food vendor, Jaq said to Meh'Lindi: 'Of course, he *let* you see him. He put himself in your way deliberately.'

She nodded. 'Question is, Jaq, dare you ignore this bait?'

'Probably not. I hardly think the aim can be to lure us somewhere to murder us.'

'Still,' Meh'Lindi said wistfully, 'the Harlequin man has the look of an assassin. Maybe even... a renegade assassin? Surely there can be no such animal!'

'Who employs him, eh?' asked Grimm. 'Or does he employ himself?'

She shrugged.

'And don't you fancy him just a jot?'

To which mischievous gambit, Meh'Lindi glared. 'Perhaps Obispal left him behind,' she suggested. 'Maybe the intention is to humiliate you somehow, Jaq? I did betray our presence to Obispal.'

'And splendidly so indeed!' agreed the squat.

'Be quiet,' said Jaq. 'If Obispal decided that a secret inquisitor was watching him, surely he'd be a fool to seek vengeance – especially when he hardly put a foot wrong. I think the idea has to be to show me something, in case I miss it.'

'Yeah, what is the hydra?' said Grimm.

'I find this somewhat galling, don't you?' Jaq asked his pretend-mistress. 'To be manipulated!'

Really, they had no other option but to board the next train bound for Kefalov.

As THE PASSENGER capsule whisked through the crystalline tube above the blurred green hell of jungle, Jaq scrutinised his personal Tarot card and recalled his trip to Terra as a boy aboard the Black Ship.

Only en route had he understood the true implications.

To his keen senses, that cavernous crowded ship had been awash with psychic turmoil – despite the dampening field projected by a suppressor adept linked in to arcane machinery. This deadening field was subtly nauseating, a psychic equivalent of the stale, rebreathed air. In spite of it, Jaq easily read raw talent, hope, muted dread; and on the part of some of the officers boredom mixed with disgust, on the part of others fierce dedication, occasionally mixed with regret.

The suppressor field seemed to work perversely on Jaq, who already knew how to hide his own light. He hadn't read moods before, but now almost everyone on board appeared to broadcast sludgy feelings.

Stray whispers in a hundred distant-cousin tongues twittered through the ship, as if voices were trying to inform him of his fate, the ghost echoes from a million previous passengers, ten million down the centuries that this ship had been in service.

Of course, the ship was rife with ordinary gossip too, in various versions of Imperial Gothic, some halting, some fluent, in a waveband of accents from mellow to harsh, sibilant to guttural.

'A great fleet of ships like this tours the galaxy–'

'They trawl for promising psykers–'

'Wayward, twisted psykers are hunted down ruthlessly on a host of worlds. They're preached against and purged. The Inquisition scourges them. Planetary governors destroy them–'

'At the very same time fresh, uncorrupted psykers are being harvested. They're sent to Earth in Black Ships such as this–'

Psychic talent was the floodgate by which the malevolent lunacy of powers in the warp could invade and ravage worlds, could corrupt the human race into polluted slaves of evil.

Yet psychic talent was also the hope of the future, of a galaxy in which the human race, free and strong, could defend itself mentally.

Meanwhile, the God-Emperor must defend all his scattered multi-billions of subjects by ruthless sacrificial force. For a terrible equation prevailed: that which would ultimately save the human race – the evolution of a higher consciousness – was, in its long and vulnerable gestation, exactly what could so easily destroy humanity by letting it be corrupted, polluted, warped and ruined. Only the utter ruthlessness of one ravaged, machine-sustained tyrant and the overstretched forces of his fierce yet fragile Imperium kept the human race tottering along its fraying tightrope.

'Sacrifice–'

Sacrifice on his own part, yes indeed. Was not the Emperor tormented and exhausted by his own ceaseless vigilance?

'Sacrifice–'

But also by the sacrificing of his own subjects...

Of the gathered talents on board the Black Ship, a fraction – the brightest and the best – were destined to be recruited as psykers in the service of the Imperium. Most of this fraction would be soul-bound to the Emperor for their own protection.

'Soul-binding is agony–'

The ghastly mental ritual would burn out optic nerves and leave those chosen psykers blind forever.

'Sacrifice–'

Many of those on board who were of merely ordinary calibre would serve by yielding up their vital force to feed the Emperor's insatiable soul, so that he could continue to be a watchful beacon and protector. After suitable lengthy training for the sacrifice, these psykers would be consumed

within a few scant weeks or months, drained of their spirits until they died.

'SACRIFICE!'

Which did not pleasure the Emperor. Oh no. Each soul
he devoured lanced him with anguish, torment, it was
rumoured. Such was the cruel equation by which humanity survived in a hostile universe.

'SACRIFICE!'

No passenger on board the Black Ship was older than
twenty standard years. Many were as junior as Jaq. One girl
in particular... he refused to think of her right now. As the
ship's officers administered tests and counselled their
human cargo, it became evident that almost all were going
to their deaths.

Worthy deaths, necessary deaths; but still, deaths.

In what manner – other than its worthiness – was this
fate different than being slaughtered on one's home
world?

The difference was...

'SACRIFICE! TO THE GOD AND TO HUMANITY!'

Some young psykers wept. Some prayed. Some raged.
Those who raged were restrained. In later life, Jaq understood that this particular Black Ship had been carrying a
higher percentage of individualists hailing from less long-
standingly pious worlds, than most such shipments. Yet
many of the young passengers adopted an air of cool
nobility, even of passionate complicity in their own fate;
these were praised. Devout dedication was the desidera-
tum for soul-sacrifice.

Death laid a numbing hand on Jaq's heart. He bargained
in his soul with fate, promising to dedicate his life to
Imperial service without scruple – if only a life was left to
him to dedicate.

Jaq still clearly remembered his reprieve and how
annoyed he had been not to have foreseen it.

'You can blank out your light, boy,' the goitrous officer
had told him, almost respectfully. 'Without training,
that's rare. You'll certainly be recruited. I suspect you

won't need soul-binding. I may well be addressing a
future inquisitor–'

To hunt down those who resembled him, yet who had
gone astray? To purge his – cousins – who had been twisted
askew? To destroy his diseased psychic kin without a qualm?

Yes.

Jaq had spent the remainder of the voyage feeling
exalted, yet pitiful. Sad for the bulk of his travelling companions; glad that his own destiny was different. His
fellow travellers saw him praying to the Emperor, as he had
been schooled to. They presumed that Jaq was honing his
soul serenely in expectation of sacrifice. His example had a
calming effect on others. Already he was mentally a secret
agent, privy to hidden knowledge.

'YET SEEMINGLY THE Harlequin man can pierce my cover,' Jaq
murmured under his breath. 'What manner of man must
he be?' He tucked his Tarot card away.

Presently the city of Kefalov loomed ahead. From a distance Kefalov was a grey brain bereft of a skull, ten
kilometres high at least. Its tiers of convoluted ridges
would be harder than any bone. As the train neared, great
windows, air-vents and portals became visible. Seeming to
be merely speckles and punctures at first, actually they
were as tall as the highest trees.

A stream of military ram-jets flew from one such vent,
into a sky the hue of bruised blood in a badly beaten body.
Dirty clouds glowered and snake-tongues of lightning
flickered. Soon bombs would rip the surging vegetation
somewhere, punching holes which would rot and quicken
with parasitic blooms.

The petrified brain smoked and steamed lazily, venting
effluvia. Kefalov leaked effluent into the jungle, poisoning
the vicinity, forming a deep sickly vaporous swamp over
which the train raced, insulated in its tube.

SCARCELY HAD THEY left the station concourse than 'Rogue
Trader Draco' was voxed to a public comm-screen.

From the viewplate in the open booth *that face* looked out at Jaq, eyes twinkling like ice in chartreuse, a playful and predatory smile puckering the lips.

'Zephro Carnelian at your service!' announced the Harlequin man.

This call just had to be an act of purest derision, a flaunting of how well this enemy had foretold Jaq's actions – or even was psychically alert to Jaq's whereabouts.

Enemy?

Most likely. Stalinvast couldn't very well be hosting a second secret inquisitor, could it? Surely Proctor Firenze would have advised Jaq of the presence of another Malleus man? If Baal Firenze *knew*; if he knew!

This mysterious man had penetrated Jaq's Tarot. He was dangerous, dangerous. He was playing with Jaq, as though Jaq was a card in his own paw.

'Do you imagine you have some business with me?' Jaq asked the image non-committally. Meanwhile, his mind raced.

With a giggle, Carnelian tipped his foolish foppish cockaded hat to Jaq.

'Business? Oh yes: *hydra* business. A terrible menace, hmm? Thought I'd draw your attention to it. Good specimen here in the undercity. Fancy a spot of big game hunting with me?' The man spoke Imperial Gothic with no trace of the local husky accent, but rather with a kind of spooky affectation – almost, thought Jaq, an alien affectation.

At Jaq's back, Meh'Lindi and Grimm warily eyed loitering beggars, pedlars, riff-raff. Naturally, passers-by eyed Meh'Lindi. In particular two small groups of vigilantes wearing diversely blazoned combat fatigues seemed to be sizing up Jaq's trio, either with a view to offering their services or with less savoury intent. One group, decorated with motifs of gaping, dagger-toothed mouths, had tattooed their shaved skulls with leering lips and a view of the brain tissue below. The other, adorned with green toad-badges, wore steel skullcaps piled with simulated excrement. Or perhaps their own hair, waxed solid and stained, coiled through a hole in the cap.

Tension brooded in the air. Décor was at once oppressive and lurid. Brown entrails seemed to bulge from the walls, sprayed with pious mottos. Dingy pillars were subtly phallic. It wasn't so much that Kefalov appeared already to be a more sordid city than the capital, as that this particular city hadn't been devastated at all. Thus aggressions and desires bubbled and brooded, as yet unpurged.

If the brain was letting off steam and smoke into the sky while filth flowed down its flanks, it remained a pressure vessel of packed humanity, a vat of frustrations, oppressions and twisted longings.

'Do you fancy potting a fine trophy, sir inquisitor? Oops! My apologies, honourable *trader*.' Carnelian chortled hectically.

Jaq peered at the face in the screen – especially at the eyes – for signs of a daemon rooted within the man's psyche. Those eyes seemed rational and unhaunted. Was this clownish farrago all a pretence?

'Whereabouts in the undercity?' asked Jaq.

'Why, everywhereabouts. That's the nature of the beast.'

Jaq made a guess. 'And I suppose the death of so many millions – the psychic shockwave – conjured up this new abomination, whatever it is?'

'You're catching on, Sir Jaq.'

'Why should you tell me? And what do you have to do with this hydra? Well?'

'Ah, tetchy, tetchy... *You're* the adept investigator! Must I dot every eye and cross every tee?'

'Damn you, Carnelian, what's your game?'

'Do call me Zephro! Please! Shall I show you some of the pieces and let you try to guess the rules? Pray to visit sub-level five in the Kropotnik district of this fair burg.'

Meh'Lindi hissed. The hesitancy of the vigilantes seemed only due now to mutual dislike, which would soon resolve itself one way or another. Jaq quickly cut the connection.

* * *

POXED, DISFIGURED SCAVENGERS scuttled across hillocks of debris which rained into this underworld from a low steel sky by way of chutes and grilles.

Once upon a time this plasteel cavern with its ranks of mighty support pillars must have seemed spacious, voluminous, gargantuan. Now it was merely extensive horizontally, connecting to other such caverns through vast arches in its barrier walls a couple of kilometres distant. In places the dross almost brushed the roof. Feeble illumination came from phosphorescent lichens mottling the ceiling and from the furnaces of the many tribes of recyclers whose smelting activities and whose upward export-trade in reusable elements to higher zones of the city alone prevented their home-space from filling as full as a constipated bowel.

Perhaps these inhabitants of the underworld were slowly losing the struggle. On the other hand, nourished on the synthdiet they must exchange for their impure ingots, maybe the tribes were breeding fast enough to fend off being buried alive in swarf and shavings and other detritus.

Just as a queen bee unwittingly hosts tiny mites that have specialised to graze on her mouth parts, so at the bottommost end of the city did Kefalov house its recycler and scavenger tribes. Nay, they were useful – some might say vital – to the economy of the city.

They weren't such people as would, or could, send reports to the administration high above, not even of anything monstrously peculiar. Given their foreshortened horizons, and their own abnormality, how could they really think in terms of something as being significantly abnormal?

They scuttled like crabs. They burrowed like worms. They rolled balls of wire about like dung-beetles. Jaq suspected that their recycling and export trade had practically become instinctive. What did these know of the rest of the city, let alone of planet or galaxy? As much as the mite on the bee's mouth parts knew about the rest of her body, or about the throbbing hive.

'How must it seem,' Jaq asked, 'to live one's whole life
down here?'

He already knew the answer. Blessed are the ignorant;
cursed are those who know too much.

'At least it's warm enough down here,' remarked Grimm.

From the catwalk they surveyed this choked cavern
which lay beneath even the underbelly of the city. Furnaces
winked like fireflies. Holding a lens to one eye, Jaq
scanned tunnel mouths that were almost buried.

Sprawling out from one tunnel, glassy branching tentacles pulsed as if they were huge muscles dissected out of
the body of a leviathan.

As soon as Jaq noticed those translucent, almost immaterial shapes, their extent appalled him. They wove across
the metallic dunes, submerging themselves like roots, sur-
facing again, twitching, throbbing sluggishly. Tendrils
coiled and uncoiled, seeming to exist one moment yet not
the next.

What did the scavengers think of this intrusion into their
domain by a rubbery multi-octopus? The human crabs
scuttled clear of its feelers.

Or should that be: *their* feelers? Jaq couldn't tell whether
the hydra was single or plural, connected or disconnected.
Or how much more of it existed out of sight, packed
within the tunnel complexes.

Those tentacles did not appear interested in trapping the
denizens of this underzone. Rather, the hydra seemed to be
waiting. Meanwhile, it signalled a menace that alarmed
Jaq's psychic sense.

'Yuck,' said Grimm, as he too became aware of it. 'It's like
those pesky jelly strings in eggs that stick between your teeth
– really monstrous ones from an egg the size of a mountain!
It's like umbilical cords and nothing but. Yuck, yuck.'

'Shall we see how it reacts to laser and plasma?' suggested Jaq.

'Oh yes, let's slice it and fry it.'

Meh'Lindi sniffed the stale, hot, ferrous air like a fretful
horse.

The three headed along the catwalk, descended a rusty ladder on to the dunes of debris. They waded across until they reached a vantage point fifty metres short of the closest tentacle.

Jaq aimed his ormolu-inlaid laspistol and squeezed. Hot light leapt out from the damascened chromium steel nozzle in a dazzling silver thread. He drew the sliver of light across that limb of the hydra as if slicing cheese. He sliced and resliced. Severed portions writhed. Gobbets seemed to wink in and out of existence. Though chopped every which way, the whole tentacle squirmed towards where they stood as if still joined together, glued by some adhesive force from outside the normal universe.

'Plasma,' Jaq said to himself and switched weapons. The frontal hood of the plasma gun was gilded with safety runes. Ventilator holes in that hood doubled as the hollow pupils of slanting crimson eyes that focused faithfully on the chosen target, since a single discharge of super-heated plasma would completely exhaust the capacitor. A couple of minutes must pass before the accumulator vanes behind the hood re-energised the conductors and insulators. This target, though, was large and various.

The gun bounced in his grasp as incandescent energy leapt to evaporate a stretch of that many-times-severed, yet still tenacious limb. Its boiling substance sprayed across the dune beyond, lacquering the metallic hillock. A backwash of heated air caressed Jaq's face. He smelled the bitter fragrance of ablated chromium steel. And he sensed... eagerness.

Of a sudden, the Harlequin man sprang up from behind the dune beyond.

'Yes, yes!' he shrieked, capering and applauding. 'Shoot it to smithereens!'

Jaq jammed the discharged plasma gun away and was about to aim his laser.

Blessed are the ignorant.

But not if they are inquisitors!

'Meh'Lindi...'

'Yes, Jaq, I'll take him for you.'

'Unharmed,' he called after her.

She had already started down the scree of debris in pursuit.

'Or reasonably unharmed!'

He need not have bothered.

SIX

ONCE MORE THE turbulent bilious jungle rushed by beneath the plascrystal train-tube.

Jaq said patiently, 'Let's recap what happened just once more.'

In truth he felt far from patient. Vitali Googol had failed to answer vox messages sent from Kefalov; again and again, no reply from the Navigator. This enigma demanded their return as soon as possible. Jaq felt extremely irked to be manoeuvred thus – in addition to the fury he felt on Meh'Lindi's behalf because of the way she had been used.

Her emotions, her nervous system, tampered with! She who could transform herself by force of will into a passable semblance of a genestealer. She who could kill with a single fingertip. For her to be subjected to the whimsical will of a clown! To be twisted, as it were, around Carnelian's little finger: that was abominable.

The assassin said softly, 'I request permission to commit exemplary suicide. I'm dishonoured.'

Jaq sensed the distress behind the expressionless face
and the profundity of her request.

Not so Grimm, apparently. He thumped his fists on his
knees. 'Huh,' he jeered. 'Exemplary suicide, indeed? What's
that? Suicide that sets us an example of useful behaviour?
Such as a solo death-charge against a whole renegade
army? A wrestle to the death with Titans? An unarmed hike
across a deathworld? Huh.'

Meh'Lindi growled deep in her throat.

'Huh. Growl away. You'd be snapping, "Don't scorn
me!" – if you weren't so busy scorning yourself.' Maybe the
little man did understand, after all, and this was his rough
form of therapy. 'I don't scorn you, you know,' he added. 'I
could never scorn you, whatever happened.' Did the abhuman blush at this avowal?

'I request permission, nevertheless,' repeated Meh'Lindi,
still poker-faced.

Jaq sincerely hoped that she felt obliged to make such a
demand by her own code of honour rather than that the
demand was due to an abrupt, intrinsic sense of genuine
worthlessness. If the latter, then the Harlequin man would
really have hamstrung her, sowing self-sabotage within her
heart.

'Refused,' he told her firmly. 'I was to blame for ordering
you not to harm him. I tied your hands.'

Her eyes widened ever so slightly and Jaq regretted his
phrasing. Grimm smirked. Did he suppose that Jaq had
made a joke? Perhaps Grimm devoutly wished that joking
was possible in the circumstances; and would do his best
to make it so.

'Just tell me the facts again, Meh'Lindi. We may be overlooking some vital detail.'

Did not everyone, of necessity, overlook a large part of
what might be termed, for want of a better word, the truth?
Those scavengers living their entire lives in those caverns
underneath Kefalov were merely an extreme example of
segmented vision – their whole cosmos reduced to a few
cubic kilometres of debris. Even the rulers of this planet of

Stalinvast, luxuriating high up in their hives, must take a very partial view. Even an inquisitor such as Obispal suffered from – well, tunnel-vision.

Jaq struggled to see like the Emperor. He strove to think on a different plane of reason and insight. Only thus could he step outside of the present situation and hope to puzzle out the riddle of Zephro Carnelian – even while being forced to react predictably...

'I RUN TOWARDS CARNELIAN,' Meh'Lindi related. 'I run through the gap you blasted in the tentacle. Already the wounds sprout new growth. Each severed section seems alive independently. A few loose slices quiver with intent. As for the atomised material – well, I don't know. That is not ordinary matter.'

'I realise,' said Jaq.

The substance of the hydra must be partly normal matter and partly immaterium – partly the stuff of the warp, which was raw Chaotic fluid energy.

Where warp substance flowed into the world, daemons could follow presently.

'He darts away across the wasteland, cloak flapping. I chase. Bold Grimm tries to keep up but flounders.'

How Grimm basked in that word 'bold' – not from pride, Jaq sensed, but because to utter such a compliment Meh'Lindi could not be wholly filled with self-loathing.

'Carnelian is swift. "Follow and find!" he hoots. "Follow and find!" I follow. Far. Exactly in his footsteps, in case of some pitfall.

'Then a nest of tentacles writhes from the swarf, trapping my feet in a grip so strong. Even as I snatch for weapons, whip-tendrils seize my wrists and my neck. I am pulled down, spread out.

'Carnelian doubles back. I could crunch a tooth and spit death–'

'I forbade that, Meh'Lindi.'

'Yes. Now a tendril gags my mouth. He kneels by my head, grinning. I flex, but can't break free.

'He whispers in my ear: "This'll soon be everywhere on Stalinvast and when it's everywhere, ah then..."'

'I don't know whether he uses a slim feeler of the hydra – I can't see if he does – but I suppose he does. An immaterium feeler, used as a probe.

'He reaches into my head, into my brain. He finds the pleasure centre there. He stims it again and again. I am hating him, but I writhe in a betraying ecstasy, an agony of pleasure. Hating him still, I burn with utter delight.

'He says, "Sir Jaq's correct in his supposition that all the slaughter brought it to life – exactly like a conjuration."

'I am hardly able to think, only feel. But I gasp, "What is a hydra? What's its purpose?"

'"Dissect it and see," he says. "Cut it into little bits." I cannot block the stimming. If he stims me much more, I know that I may seek such stimming again, however unwillingly. I imagine killing him. I link that image to the hot ecstasy.

'We are taught to resist pain. We are taught to block pain. But to resist ecstasy: who would have thought of such a thing?

'He laughs and stops his probing of my pleasure centre. "Enough!" he cries. "Your little friend is coming clumpingly along. He can never – and Jaq can never – make you feel the way I have made you feel today. Should you ever wish them to! So remember the *ideal*. Remember Zephro Carnelian, master of the hydra!" And off he flees, out of sight.

'I am still moaning. Kindly Grimm cradles my head, as I cradled him. I snarl at him. He blasts me free. I roll away. The cut tentacles and whip-tendrils sprout anew, budding and stretching elastically. Grimm has collected Carnelian's hat, which fell off as I chased him. We return. I am disgraced. I lust. I beg permission.'

'No, Meh'Lindi. Carnelian is guilty of psychic rape. You aren't guilty, believe me.'

'Huh,' said Grimm, 'a different case from physical rape, which principally *hurts*, so I hear. Why should an enemy inflict *pleasure* on you?'

'To insult,' she replied distantly.

'To undermine you,' the squat said briskly. 'To make you doubt yourself – just as you are doubting now. I don't doubt you.'

Jaq frowned. Could that have been Carnelian's prime motive? Perhaps it was. Jaq felt that he was missing something. He strove to analyse events...

Carnelian's scheme couldn't have been to expose Jaq to whatever type of recycling of human bodies occurred in that underworld. True, the crab-men had begun to take an unhealthy interest in him once his companions had rushed off after the Harlequin man. He had needed to shoot two or three. By the time Grimm and Meh'Lindi returned, a tribal attack seemed imminent. However, they evaded this easily enough.

No, Carnelian definitely seemed uninterested in killing or injuring Jaq and companions; aside from the injury to Meh'Lindi's esteem, and Jaq's own, which might have been purely incidental...

Assuming that agents of Carnelian had interfered with the Navigator back in Stalinvast, therefore Vitali was probably still alive.

The Harlequin man had entered Meh'Lindi's head. After a fashion he had controlled her – not exactly in the way that a slavering daemon from the warp might control a victim.

Was his psychic ravishing of Jaq's assassin and his blithe withdrawal some kind of message that the true purpose of the hydra was a similar ravishment?

If so, why should he show Jaq this?

'Let me see his hat,' said Jaq.

Grimm tugged a crumpled purple handful from his pocket and restored some shape to the hat.

Jaq examined the cockade. It showed a naked infant seated upon a stylized cloud against a starry background, each star being a tiny red carnelian stone. The infant was either blowing or hallooing through chubby cupped hands.

The child was a zephyr, a wind-spirit. Hence this was Zephro's personalised hat. Apart from those blood-hued stars, the image seemed curiously benign and harmless.

'Well?' asked Grimm eagerly.

Jaq tore the cockade loose and pocketed it, for the minor satisfaction of having at least a scrap of the Harlequin man in his grasp.

'He dropped his hat, that's all. Not so that you could find it as a clue. It simply fell off.'

'Huh. At least he isn't perfect. Eh, Meh'Lindi?'

'Is that,' she asked icily, 'meant to console me?'

The squat withered somewhat. When it fell to his lot to cut her free from the coils of the hydra, had his poignant fixation received a body-blow – or a boost? For a while, did she seem almost within his reach? And was she now an absolute stranger again?

Jaq wondered how much effort of will it had cost her to resist ultimate, engulfing pleasure so as to gasp out a question or two to her tormenter and enchanter. How much might that experience have twisted her within?

On that doleful Black Ship on the way to Earth years ago, Jaq had kissed a girl psyker. Olvia had been her name. Her unformed talent was for curing injuries; and she was destined to die.

Olvia thought that Jaq would die too, and he had not disabused her. They had embraced for mutual comfort. They had kissed, though that was all.

Afterwards Jaq had felt that he had betrayed Olvia. Maybe his self-denial in the matters of the flesh had begun then and there. What of the woman to whom he had recourse subsequently, on an icy world, as a fledgling inquisitor? The woman whom he paid for her favours so as to learn of that enchantment that could fuddle men and women? He never asked her name. The experience had cheated him.

He would only ever, he sensed, be able to pair with a woman who was his own match – professionally, as it were. How few human beings in the entire galaxy could

fulfil that criterion! If they did fulfil it, surely they must be
potential rivals, competitors even in the guise of colleagues.

So therefore: loneliness and duty.

He had begun to think of Meh'Lindi as someone who
might... As someone who was strong enough, strange
enough...

Jaq staunched the thought, like an open wound.
Carnelian had dealt that wound with devastating accuracy.
Not because the Harlequin man had sullied Meh'Lindi in
Jaq's eyes, oh no, no question of such a despicable thought
– but because Carnelian had used pleasure as a weapon,
therefore Meh'Lindi must reject dalliance with any such
delights; even if she had felt the faintest inclination to
dally in the first place, and that was a dubious proposition.

Folly, thought Jaq! I'm reacting to her as dotingly as
infatuated Grimm or mooning Vitali. Double folly, now.
Carnelian's attack on Meh'Lindi has fuddled me.

And her too...

'We must both think very clearly,' he said to her. 'We
mustn't indulge our feelings at all.'

There in the train, Jaq prayed for clarity.

THEY FOUND GOOGOL tied up securely in the Emerald Suite
with a leather hood over his head. The Navigator ached
almightily with cramps and had soiled himself. The eye-
screen was missing.

Grimm released Googol, cleaned him, massaged him.
Then Googol sprawled wretchedly on a couch, whispering
of how a power axe had sliced a hole through the door and
how stun-gas had billowed into the suite, all within seconds. Googol glanced perplexedly at the door, which was
perfectly intact. The assailants had replaced it. Was that so
as to cast doubt on Googol's word? Or only to prevent
prior discovery?

'Three of them, I'd say. Never saw their faces. Only heard
their voices when I woke, all trussed up. I pretended to be
still unconscious.'

'Let's assume they realised you were awake,' said Jaq.
'They probably saw you twitch. Let's assume they waited
around so that you could overhear them talking.'

'That didn't occur to me.'

'No? Well, I'm cultivating suspicion, Vitali.'

'Surely not of me, Jaq? You don't think that... They did
cut through the door, I swear it!'

'Yes, yes, I'm sure they did. As well as blinding me by
stealing the screen, what did they want me to know?'

'Ah, let's see... It's coming. "Now Draco won't be able to
see how Vasilariov is infested." Something along those
lines. They mentioned names of lots of other cities too, but
I couldn't hear what they were saying about them clearly
with that leather over my lugs.'

'Meh'Lindi.' Jaq spoke with a casualness which, in the
circumstances, brought her to full alert. His gaze flicked.

It only took her moments to locate the spy-fly roosting
in a shadow, to aim her digital laser and evaporate the tiny
surveillance device. Her accuracy was unimpaired.

'Spider time,' said Jaq. He fetched a detector from his lug-
gage. This chittered in his hand as he swept the suite,
uncovering four further spy-flies, which Meh'Lindi
despatched.

'Now that Carnelian can't overhear us,' he said, 'I can
perhaps plan something *un*expected.'

'Outside of here: more flies? Wherever we go?'

'Undoubtedly,' he told her.

'Use jumblespeech?'

'Carnelian may understand it.'

'He reached you through your Tarot before. Can he eaves-
drop through a card, Jaq? Sense what you're thinking?'

'When I activate them. Maybe! Otherwise, I strongly
doubt it. I shall leave them inert, even if that closes off the
currents of the future. Any more gossip, Vitali?'

'Not that I recall.'

'By the way, trusty watchman,' said Grimm, 'how fruit-
fully did you occupy yourself while you were lying there
with nothing to do and a hood over your bean?

'I contemplated ways of killing my attackers.'

'Huh, that isn't very grateful, seeing as how they left you alive. Don't you mean that you replayed the episode with yourself as hero? Didn't you fantasise about what might have occurred if only you'd been holding your breath at the time and a gun as well? Ah, I bet by the end of it you were quite amazed to find yourself still inexplicably tied up.'

Googol sighed. 'I *would* have killed them, hot-shot. No coward navigates the warp. As to my... period of meditation, there are mental disciplines in which I fear you're sorely lacking, Grimbo, though I thank you for rubbing life back into my limbs.'

'And changing your dirty underwear.' Grimm sniffed at his blunt, though nimble, fingers. He disregarded the Navigator's diminution of his name, perhaps sensing the undertone, this time, of almost fond indebtedness. Almost.

'Actually,' confessed the Navigator, perking up, 'I composed a poem and quite a good one.'

'What?' said Grimm.

'Did you really do that, Vitali?' Meh'Lindi asked, with more than a note of admiration in her voice. 'I salute you.'

'What for?' asked the squat, perplexed. Meh'Lindi's reaction was her first really affirmative one since her humiliation at Carnelian's hands. 'I like poems, too,' he ploughed on hopefully. 'We sing many epic ballads – about our wars with the foul orks and the deceitfulness of the eldar. Our ballads are all quite long. Take a day or so to recite.'

'Mine are generally quite short,' said Vitali. 'Verses should aim to be gems, not gasbags.'

'Huh! Let me tell *you*–'

Were the squat and the Navigator on the brink of a poetical competition with which to court Meh'Lindi? But then she interrupted.

'One's whole previous life becomes a poem by means of the suicide-ode.'

Jaq didn't wish to hear any more. 'Grimm,' he said, 'I want you to go deep into the ruptured entrails of Vasilariov to search for another hydra. I'm sure you'll find one down where the dross and scum gather.'

'If I find it, should I slice it up a little?'

'Absolutely not! Just report back here.'

'I should go,' Meh'Lindi said disconsolately. 'I could atone.'

'The role of an assassin,' Jaq reminded her, 'is not to feel remorse in any respect. I'd prefer that you stay here. I need to think.'

'Her presence assists you to *think*?' enquired Googol. Irony was returning to his voice. Consequently he was recovering from his minor ordeal.

THINK.

'Search for another hydra.' That's what he had told Grimm.

As Jaq questioned Meh'Lindi yet again so as to compare her impressions with his, a sickening realisation about the probable nature of the hydra dawned on him.

'Dissect it. Pot a trophy.' Thus Carnelian had goaded Jaq, wishing him to do exactly that, wanting him to attack the hydra in the axe-swinging style of an Obispal.

Not only would the creature regenerate severed scraps of its body into new limbs, not only would gobbets of its substance give rise to more of it, but in some fashion – through the medium of the warp – its substance could remain connected together, could still function as a unit even when slashed apart.

And therefore, *therefore*, the hydra that lurked under the city of Kefalov and any hydras roosting in the underbelly of Vasilariov and other cities on this planet were all *one and the same*.

Had even Jaq's plasma blast truly damaged the beast – or simply stimulated it, spraying elements of it hither and yon?

All the millions of deaths resulting from the genestealer rebellion – a great psychic bellow of rage, pain and extinction – had served to trigger the growth of this creature.

The rebellion had been sparked deliberately, primarily to feed the creation of this creature. To forge that strange blend of protoplasm and the fluidium of the warp – or more exactly, to quicken it, since its ultimate origin must surely lie elsewhere, in some dire biological crucible.

Why here, why Stalinvast, and not some other world? Jaq imagined arcane astromantic calculations and perversions of Tarot divination – conducted by Carnelian, the Tarot-sneak? – before this planet was chosen for the first emergence of the entity.

The first. There had to be a first emergence somewhere. And this world harboured enough infesting furtive stealers to cause a huge conflagration of lives – the calculated level of obscene sacrifice – without leading to really major devastation.

All to what end? If guided by an adept, the hydra could enter people's minds on a deep-down level where the ultimate biological controls of behaviour existed, the pleasure centre and the pain centre...

Daemons did not seem to be involved at all. *Someone* – human or alien – had engineered a mighty and sinister living tool for an unknown purpose.

Jaq had been chosen as a dupe.

On discovering a macabre entity such as the hydra, any inquisitor worth his salt would call in the nearest available force of Space Marines – Blood Angels, Space Wolves, whichever – to root out the malevolent lifeform.

The result of this obvious strategy would be to spread the hydra around still further, so that more and more of it grew from the savaged fragments left behind. As soon attempt to slice water with a sword, or chop up the sea.

Jaq had been blinded – had his eye-screen stolen by agents of Carnelian – so that he would see even less of the picture than before and would be the more likely to call in such a vigorous and essentially useless assault. Carnelian even teased him with the truth, assuming that Jaq would fail to perceive it.

Therefore, Jaq would not call in a Space Marine unit to assist him. Would not, must not.

That only perhaps left him one alternative – an ultimate alternative which no one, not even Carnelian, could reasonably expect him to invoke, let alone soon...

The name of that alternative was *exterminatus*.

'In an Imperium of a million worlds,' he repeated to himself, 'what does the death of one world matter in the cause of purity?'

For such was *exterminatus*: the total destruction of all life on the surface of a planet by means of virus bombs delivered from orbit.

The life-eater virus, spreading at amazing speed, would attack anything whatever that breathed or grew or crawled or flew as well as anything of biological origin: food, clothes, wood, feathers, bone. The life-eater was voracious. The jungles of Stalinvast would swiftly rot into sludge that would form shallow festering inland seas and lakes, where rot continued to feed so that the very air burned planet-wide, searing the whole surface to ashes and bare rock.

In the cities all protein would eat itself and ooze in a tide into the underbelly, rot eating rot, until the firegas detonated, leaving the cities like mounds of dead, blasted coral.

What if the hydra was not... life exactly? No matter. What would it have left to prey upon, if such was its design and its destiny?

Exterminatus.

The word tolled like a woeful bell.

'What does the death of one world matter...?'

When one person dies, that person's entire world – their whole universe – vanishes for them. A cosmos is snuffed out and quenched. Any individual's death essentially involves the death of an entire universe, does it not? The death of a planetful of people could hardly involve any more than that.

Yet it did.

By now Jaq was on his knees, praying. He yearned to consult his Tarot so as to connect himself however tenuously with the spirit of the Emperor. He dared not, lest his inner thoughts might be snooped upon by an interloper.

Exterminatus.

It did matter. He would be sacrificing a rich industrial world, a bastion of the human Imperium. He would also be slaying a part of himself, burning out certain aspects of... sensitivity, of scepticism. Aspects which made him remember an Olvia and mourn the death of that comparative stranger. Yet was not everyone essentially a stranger? Maybe he should have cauterised those aspects of himself long since.

To contemplate causing the death of a world was, he realized, akin to contemplating one's own suicide. A harsh, chilling light shone through the soul, and where it shone, in its wake the ultimate darkness began to gather.

His knees ached as he had knelt there for hours. Googol had gone to sleep and was snoring gently. Meh'Lindi sat cross-legged regarding Jaq expressionlessly all this time. She had become a statue; he hardly heeded her. An inner light shone upon his wounded, confused, hopeless feelings for her; and soon in its wake a healing shadow swept across those feelings, obscuring them.

Exterminatus.

SEVEN

FAR BELOW THE windows of the suite, the jungle exhaled mists of early morning to dazzle the eye as the sun brightened. Along the horizon dirty clouds were already bunching up, to suffocate the radiance falsely promised by the dawn.

Jaq had prayed all through the night and felt giddy but purified.

At long last Grimm returned. 'There's a hydra down below all right,' he reported. 'All over the place! Appears to be influencing the human rats and roaches down there not to notice it. No, not to be properly *aware* of it; that's how it seemed to me. Now you spy it, now you don't, like some mirage. Its jelly shifts in and out of reality.'

'I dreamed about it,' said Meh'Lindi. 'Attacking it increases its vigour. Is some of it still in my head?'

Jaq arose at last, staggering slightly. Crossing to her, he placed a palm against her brow. She flinched momentarily. Extending his psychic sense, he spoke words of power in the hieratic ritual language.

'In nomine imperatoris hominorum magistris ego te purgo et exorcizo. Apage, Chaos, apage!' He coughed as though to banish a clot of phlegm, the taste of Chaos. 'I exorcize you,' he told her. 'You're free of it. I'm a daemon-hunter; I should know.' Though truly the hydra was no daemon.

Meh'Lindi relaxed. How perceptive of her to realize that the entity might thrive on violent opposition.

Nothing could thrive after the wholesale scouring of the planet.

Googol had risen earlier to consult the comm-screen. 'I've checked with spaceport registry, Jaq. Zephro Carnelian has his own interstellar craft in a berth. It's registered as belonging to something called the Zero Corporation.'

'Meaning that no such corporation exists.'

'Ship exists. She's called *Veils of Light*.'

'How did you confirm it belongs to Carnelian?'

'Ah... we Navigators have some influence where matters of space are involved.'

'The famous Navis Nobilitate spider's web?'

'Depending on our particular family allegiances...' Googol seemed pleased with himself.

Grimm yawned, and yawned again.

Jaq wished that he himself could slumber. He musn't. He must act in the purity of the moment. He located a powerful stimulant.

'I shall pay a call on Governor Voronov-Vaux,' he announced. 'Dawn is a good time to do so. I shall reveal myself. He will be less alert, more pliable. I need his astropath to send an interstellar message.'

'If I was a lord,' observed Grimm, 'I'd be tetchy first thing in the morning.'

'Be glad you aren't a lord, then, my buoyant mankin,' said Googol. 'May I come along too, Jaq? Leaving me seems to lead to embarrassments. I'm restless. I've been cooped up. A Navigator needs... to explore space.'

Jaq nodded. If they needed to leave Stalinvast rapidly, the pilot musn't be languid. A false, drug-induced vitality coursed through Jaq's blood and muscles and illuminated his mind harshly, sweeping away fatigue and any remaining perplexity. In such a state, he knew, he could make judgments which were almost too pure, too unrelenting. Perhaps he needed an ironist to accompany him – at his left hand; and at his right hand, his assassin.

'We eat first,' he said, 'and we eat *well*.'

THE VESTIBULE LEADING to the governor's quarters was the mouth of a toothed monstrosity. Sculpted from marble blocks, the vestibule was capacious enough to gulp all but the bulkiest of actual jungle monsters whole. Jaq wondered whether this menacing foyer was designed to close up exactly like a mouth, using hidden plasteel muscles to move the marble blocks.

Certain ancient stains along the approach corridor – which resembled the rib cage of a very long whale – had suggested that those ribs could clash shut at any sign of unwelcome visitors, imprisoning or crushing intruders.

Within the vestibule, red lighting ached drearily on the eye. It stole away all other colours or rendered them purple, black. Air puffing from the ventilator gargoyles, styled after lizards of the jungle, smelled musky rather than fresh. Despite his drug-boosted clarity, Jaq felt half-blinded and stifled.

'How strange,' the majordomo was saying, 'another honourable inquisitor presenting his credentials so soon after we have seen the last one off!'

The fat man fluttered chubby, ringed fingers. He wore corrective goggles which must translate the rubicund gloom of this vestibule into the true spectrum. A seemingly black Voronov-Vaux monogram emblazoned his silk robes.

'Our world has just been cleansed, sir, at enormous cost – and with the whole-hearted co-operation of his lordship. Our population is culled. The economy will boom.'

'Ah yes, the economic stimulus of slaughter!'

Jaq held up his palm once more, activating the electronic daemon-head tattoo of the outer Inquisition. The guards in saurian leather and goggles, who manned this last of many checkpoints, stiffened. An Obispal had recently reinforced the Inquisition's authority.

'I simply require the use of your master's astropath,' said Jaq.

'Ah, you need to send an interstellar message? His lordship will be curious. You'll be reconfirming that our whole world is cleansed, I take it?'

'The message is *my* business.'

'Our astropath might mention the content to his lordship later on, so why not divulge it now?'

Unlikely, thought Jaq, that the astropath would mention anything at all ever again... He doubted that the astropath would wholly understand the message that Jaq intended to send. If at all, if at all. The message would be couched in Inquisition code; the astropath would parrot the words out telepathically.

Still, the astropath would remember, and some scholar on the governor's staff might construe the meaning.

On this occasion the astropath must seem to succumb to the pressure of his work. Meh'Lindi would see to this subtly. The astropath must suddenly appear to be possessed – with lethal consequences.

The astral telepath would die in any case when *exterminatus* arrived. So this would almost be a mercy killing. A grain of dust to set beside the mountain of several billion other deaths...

'Ah,' said the majordomo, 'I'm well aware that the college of the priesthood here in the capital was destroyed during the rebellion. You can't use their astropath. What of commercial ones?

'Less reliable.'

'Reasonably reliable.'

'Reasonably is not enough. Your master's astropath will be the very best on this world.'

'Oh yes. Granted. Utterly true. Only the best for an inquisitor. Still, the priestly colleges in other cities boast of some fairly excellent specimens...'

Such would die too, along with many good priests. Was the *cause* sound enough, when the true nature of the hydra remained so opaque and ambiguous?

The hydra *had* to be sinister. The obvious response – of summoning in an exterminator team – just *had* to be wrong. Briefly Jaq entertained the notion that he was being tested by some Hidden Master of his secret order who had instructed Baal Firenze to send him to Stalinvast to assess whether Jaq possessed supreme courage and insight – enough for him to become a Hidden Master himself.

If so, that master must already have known about the hydra. Would even such a power squander a whole planet simply to test one individual? Maybe Jaq would send the signal for *exterminatus* – and that command would already have been countermanded, light years away. The red light grated on Jaq's eyes as if his own eyes were bloodshot, dazed with the blood of billions.

He tried to spot any spy-flies lurking in this foyer, little spies which so recently had been his own to command, until they were stolen. The dire light and dark shadows foxed him. A spy-fly might be hiding in the open mouth of any gargoyle. It could be peeping from the eye-socket of any of the saurian skulls with jewels atip their horns mounted on the walls.

Jaq hadn't told either of his companions exactly what he intended to do, and just then it occurred to him how Googol might resent the deaths of fellow Navigators caught on this world when the flesh-eater came.

'Thus,' said the fat man, 'your message must be distinctly *urgent*...'

Aside from the pre-eminence of a governor's own astropath, Jaq had one further reason for visiting Lord Voronov-Vaux's domain. He would have felt it demeaning to condemn this world utterly without first paying a visit to the vicinity of its ruler.

Just so, did an assassin care to leave a calling card...

Nor had he wished to leave the capital a second time.
Nor had he wanted to... The thought tried to elude him.
He brought it into sharp, cruel focus.

Nor had he wanted to have recourse to the services of an
astropath belonging to a pious and loyal fraternal organisation. Whom, and which, he must sacrifice to the
flesh-eater.

Had he come here to the governor's court out of cow-
ardice? Out of craven abdication of his moral duty
masquerading as brazen confrontation?

'Don't hinder me,' said Jaq. 'I demand access in the
Emperor's name.'

What name, Jaq wondered fleetingly, was *that*?

Meh'Lindi moved closer to the majordomo, her fingers
flexing. Googol fiddled ostentatiously with the bandana
round his brow as if toying with the idea of removing what
masked his third eye, the warp-eye, a hostile glare from
which could kill, as was widely known though seldom
tested.

'Of course you must be admitted to His Lordship,' burbled the majordomo. 'An inquisitor, oh yes! Though it's
inconvenient.'

'If so, I don't need to see the governor – only his
astropath.'

'Ah... His lordship must needs give consent. Do you see?
Do you see?'

Not very well, thought Jaq. Not in this ruddy obscurity.

THE GOVERNOR'S SANCTUM was a leviathan suffused with the
same dreary red light. Above the tenebrous vault of the ceiling, sunshine must reign. Jaq doubted that even the most
towering of storms could engulf the uppermost reaches of
Vasilariov. Of that outside brightness, no hint existed.

Now Jaq understood the function of that helmet he had
seen the governor wearing out at the spaceport under the
open sky. Voronov-Vaux must see best at red wavelengths.
Probably in infrared too. The governor must see the heat
of bodies as much as the physical flesh.

That was a mutation, a deviation. Since this affected the ruling family, no one might dare oppose it. Conceivably it contributed to the family's mystique.

Censers burned, further hazing the air. Goggled officials hunched over consoles around tiers of cantilevered wrought-iron galleries, listening to data, whispering orders. A string orchestra wailed as if in torment. Caged mutants with abnormally large eyes played complicated games on three-dimensional boards. Were those bastards of the Voronov-Vaux clan? Inbred freaks? Talented advisers, held in permanent captivity?

Jaq smelled the whiff of genetic pollution.

The busy galleries were attached to the ribs of the leviathan. Between those ribs, at floor level, sub-chambers formed deep caves. At the heart of the enormous room an ornate marble building shaped like a pineapple squatted on a disc of steel. That disc must be a lifting platform which could raise and lower the governor's sanctum sanctorum, his travelling tabernacle. Up into his government's headquarters; down into his family apartments and bunker.

Give thanks that the sanctum sanctorum was present, not sealed away below.

Liveried guards admitted the majordomo and those he escorted into the marble pineapple. The fat man loudly prattled unctuous apologies. From a dim inner room Jaq heard flesh slap flesh. With a squeal, a scantily clad girl whose eyes were twice the normal human size scampered out, to be caught by one of those guards and led away.

Lord Voronov-Vaux followed bare-footed, adjusting a black robe on which dragons of seemingly purple hue writhed at the edge of visibility.

'YOU'RE THE HEREDITARY lord of a whole world,' Jaq found himself saying presently. 'Whereas I'm the emissary from the lord of the entire galaxy.'

'Lord of parts of it,' growled the governor.

'Of the human parts.' Jaq stared at those mutant, red-seeing eyes accusingly.

'True. Well, I'm hardly rebellious! I placed all my loyal guard at the previous inquisitor's service, did I not? Did I not sustain terrible losses?'

'Much to your benefit, may I remind you? Otherwise, within a few decades genestealers would have begun to infiltrate your own family, polluting and hypnotising.'

'I realise.'

'Now I only wish you to place your finest astropath at my service.'

Standing before the man, Jaq's various rationalizations evaporated. In coming here, he was actually following psychic instinct, an indefinable but insinuating impulse to visit the court of Governor Voronov-Vaux.

In the psychic economy of the universe a compensation must exist for the reverses Jaq had suffered at the hands of the Harlequin man. Something was going to balance his previous contretemps. Because he had prayed with a pure heart throughout the night, a tendril from the God-Emperor was now nudging him like a guardian spirit.

The monstrosity of the *exterminatus* he contemplated had eclipsed that thread of instinct until now, all be it that *exterminatus* was the correct course of action. Exhilaration keened through Jaq. Could the drug alone be responsible? No. He felt subtly in touch with higher forces, as though he had become the Tarot card that represented him.

'Hmm,' said the governor, 'but why? What have you discovered?'

Voronov-Vaux, a stout, balding fellow, was plainly a sensualist. To rule a planet he must be capable of severity. Yet his curiosity as to Jaq's request seemed to proceed from reasonable concern rather than from the paranoia which often afflicted rulers. Actually, the governor would have ample reason to feel paranoid if he did but know the gist of the message Jaq intended to send.

Led by the tendril of intuition, Jaq said lightly, 'Let's hope that, after all your loyal assistance, Inquisitor

Obispal doesn't report adversely to the Imperium about your mutation... I certainly shan't.'

What need to? Voronov-Vaux and everyone else on this world would soon be dead.

The governor twitched. 'Harq wouldn't. He swore on his honour.'

There was the key! Obispal had virtually blackmailed Voronov-Vaux to allow him to root out the rebellion with wanton use of force, resulting in all those millions of deaths.

Voronov-Vaux's red vision was his vulnerable flaw; for the Imperium might just decide puristically that a mutant should not continue as governor. His lordship was glancing askance at Meh'Lindi. Did he detect the heat-profile of an assassin?

Did he imagine he had already been judged and condemned? Lesser lords would be only too eager to step into his shoes.

'So do I also swear on *my* honour,' Jaq assured the man. 'A good governor does as he pleases on his world, just so long as he pays his tithes in treasure and people. Or in your case, weapons. A minor mutation should be deemed an eccentricity and nothing more. Out of curiosity, how long has this variation been in your family?'

'Since my grandfather's time.'

'May it endure until the end of the world! I promise. Harq promised. I suppose Zephro promised too?'

'Carnelian, yes... A peculiar individual... He almost seemed to regret the necessary slaughter of my people as much as I did.'

Ha, it was proven. The Harlequin man was Obispal's associate, utterly. Could Obispal really be loyal to the Imperium? It hardly seemed so. Surely here was the evidence that Jaq's Emperor-sent impetus had been leading him toward.

'Now may I use your astropath without further ado?'

'Yes. Yes, inquisitor.'

'I'm glad you are so loyal.'

Your reward, thought Jaq grimly, will be *exterminatus*.

As soon as Jaq met the astropath he guessed that there was more awaiting.

EIGHT

THE PRIME ASTROPATH of Stalinvast was a small, thin, dark-skinned woman. And she was old, *antique*. Deep lines grooved her prune of a face. Her hair, which shone so brightly red, must really be purest white. Due to the long-past agony of soul-binding her blind eyes were opaque and curdled.

She leaned on a staff as tall as herself, and could not see the visitors to her fur-lined chamber, but her nearsense informed her.

'Three more come,' she sang out. 'One with the vision. One with the sense. And one who is more than she seems!'

Momentarily Jaq imagined that the majordomo had led them, in error of mischief, to a soothsayer. However, the old woman's dark purple habit would, in true lighting, be some hue of green appropriate to an astropath.

'I'm the one with the vision,' agreed Googol. 'It's warp vision – the Navigator's eye.'

And I, thought Jaq, am the one with the sense. Whereas Meh'Lindi... she's the one who will presently cause this old woman's heart to stop.

The astropath reached towards a fur-cloaked ledge; and the fur shifted. Glowing eyes opened. Sharp small claws flexed. She toyed with an animal, which must be her companion. The creature looked both voluptuous and savage. Would it defend its mistress fiercely?

'What is that?' whispered Jaq.

'It's called a cat,' Meh'Lindi told him. She also answered his deeper question. 'It will merely look on, observing what it sees. Who knows what it understands? Its actions are usually self-centred and autistic.'

'Why do you keep such a creature?' Jaq asked the old woman.

'For love,' she replied bleakly. 'I have kept at least a score of them during my life here, until each decayed in turn. They are my consolation.' She held up a wizened hand. 'Look, here are some of its recent scratches. I can *feel* those.'

'Leave us now,' Jaq told the majordomo. The fat man withdrew, drawing a baffle-curtain across the mouth of the astropath's furry womb-cave.

Meh'Lindi whisked an electrolumen from her sash to supplement the dull rubescence of the single glow-globe. In true light the old woman's skin was brown and her hair indeed was white as cotton, while her eyes were the boiled white of eggs. The fur lining the cave was a brindled orange; that of the cat creature too. The animal's pupils widened into black marbles at this sudden intrusion of a wholly novel radiance, then narrowed to slits. Its jaws widened, baring sharp little teeth.

It was, however, yawning. A yawn, in the face of a whole new world of light!

'Your name?' Jaq asked the old woman.

'People call me Moma Parsheen, perhaps because I have no children except for...' She stroked the cat creature.

'I'm Inquisitor Draco.'

'An inquisitor? Then you probably know how much was burnt out of me. I neither see nor smell nor savour any tastes. I only touch.' The cat writhed sensuously, throbbing. To kill this woman might indeed be a blessing to her...

'Moma Parsheen, I wish you to send a message to the Imperial Ravager Space Marines' headquarters, orbiting Vindict V.'

That fortress-monastery was the nearest roost of ultimate warriors capable of obliterating a world. Jaq already had his fatal signal concisely formulated: *Ego, Draco Ordinis Mallei Inquisitor, per auctoritate Digamma Decimatio Duodecies, ultimum exterminatum planetae Stalinvastae cum extrema celeritate impero.* The triple-D code phrase, sometimes vulgarised as Death-Destruction-Doom, would itself suffice to launch *exterminatus*. Thus the Inquisition mission stationed on the orbital fortress would advise. Jaq had included the phrase *Ordinis Mallei* by way of double indemnity; the mission was almost bound to include a covert member of his own Ordo. Never before had he sent such an order, never. This weighed on him like an inactive dreadnought suit of combat armour, imprisoning him; and he sought his enhanced clarity, as it were, to restore power to that suit.

'Listen to me carefully, Moma Parsheen.' He recited the words. She might not understand them, but she repeated them back faithfully.

'Now commence your trance.'

The blind woman quivered as she skryed light years outward through the warp, obeying the disciplines of the Adeptus Astra Telepathica, seeking contact with the mind of some other astropath serving the fortress-monastery at Vindict V.

Yet then she hesitated. 'Inquisitor?'

'What is it, old woman?'

'Such a resonant message... '

'Send it *now*.'

Now, before the Harlequin man could intervene. A spy-fly could be nestling in these furry walls. An agent might be poised nearby, prepared to burst in here on a suicide mission.

'Inquisitor... I'm sensing warp portals opening deep down in our city. And yes, in other cities across this world...'

'You must send my message immediately!' To sense portals in distant cities, she must possess impeccable talent...
'What is entering through these portals?'

The astropath shook her head. 'Nothing is entering. Strange... substances are departing from this world.'

'*Leaving*? Are you sure?'

'I am. A life that isn't exactly life. A creation... I can't really tell. There's so little mind. It's as if its existence is almost blank as yet. Embryonic... awaiting. I sense it all passing away through those portals. So many little portals! What is happening?'

'Don't send that message, Moma. Absolutely don't.'

'No?'

'New circumstances. Meh'Lindi, there's a spy-fly somewhere in here with us—'

'Who are you, inquisitor?' asked the astropath, relaxing from her trance state. 'What is happening?'

'Our hydra's withdrawing into the warp whence it came,' Googol murmured, half in answer to her. 'Never find it again, I don't suppose.'

'Can't you track it with warp vision, Vitali?'

'I'm a Navigator, not a magician. In case you hadn't noticed, I'm not in the warp at the moment. We're a week's travel away from the jump zone.'

'Exceptional Navigators can see into the warp from the normal universe!'

'Yes, yes, yes, Jaq. But the hydra isn't flying away *through* the warp. It's using portals to leap directly from here – to Grimm knows where.'

'Damnation...'

For a short while Jaq had believed he had achieved something admirable. The draconic decision to declare *exterminatus* had been exactly right, a model of resolute courage and pure thinking. Carnelian, spying through the eye-screen from wherever, had immediately begun withdrawing the hydra into the warp of Chaos to save it from extinction. Thus Jaq was saved from the consequences of his pronouncement. Now he had no way to track the cursed creature.

How very quickly Carnelian had acted! Surely the Harlequin man understood that *exterminatus* wouldn't arrive instantly? Time for the Space Marines to equip and load virus bombs... warp-time versus galactic time... Ten local days at the earliest. It was almost as though Carnelian hoped charitably to save this planet...

'Damnation, it's escaping...'

The old woman lapsed into a semi-trance. 'If the... existence... possessed a higher consciousness,' she mused, 'I could place a psychic homer in it for you, a little beacon. Though only I could follow such a trace.'

'Well, it doesn't,' snapped Jaq, 'and meanwhile it's sliding away like slops down a drain.'

Outcry assaulted his ears. As Meh'Lindi doused her electrolumen, Jaq whirled and tore the baffle-curtain aside.

Through the crepuscular afterglow, from behind the marble pineapple, there came skipping a true-light figure. Aglow, the intruder radiated his own natural wavelengths luminously like some alien eldar attired in a holo-suit. He pirouetted. He bowed.

'Carnelian!' Meh'Lindi hissed and tensed.

'Sir Draco,' cried the figure. 'Nice try, but not nice enough, so it seems. Follow me, find me! Follow me, find me!' Did Carnelian think he was playing some childhood game?

'No one is really there,' warned Moma Parsheen. 'The space he speaks from is empty.'

Jaq understood. The figure was holographic. Spy-flies hovering beside that astral shape must be projecting it, weaving it of light.

To reverse the mode of operation of the jokaero spying device in this manner, the Harlequin man must understand the technology better than Jaq did. Carnelian must know special runes to inscribe around the eye-screen and arcane litanies to incant, to make it serve this two-way purpose, which perhaps had been the true purpose of the device in the first place...

'I'm listening,' Jaq shouted. 'I'm all ears!'

Did Carnelian hope that Jaq or Meh'Lindi would rush, or fire, impetuously – only for their laser beams or needles to pass through the phantom without effect, until they hit some bystander or the governor's tabernacle? As soon as Jaq realised how Carnelian was accomplishing this intrusion, he knew that he hadn't lost.

'Moma Parsheen,' he whispered, 'place your tracer in the man that sends this illusion. His tiny toys are nearby, linked to the real man somewhere in the city. Feel out those links. Snare him.'

'Yes... yes...' she mumbled, en-tranced.

'What do you want with me, Carnelian?' Jaq shouted, to persuade the illusion to linger long enough.

If only the governor's guards refrained from opening fire... Obviously they had seen Carnelian before in this sanctum, though not in that eerie, invasive guise. They were leery of the figure of light who had appeared as if by magic yet who looked so solid.

'Ask not,' Carnelian taunted, 'what you can do for me, but what I can do for you.'

'And what might that be?'

Once more, Jaq surmised that he was being tested, his every action scrutinised by a cunning, manipulative intelligence.

'Follow me, find me. If you can!' The figure levitated, spinning, darting out its arms menacingly, hands crackling with light – and vanished, just as the guards opened fire in alarm. Ruby laser light stitched the interior of the sanctum like thinnest threads of stronger flame within a dully glowing oven.

In vain.

Worse than in vain.

Screams rang out from the galleries, where spectators had been gazing down instead of hiding. Some data screens exploded. The laser fire ceased too late.

'Did you succeed?' Jaq asked the astropath urgently.

'Oh yes. I marked him without him knowing. I can track him, and he won't know. You'll have to take me with you,

Inquisitor Draco. Take me from this place. I have been here for decades untold in this court, never leaving it except in my mind, ranging to far stars yet never truly experiencing those elsewheres. Only terse commercial messages. Is it one and a half centuries, is it two? I was rejuvenated... was it twice, was it thrice? Because I'm so valuable. Oh I am sightless but I can sense my environs and weary utterly of them. Food is always ashes in my mouth. Incense only stifles me; it has no aroma. I can only touch. Take me far away.'

'If Carnelian leaves Stalinvast,' Jaq said bluntly, 'we may need to take you a vast distance.'

Oh yes, Jaq's intuition to visit Voronov-Vaux had been right. She, Moma Parsheen, had been the true goal of his guardian spirit, of the tiny fraction of the Emperor's potence that walked with him.

'Why should I have feared the sending of your message, inquisitor? Because I feel any tenderness towards my prison where all luxuries are insipid? Because I feel any attachment to this city or this world where I have laboured?'

She must indeed have plumbed the general sense of Jaq's message.

'Ah, but to be released by death before I could ever sense somewhere else directly! That would have been cruel comfort.'

'From an inner sanctum to the inside of a ship,' said Googol. 'You mightn't find the contrast all that stunning.'

'Even the brief journey to your ship will be a great liberating expedition for me.'

'Yes, we must go to the *Tormentum* right away,' said Jaq. 'Now that the hydra has gone into the warp, where else would Carnelian head?'

'You are old, Moma Parsheen,' Googol observed doubtfully.

'I will *stride* out with you,' she promised.

'What of your cat-animal?'

'Ming will cling to his home, not to me.'

'Yet you loved such a creature?'

The old woman ducked quickly back into her soft cave, to linger for a few seconds by the animal. She fondled its scruff, then snatched up a simple sling-bag of possessions embroidered with fidelity emblems.

'I'm ready.'

'Now's the best time,' said Meh'Lindi.

The injured were crying out up above. A console sprayed electric sparks and began to blaze. Distraught, the fat majordomo was bustling into the chamber. Guards were arguing. The Harlequin man couldn't have provided a better distraction.

EN ROUTE TO the train-tube terminal Jaq voxed Grimm to carry away as much as he could from the hotel suite, settle their account if challenged and rendezvous at the *Tormentum*.

At one point in their journey, Moma Parsheen was overcome by frailty. Limp and detached from her fast-shifting surroundings – maybe overwhelmed by those – she needed to be guided, almost carried along by Meh'Lindi for a while. Then the old woman recovered vigour and strode, favouring her staff.

EVEN BY THE standards of ships that could set down upon the surfaces of worlds, the *Tormentum Malorum* was singularly sleek and streamlined for rapid departure or arrival through atmosphere. Only warp-vanes jutted notably from the hull, and those were contoured cleverly as wings.

Within, the vessel in no wise resembled a rogue trader's treasure den or seraglio. The *Tormentum* was a sepulchral temple to the Master of Mankind, atrabilious and funereal.

In its layout the interior resembled black catacombs. Narrow corridors linked cells housing bunks or stores to crypt-rooms housing instruments or engines. Walls, ceilings and floors were clad in smooth obsidian and jet carved with runes, sacred prayers and holy texts. In niches, each lit by an electrocandle, images of the distorted enemies of humanity seemed to writhe in flames. The dark glassy surfaces reflected and re-reflected these flickering lights so that walls seemed to be the void – solidified – with stars and smeared veils of nebulae glinting within. Portholes were few and usually hatched over with leering daemon masks.

One bulkhead was a great bas-relief representing the heroic features of the Emperor stood astride the cowering form of the arch-traitor, Horus. A far cry from the shrivelled but undying form, embedded in the very centre of his throne amidst a forest tubes and wires. A virtual mummy, a living corpse that could not twitch a fingertip – though did any fingers or even fingerbones remain within that mass of medical machinery? Yet the Master's mind reached out afar.

Jaq often prayed to this bas-relief. The whole décor of the ship reinforced his faith.

As to Jaq's companions... Meh'Lindi's attitude to the *Tormentum* was impassive, inscrutable, while the corridors and crypts reminded Grimm nostalgically of mine workings and coaly caverns. The little man would trot around, mumbling contentedly, reenacting heroic skirmishes with rabid orks in cramped subterranean strongholds.

Googol talked to himself in a muffled manner or merely droned – hard to say which – whenever he was in space. At first Jaq had assumed the Navigator's idea was to sustain, sympathetically, the pitch of the ship's engines which sometimes skipped a beat, by chatting or humming to them. Jaq now surmised that Googol was reciting his own verses under his breath, polishing old ones, composing new ones. *Gloom. Tomb. Doom.*

Moma Parsheen embraced her new surroundings intently. Though more restricted, she declared them to be 'charged with potential space' – the potential to be elsewhere, anywhere else, in the galaxy.

Grimm, when he arrived, treated the old woman with a teasing reverence.

'A century or two? That's not so old! Me, I'll live at least three hundred years–'

'And still be none the wiser,' Googol said airily.

'Huh. You shorten the body, you increase the length of lifespan, I'm thinking.'

'Maybe we should breed men a span high so as to live a million years.'

'Sour grapes, Vitali! You're prematurely aged. It's all this warping you do.'

'That's my talent, sprat. Doesn't mean I'm going to die prematurely just because my face has character.'

'Wrinkles is the word. Anyway, I thought you wished to retire to some asteroid to be a bard. When will you entertain us with one of your effusions, by the by?'

Googol scuffed the abhuman lazily.

'Do you ever compose elegies?' Moma Parsheen asked unexpectedly. 'Dirges? Songs of lamentation?'

'For you, dear lady,' Googol replied gallantly, 'I might attempt such a challenge, though that isn't my usual style.'

'Huh, what about me?' protested Grimm. 'What I'm saying, Vitali – what I've been driving at in my own bluff way – is that I would very much appreciate, that's to say, well...'

The little man tore off his forage cap and twisted it in his hands. 'Ahem. The epic ballad of Grimm the squat who helped trounce the hydra. For my old age. I will teach you the modes, the verse form. If I live past three hundred or so, you see, I become a living ancestor; and an ancestor needs an epic under his belt. If I live past five hundred...' He grinned lamely. 'I reckon I'll become psychic then. Oh Moma Parsheen, in that respect you're a living ancestor already. I guess for a true human you've reached a decent age.'

'Decent?' she echoed disbelievingly. 'To be psychic is a blessing? My talent has robbed me utterly.'

'Would that robbery be the subject matter of your elegy?' Googol asked.

'Oh no. Oh no.' She didn't amplify further. 'How old are you, Grimm?'

'Oh, no more than fifty. That's standard Imperial years.'

'And bouncing along like a rubber ball.' Googol laughed. 'Maybe you do need an epic – of naivety.'

'I'm a sprat, it's true. A clever sprat; that's true too. *But,*' and he eyed Meh'Lindi puppyishly, 'my heart can be heavy at times.'

Meh'Lindi frowned. 'Mine too. For other reasons.'

She had quickly abandoned her sensual mistress's garb and was attired in a clingtight assassin's black tunic.

Jaq had likewise divested himself of his trader's gaudy gear and now wore the black, ornamented, hooded habit of his Ordo.

Along with Googol in his affectedly fluted black silk on-board suit, these three seemed to be a trio of tall-standing predatory bats who eclipsed the false star-void of the walls, wherever they stood, like dense hungry shadows eating the fire-flies of the night.

Moma Parsheen sank into a semi-trance.

'I warn you: the man called Carnelian is hurrying towards this spaceport.'

A WEEK LATER, in pursuit of the *Veils of Light* – not trying to catch Carnelian, only follow him – the *Tormentum Malorum* entered the ocean of Chaos which was warp-space.

Only then did Moma Parsheen say to Jaq, 'I sent the message anyway.'

'Message?'

'Your message to Vindict V. I sent it while we were still in Vasilariov.'

'Unsend it!' he cried. 'Cancel it!'

Sightless, she smiled thinly and inhumanly; she who had not seen a smile with which to compare since her girl-hood, nor a mirror either.

'From here, in the very warp? Impossible.'

Was she telling the truth? *He did not know.*

'In that case,' said Jaq, 'let us drop back into true space.'

'And lose the scent of Carnelian? While we dilly-dally in

the ordinary universe, his ship will forge onward through the warp out of my range.'

'Surely you can transmit from the warp.'

'I'm sure I wouldn't know how, inquisitor. That's quite outside of my experience. If I was trained in that, I've forgotten long since. Please recall how I've been penned in a sanctum on a planet for most of my days. I haven't known the pleasures of star-cruising. So, supposing I tried, the task would demand *total* concentration. I might easily lose my sense of our quarry.'

'You're lying.'

'The application of torture,' she said idly, 'would certainly distort my talent.'

Jaq wished she had not alluded to any such notion. To administer torture while within the warp – to a talented astropath of all people – would be plain lunacy. *Tormentum* mightn't be heavily screened against evil; what would be more likely to pierce the membrane between reality and Chaos than mind-screams of pain? What more likely to attract the attention of... the hyenas of Chaos?

From his Navigator's couch, Googol looked on anxiously. He fingered some of the amulets and icons that dangled around his neck now that he was in the warp.

'Jaq?'

'We carry on,' Jaq said anguishedly.

Time passed faster in the warp than in the real universe, but was also inconstant, unpredictable. Moma Parsheen had sent the *exterminatus* signal just over a week earlier. The Ravagers might already have sailed towards their jump zone, or be on the point of sailing. Once in the warp, how quickly would they arrive in the vicinity of Stalinvast?

Jaq imagined the priests of the squadron instructing the ultimate warriors righteously and reverently, honing their spirits for a task that was awesome – and yet almost abstract. How much more eager those warriors would have been to contact a foe face to face.

If the government of Stalinvast realised the import of the death-fleet's arrival, the orbital monitors might resist for a while. A day. A few hours. Armageddon would soon enough descend – enforced almost with a sense of regret.

Out of a million worlds, what did one matter?

Yet it did. For this would be one more loss suffered by the Imperium. The granite rock of the Imperium, which rested upon shifting sands of malevolent Chaos, could not endure an infinity of such cracks in its fabric. Indeed that rock was already much riven.

It could crumble, and all human culture could collapse, just as it had collapsed once before, but this time never to rise again. It must not crumble. Or daemons, loosened from Chaos, would feast.

Yes, it did matter! For Jaq called to mind the fat, fussy majordomo and Lord Voronov-Vaux of the red vision, but not a bloodthirsty vision, and the great-eyed girl who had scampered from his bed, and all the survivors of the gen-estealer uprising who had dolefully expected that their lives would at least continue after the disaster.

All were to die, all.

Not even in the way that Olvia must have died years ago to serve the Emperor – but to sate one mad woman's vengeance. When the time came, would Moma Parsheen tune in to the deaths of fellow astropaths on Stalinvast?

Jaq could order Vitali to drop back into normal space and no doubt could force the old woman to comply. He himself. He wouldn't order Meh'Lindi to do the task.

Yet then a terrible, enigmatic conspiracy might succeed...

'You have murdered a world,' he accused her.

'And now that world needs an elegy,' she said. 'Our resident poet could sing of Stalinvast's lethal festering jungles which I never saw; and of viscous scabs blasted in those jungles by a host of weapons; and of all the reef-cities which I never saw either, infested with their slaving grimy weapons-makers. He could sing of lizard-clad nobles hunting for trophies, and of body-heat orgies and mutations of the eye, and of a lone white-haired woman whose senses had been scarified, locked in a sanctum forever, her mind reaching to the stars; and out among all those stars and worlds that she spoke to in her mind, no fellow spirit yearned towards her or was able to express any such feeling–'

'Enough! Later, I will – I *ought* to execute you.'

'I do not much care if you do.'

'Oh you will, Moma Parsheen, you will. When it's too late, near the end, everyone cares. They may even wish for death, but they still care.'

'Perhaps,' she said, '*yours* should be the ballad of naivety? I shall have travelled away in the flesh from that wretched court – light years away by then, light decades. With every light year I redeem a year of my lost life.'

'And how about your cat-creature?' Meh'Lindi asked the old woman softly.

At that, in Moma Parsheen's visionless eyes a few tears welled.

For several minutes a sense of utter paralysing futility overwhelmed Jaq.

ΠΙΠΕ

SHOULD ANYONE BE foolish enough to don space armour and climb through the airlock, nothing whatever would be strictly *visible* – save for what had already come from the ordinary universe.

No stars shone in the realm of the warp, for no stars were present, nor any nebulosities of gleaming gas. Neither did darkness absolute prevail, as at the bottom of a well at midnight; for even blackness – the opposite of light – was absent.

On other wavelengths of perception than the visible, the warp was far from empty. It was super-saturated with virtual existence. Vitali Googol's warpscreen displayed an iridescent soup of energies riven by currents both swift and sluggish, poxed with vortices and whirlpools.

Here was the domain which glued the Imperium together since ships could slip through it to distant stars within days – or months at most – instead of taking impossible thousands of years over such voyages.

Yet here too was the realm where Jaq's special foes coagulated. Here was the infinite region where powers of Chaos achieved a twisted consciousness and a purpose anathema to all that was real and true.

Yes, the standing waves of warp storms became animate as great Powers. They drank the rage or the lust or the caprice of mortals whose souls returned to dissolve in this sea of energy.

These bloated Powers dangled lesser daemons. Avatars, made out of their own perverse essence, would hook into the spirits of vulnerable psykers, into greedy, heedlessly ambitious mortals, and would offer those dupes a little power – playing them like living puppets on intangible strings – before twisting them into tools of evil and eventually consuming them.

Thereby did the diabolical Powers seek to mutate the substance of the universe and to destroy Man's far-flung yet ultimately frail empire of sanity – a sanity that must needs defend itself with unrelenting savagery...

Jaq had learned all this during his training in the headquarters of his Ordo, that labyrinth many contorted thousands of kilometres in extent which cut through the bedrock deep beneath the massive concealing ice-cap of Terra's south polar continent.

'ASTRONOMICAN STRONG AND clear,' reported Googol. 'South declination eighty-two point one, ascension seventeen point seven. No significant warp storms evident.'

The warpscreen might have been a tank choked with bubbling prismatic frogspawn. Through that viewer they could all peer into the warp as if through one-way mirror-glass. Nothing from the warp could intrude into *Tormentum Malorum*, for the ship – this bubble of reality – was strongly shielded with force-fields and prayers.

Of course, with his warp-eye Googol saw far beyond the portion of warp space shown in the viewer – clear to the Emperor's aching beacon.

Starfarers in less well-protected vessels might hear the scrabbling of claws upon their hulls, or wailing incoherent voices, lascivious enticements, rumblings of wrath. If a vessel's force-skin was penetrated, daemons might congeal ectoplasmically within.

Let those be sirens of Slaanesh rather than harpies! Perhaps the death was sweeter. Or merely more prolonged.

THE INQUISITION SCHOLA was a vast, almost deliberately confusing maze of baroque halls, dormitories, sanctums, reclusia, libraria, scriptoria and apothecaria, dungeons, theological laboratories, psychic gymnasia and weapons arenas.

Fierce, sourly wise old adepts, who had retired from the field of stars, coached the intake of novices in the outer secrets of the art of the inquisitor, his ken and practice.

Jaq thrived at acquiring the necessary skills; yet already it was plain that he would never be a dogmatist, nor a flamboyant practitioner of the art of suppression.

'Why?' he would ask; and, 'Wherefore?'

He voiced such questions reverently, righteously, but voiced them nonetheless.

One day an instructor said to Jaq, 'We have our eye on you.'

Jaq feared being marked as a heretic; but that was not the reason why he was being specially scrutinised.

'CARNELIAN IS AT two-thirds of my tracking range,' commented Moma Parsheen, the murderess of a world.

Aft, Grimm was labouring in the stygian engine crypt by electrocandle and lantern light, tuning the drive that bore them through the warp. He only used spanners and gauges, scorning the runes or litanies which all other techs deemed so essential to woo the spirit of a machine.

Jaq lit incense sticks – frangipani, myrrh and Vegan virtueherb – in the obsidian control room. The air gargoyles gently sucked and puffed the aromatic smoke into strange curlicues as if sketching the features of potential daemons which might lurk outside the hull. His thoughts drifted forward in time from his novitiate. Years elapsed in his memory just as light years were elapsing in ordinary space as they fled onward.

HE HAD TAKEN all his oaths as a journeyman agent. He had served on a dozen worlds, rooting out aberrant psykers and heretics scrupulously and astringently – never succumbing to excess of zeal, though zealous none-the-less.

He was always willing to entertain a doubt – before, as was so often sadly the case, needing to crush all doubt. He never destroyed a witch simply on the say-so of vindictive enemies.

Came the day when a robed elder inquisitor activated a palm-tattoo that Jaq had never seen before, and spoke to him the words: 'Inner Order.'

A wheel within a wheel...

MEH'LINDI COMMENCED SOME isometric combat exercises as if to repel the oppression of being in the warp, which at times could generate a spiritual migraine, an ache of the soul.

She flexed. She tensed. Presently she danced – slowly. Each gesture, each step, each posture and nuance of limb or finger was part of a complex killing ritual. For a while she became the priestess of her own cult of Assassins, carrying out a deadly ceremony which appeared suave and innocuous, but was not.

Moma Parsheen took heed. Perhaps her nearsense completed for her – in her mind's eye – those abbreviated gestures so that she perceived the weaving of a skein of death. The old woman smiled distortedly, her brown, lined face a mask dropped into rippling water.

Vitali Googol began to recite:

'Lovely lady of death
Steals away my breath
With kisses that kill
Or ensorcel the will.
Her limbs mock my bones.
My squeezed heart moans.
The endearment: begone.

Lovely lady of death...'

The Navigator shuddered and focused himself more acutely on the immaterium without, alert for maelstroms. Presently he began to hum, somewhat tunelessly, a Navigator song, *The Sea of Lost Souls.*

Moma Parsheen stroked the air. In her mind was she comforting her cat-creature as the virus bombs began to rain down?

JAQ DAYDREAMED ABOUT a subsequent year when Baal Firenze had first made himself known. For there existed wheels within wheels within wheels. The Inquisition was by no means the be-all and end-all of the fight against corruption; nor was the secret inner order of the Inquisition the ultimate either.

The order of the hammer, Ordo Malleus, had been founded thousands of years in the past in deadliest secrecy – before the wounded Emperor had even entered his life-support throne. One of its mottos was: *Who Will Watch the Watchdogs?* The Ordo had even executed masters of the Inquisition when those mighty figures had shown signs of straying from true purity or diligence.

Yet its main task was to comprehend and destroy daemons. Jaq learned the appellations of those great entities of Chaos: Slaanesh the lustful, Khorne the blood-soaked, Tzeentch the mutator, Nurgle the plague-bearer. He would not utter those names lightly. All too often, human beings showed a literally fatal attraction towards such poisonous powers and their sub-daemons; as indeed perhaps people must, since those selfsame entities had agglutinated from out of the foul passions of once-living souls.

The training and conditioning of a Malleus man quite eclipsed the rigours of Jaq's training as a regular inquisitor. At the climax of a blood-chilling ceremony he swore even more secret oaths.

How could he forget the first daemon he had combatted in full knowledge of its nature? A lurid tattoo on his thigh commemorated his victory.

By now, underneath his garments, his frame sported a tapestry of such tattoos, though he kept his face clear, for secrecy.

ZEUS VI THE planet had been a farming world.

Peasants tilled the soil and herded sheep. They thought that the stars were holes in a blanket which the fabled Emperor draped across the sky each night. An outstretched fist could eclipse the sun that burned them by day. How fiercely they would be incinerated by a whole skyful of such light! This evidently existed, since from one horizon to the other dribs and drabs leaked through the little frays in the Emperor's blanket.

The peasants sacrificed lame children in honour of the celestial blanket-holder. If such propitiation did not result in the sewing-up of any chinks, at least it stopped new chinks from showing through.

A well-armed little colony had settled in this ignorant hinterland, calling themselves the 'Keepers of the Blanket's Hem'.

Spurious preachers began to declare that the peasants were going about matters in a foolish way by sacrificing crippled infants. Cripples! This was the reason why the night-blanket was tattered. From now on the peasants must offer to the Keepers a tithe of more mature, and physically intact, sons and daughters who had some pretence to comeliness. Parents who objected were torn apart as heretics. A new cult established itself over twenty years, its shrine being the domed town of the Keepers, which was built up against the entrance to caverns.

In the final confrontation Jaq and a company of Grey Knights had fought through savage ranks of cultists who all showed some mark of Chaos – a tentacle, a sting, tendrils instead of hair, suckers, claws; through to the warlock of the coven ensconced deep within the caverns where young captives whimpered piteously in cages.

That warlock was a bloated, horned hermaphrodite draped in bilious green skin. Oozing sexual orifices puckered his/her slumping belly. His/her long muscular tongue lashed and probed the air like a sense organ as if to supplement his/her tiny shrunken eyes. Plainly that tongue had other uses too.

Acrid musk saturated the air. Jewel-tipped stalactites hung from the cavern roof, aglow like many little lamps. The warlock likewise was aglow. His/her foul body shone phosphorescently as if lit from within; as if his/her flesh acted as a window to a lascivious light from elsewhere.

The warlock had once been human; now he/she mirrored the warp-form of the daemon which possessed and which had remoulded him/her.

He/she fought by projecting an obscene delirium of dizzying debauched desire. Even though psychic hoods shielded the Grey Knights, they were rocked. Despite all his own psychic training, Jaq felt twisted within. A lurid miasma dazed his vision.

Blasts from weapons went astray or were turned back to their sources so that the warlock seemed to be using his/her assailants as puppets to fight themselves.

Two Grey Knights died. But Jaq girded himself with his own tormented chastity and fired true, from psycannon and boltgun.

For a few moments more the warlock held his/her shape and Jaq almost despaired. Then the monstrous green body exploded like a balloon of filth, spattering the walls of the cavern and the cages of the cowering young prisoners – the last time he/she would set a mark upon them.

On his thigh Jaq wore that warlock's image in phosphorescent green.

Other daemons, which he confronted subsequently, had proved to be – if anything – even less appealing.

'The hydra isn't a daemon,' he murmured to himself. 'Yet how can it come from the warp, and not be steered ultimately by a Ruinous Power of the warp?'

The daemonological laboratories of the Ordo Malleus – its Chamber Theoretical – needed to know about this

strange new entity. Jaq prayed that this Harlequin man
might lead him to it.

GOOGOL SLOWED THE *Tormentum* to a virtual halt. The ship
drifted in the sea of lost souls as the occupants of that bubble of reality stared at what the warp-scope showed.

A space hulk wallowed in the spangled spectral abyss, in
thrall to the random currents of the warp; and it was there
that *Veils of Light* had docked, slipping in to some gaping
port.

The hulk wasn't one single derelict craft. The hulk was
many, and more. It was a titanic conglomerate constructed
by madmen, even by mad aliens too. The hulk might be
ten thousand years old, so scoured, pockmarked and
ancient did some parts appear.

Once, there must have been a single core-vessel which
had lost its way or had lost the use of its warp-vanes so that
it could no longer jump back into truespace.

Maybe its Navigator had died, his mind disrupted by
daemonic intrusion. Maybe a warp storm had battered the
ship and broken its warp-vanes when their runes failed.

The survivors must have tried to live out their lives by
hook or by crook, descending into despair and lunacy,
their offspring – if any – mutating into warp-monkeys.

Over the millennia, other wrecks and crippled vessels
were welded to the first, in whole or in part, or were
crashed into place in what became a vast assembly kilometres across and deep.

Many of these were deep-space vessels that never landed
on worlds. Crenellated towers and buttressed spires jutted
from the hulk as if a multiple collision had occurred
between baroque flying castles.

The whole mass resembled, too, some jointed
megawhale of metal which had sprouted metastasising
cancers. Exotic cruciform antennae arose. Corbelled gargoyles bristled, as if spewing into the warp. Wrecked
balustrades hung loose below stained-glass galleries.
Heavily ornamented fins and flukes protruded. One pier

intended for shuttles to dock at was studded with statues of dwarfs, another was embellished with runes. Weapons turrets were moulded in the shape of snarling wolves and savage lizards. A portal gaped: leering vermilion plasteel lips with bared ebon teeth each inscribed with golden texts. This portal was swallowing, or vomiting a fat endless worm...

Around the hulk clung the waxen coils of the hydra like some giant wreath of spilled intestines. Glassy tentacles delved through hatches and fissures. Tendrils rippled lazily in the warp current like weed in a stream. Some parts of the creature – hugely swollen parts – pulsed sluggishly, suggestive of disembowelled organs.

Other great sections of the entity hung almost loose, huge gobs of spittle on glassy strands. The hulk was vast; the hydra possibly vaster.

Jaq gave thanks to the Master of Mankind for their arrival.

Should he give thanks to Moma Parsheen too?

'Can you take us somewhat closer?' he asked Googol. 'Whilst steering clear of any dangling hydra?'

'Question is, will it steer clear of us, Jaq?'

'We'll find out. I spy a vacant cavity. Starboard top quadrant, see?'

Indeed. The hugging, questing, gelatinous limbs did not block all possible entrance into the multiple hulk.

As the Navigator nudged *Tormentum Malorum* slowly nearer to the indicated zone, using only attitude jets, for Jaq a strange intuition of security began to percolate through the dread engendered by hulk and warp alike. Tuning his psychic sense, he strove to analyse this feeling until he was virtually positive of its origin.

Once more the *Tormentum* hung almost motionless with respect to the convoluted crumpled cliffside of the hulk. A hundred metres of the emptiness-that-was-not still yawned, separating their ship from a ragged hole large enough to admit several armoured Terminator Marines abreast. Would that such were here!

Googol fretted. 'If we push closer than this, any sudden warp-eddy could impact us...'

'Here will do, then,' said Jaq. 'We can cross the remaining space in power suits.'

The Navigator's face blanched. 'You mean, leave the ship... at this point?'

The squat's teeth chattered momentarily. 'Er, boss, you aren't by any chance pro-pro-proposing warp-walking?'

'But that's an insane risk,' protested Googol. '*Things* can materialise anywhere in the warp. Things I'd rather not try to name!'

'We'll be safe,' said Jaq. 'I'm picking up a powerful field of daemonic shielding from this hulk. The field spills out beyond. We're within the fringe. Daemon spawn won't be able to home in and manifest themselves. We can leave the shield of *Tormentum* in almost total confidence.'

Grimm hummed and hawed; he cleared his throat. 'That's what he tells us... You aren't, um, merely saying that to, um, jolly us on?'

'*Damnatio!*' swore Jaq. 'What sort of fool do you think I am?'

'Okay, okay, I believe you, lord. We'll be shielded.'

The fact that the hulk was protected against daemonic intrusion piqued Jaq's curiosity at the same time as it relieved his mind. For in that case how could daemons and evil have any connection with the hydra?

'Right,' said Googol. 'I withdraw my objection, which as a warp pilot I felt bound to register.' He affected a sigh. 'So I presume I'm obliged to stay with the ship.' He glanced Moma Parsheen's way. 'I've no desire to stay with *her*, though. My gaze can kill, but obviously not a blind woman. She's unreliable, tricky. I wouldn't even trust her under lock and key.'

Oh yes, Googol had been left safely in a locked room once; and he had been taken by surprise.

'Huh!' exclaimed Grimm. 'So you've decided to opt out of this little excursion, eh, Vitali? That's nice to know. Of course a chivalrous fellow such as yourself couldn't contemplate *shooting* that... parody of a living ancestor. If need be, if need be.'

'I do feel a profound antipathy to firing any type of gun inside a ship I'm piloting,' the Navigator said loftily.

Grimm's attitude to Moma Parsheen had altered drastically since she revealed her sabotage of Stalinvast's future.

'Do we have to be saddled with her?' demanded the little man. 'Is that it? While we fight our way through the coils? That doesn't make much sense.'

'You're to stay with *Tormentum*, Vitali, quite right,' confirmed Jaq. 'As to our astropath...'

Logic said that Jaq should execute her now – and quite justifiably too – for the murder of a world, for the sabotage of the Imperium. However, maybe Stalinvast still survived, and the *Tormentum Malorum* might yet leave the warp in time for him to compel the old woman to send a signal to save the situation. And even so, she deserved to die for attempted treason.

Meanwhile, here they stood, in effect discussing the advisability of killing Moma Parsheen. The astropath listened, wearing a faint rictus of a smile, and thinking who knew what. How could such a debate stimulate any sense of loyalty towards her travelling companions?

What sense of loyalty? Plainly she possessed none, except perhaps to her cat-creature far away, which she had condemned to death.

'I sense when warp portals open,' she remarked in Jaq's general direction. 'Your hydra is at least partly a thing of the warp, is it not?'

She wasn't pleading for her life. She was simply reminding Jaq of how she might continue to be useful.

'Besides,' she added, 'I presume you need to know *precisely* where Carnelian is within that great mass?'

If only Jaq could sense ordinary human *physical* presence at a distance, as some psykers could. The firefly of a psychic spirit gleaming in the nightscape of existence. ah, that he could pinpoint by and large. Exerting this sense, he encountered the fog of daemonic shielding which was hiding whosoever occupied the hulk.

'Are you sure you can still fix him clearly, astropath?' he demanded.

Moma Parsheen gazed blindly. 'Oh yes,' she said. 'I'm good at harking through warped spaces, very good. I'm not *looking* for him. I'm listening to the echo of my tracer.'

'Our astropath will accompany us,' Jaq said. If he could but consult his Tarot! Yet Carnelian might be alerted. Jaq dearly wished to surprise that man.

Meh'Lindi spoke up. 'We'll be wearing powered space armour all the time we're inside the hulk? That disposes of the problem of Parsheen's muscular atrophy.' Oh no, Meh'Lindi would not call the astropath Moma.

'Huh! Give a madwoman the strength of a tigress?'

'I presume, Grimm,' she said, 'you can gimmick her armour so that she can be switched off by any of us if she misbehaves?'

'No problem, lady.'

'I thought not! I could do so easily enough myself.'

'Do you suppose *thinking* of doing so requires true genius, huh? Oh damn it, I'm sorry. I bite my tongue. Give me ten minutes to insert a governor into Vitali's space gear.'

'Into *mine*?' protested the Navigator.

'Whose else do you think the hag'll wear? Did she bring her own spacesuit in that little satchel, shrunken by magic?'

'She has never worn such gear in her life.'

'You want rid of her, yet you don't want her to wear your suit.'

'No, I do not! She might taint it psychically. Interfere with the protection runes.'

Grimm chortled. 'Our inquisitor can exorcise and asperge and reconsecrate it afterwards.'

Obviously the squat didn't place much faith in any such techno-theological procedures, the efficacy of which was perfectly evident to Jaq and to most right-minded people.

Still, the little man seemed somehow to get by. Unconsecrated, he certainly wouldn't survive in the warp!

'I will bless all our armour beforehand,' vowed Jaq. 'Triply so, when we are about to undertake a short swim in the sea of souls! I will seal and sanctify. You, Moma Parsheen, world-slayer, will lead us to Carnelian. We will surprise him, net him, wring the juice of confession out of him.'

Jaq thought of the collapsible excruciator that any inquisitor carried, to extort information from the unwilling. It had rarely been his style to use that instrument. Even though the device was righteous, he felt a certain repugnance towards it. Sometimes the whole galaxy seemed to reverberate with a sob of pain, a moan of anguish.

Soon JAQ AND Meh'Lindi were donning their stout suits of power armour and Grimm his smaller version of the same, while Googol disdainfully assisted Moma Parsheen into his own suit, his lips curled, as if he was packaging excrement.

Cuisses on to thighs... locking on to the hip girdle. Flared greaves on to shanks; magnetic boots locking into the greaves...

'*Benedico omnes armaturas,*' intoned Jaq. '*Benedico digitabula et brachiales, cataphractes atque pectorales.*'

Presently they were testing their sensor pick-ups, temperature regulators, air purificators...

TEΠ

LIKE FOUR BLACK-CARAPACED beetles decorated with protective runes, fluorescent red icons, and weapons pouches, Jaq and Meh'Lindi and little Grimm – who was tugging Moma Parsheen – jetted their way into a ruptured, cavernous hold. They hoped to maintain radio silence.

Junk of aeons hung aimlessly nearby: strange knobbly skulls of some humanoids reminiscent of irregular, cratered moonlets, an antique plasma gun half melted into slag, broken crates, and a buckled cage that was still confining a corpse dressed in a spotted leotard. A tumble of yellow silken hair suggested woman, though the long-exposed flesh was purple leather.

Their light beams played around the interior. Shadows jerked about. The corpse in the cage seemed to shift as if seeking release. In the deeps grim giant ghosts appeared to swell. This was all illusion.

Jaq carried on his suit a force rod, power axe and psy-cannon. The force rod, resembling some solid black flute embedded with enigmatic circuits, stored psychic energy

so as to augment a psyker's mental attack. Unknown aliens
had crafted all such force rods which had fallen into the
hands of the Imperium, most notably the cache found in
the ice-caverns of Karsh XIII. Impervious to any probing, a
rod never needed or offered the possibility of any over-
haul, so it was perhaps the least adorned of all weapons.
By contrast, the shaft of Jaq's power axe was embossed
with rococo icons, the pommel of that halberd was a brass
ork skull, and complex purity seals embellished the power-
pack to which a cable resembling a gem-serpent ran. The
psycannon likewise was adorned with supernumerary ribs
and moulded flanges painted with esoteric, exorcistic
glyphs.

Jaq drew Meh'Lindi's attention to the bio-scanner in its
filigreed, jade-studded frame. A blotch of green light registered the psychic throb of life deep in the interior of the
hulk. However, his scanner was fogged by emanations
from the aspect of the hydra that was alive, almost mask-
ing the trace.

That pocket of life was plainly still some distance away,
yet it was apparent to Jaq that the instrument was attempting to distinguish more than the single sharp blip that
would represent Carnelian alone.

He held up his gauntlet questioningly, opening five fingers once... then twice.

Meh'Lindi signalled another ten possible presences far
ahead, in her opinion. Maybe more.

When Jaq turned up the gain on his sensor, static
flooded it. Too much interference from the hydra. To his
annoyance the sensitive instrument failed like a night-
flower wilting in too bright a light. He muttered an
invocation but the machine's soul had perished and did
not revive.

Ever since entering the hulk, Jaq had been aware of daemonic shielding. While this relieved his mind in one
regard – daemon spawn would be unable to home in and
manifest themselves – the precaution piqued his curiosity
afresh.

Jaq heartily disliked space hulks. It was well known how these sinister plasteel cadavers could house genestealer broods, adrift for centuries or millennia until a fluke of the warp vomited the derelict into truespace close to some vulnerable world.

Or they might shelter piratical degenerates who had become creatures of Chaos.

Loyal subjects of the Imperium always feared hulks. Imperial merchantmen traversing the warp would flee at the sighting of one. Space Marines were honour-bound to board a hulk, to cleanse any threat it posed, and to recover any valuable or enigmatic pieces of ancient technology from millennia earlier which might be encysted in the wreck like pearls held in a lethal clam.

Too often, the consequences of such boardings proved quite dire.

Where better, then, to hide the heart of some treacherous web of intrigue than in such a megavessel lost in the vastness of the warp, that all sane voyagers would shun?

The four intruders drifted through the hold. Half a dozen different black-mouthed corridors beckoned, angling away variously. Tentacles of the hydra protruded from two; stout soapy cables, undulating sluggishly.

Moma Parsheen pointed to a third, empty mouth. That direction corresponded with the earlier bearings for the green splotch of life signs.

HAD IT NOT been for the psychic tracer, they must surely have lost themselves in the labyrinthine entrails of what was not one vessel but many, some of these enormous in their own right.

They traversed sooty halls so crammed with long-dead machinery as to be mazes in themselves. They floated down dismal lift shafts; they mounted crazily angled corridors where friezes showed forgotten battles between impossible ships shaped like butterflies with wings of spectral energy. Other walls were gouged as if claws had ravaged them. Some walls glowed with runes.

Their lights picked out the graffiti of long-dead people –
prayers, curses, obscenities, threats – and what might have
been messages in alien script or in the calligraphy of madness. In one zone a drift of loose bones, kippered limbs,
and dehydrated heads suggested cannibalism.

At last, a functioning airlock admitted them into a section where a breathable atmosphere survived, and
warmth.

Survived? Ah no, thought Jaq. Where air and heat had
been *restored*.

He raised his visor and breathed cautiously. Oxygen
enough, a spike of ozone – and a hint of sensuous cloying
patchouli, perhaps injected to mask the undertow of
smouldering embers, as of charring insulation.

The others copied him, Grimm assisting Moma
Parsheen.

'He's very close,' the astropath commented dully.

Through a plascrystal port they gazed upon a vast hazy
hangar lit by the occasional glowstrip. *Veils of Light* was
berthed there, tethered magnetically. So were six other star-
cruisers. One, shaped like a terrestrial shark; another like a
rippy-fish; a third like the sting of a scorpion. Jaq looked
in vain through a lens for identification marks, badges, or
names. All the usual safety runes, of course. Otherwise, so
far as he could see, the vessels were anonymous, identities
concealed. Servitors – half-human, half-machine – rolled
to and fro, stepped like spiders across the hulls on sucker
pads. The haze in the hangar was exhaust gas expelled during docking.

That shark ship reminded him–

A speaker crackled to life.

'Welcome, Jaq Draco!' That was Carnelian's voice: part
merry, part crazed. 'Congratulations! You're everything we
hoped for.'

'Who is we?' Jaq shouted in response and promptly
slammed his visor shut in case of gas attack. Meh'Lindi
and Grimm followed his lead, and Meh'Lindi flipped the
blind woman's visor shut too.

Jaq drew his power axe. The assassin and the abhuman both favoured laspistols at this point. In the gravityless environment of the hulk any unexploded bolts or similar projectiles could ricochet unpredictably for a long time within a confined space.

'All will be explained!' came the voice, now over their audio pickups. 'First, you must shed your armour and weapons. Especially, your assassin must divest herself of every tiny hidden trick. Except herself, of course! She's the funniest trick of all.' Carnelian giggled. 'Do it now. You're being scanned.'

Jaq switched on the magnetics in his boots to give him purchase for possible combat. Grimm and Meh'Lindi didn't need to be told to do likewise.

'Ah, you're rooted to the spot!' mocked the voice.

Moma Parsheen still floated blindly near the plascrystal port. Jaq gestured urgently ahead, and swung a boot forward.

At that very moment, from the air-gargoyles furthest away, fingers then arms of grey jelly erupted to interlace across the corridor. Behind the little party similar tentacles of hydra burst forth, blocking any retreat.

Jaq activated his power axe and strode forward. Meh'Lindi and Grimm flanked him, firing their lasers, slicing through the impeding arms.

Severed segments writhed and melted. Globules filled the air. Still more tentacles poured into the corridor – from every gargoyle now. The hydra's substance reformed and repaired itself, recoagulating and stiffening even as Jaq hewed with his power axe and as his companions lasered.

A force greater than magnetism gripped Jaq's feet. The floor was ankle-deep, knee-deep soon in viscid, melted and disjoined hydra which sought to set like glue. Jaq powered a boot free, then the boot was trapped once more.

Quite quickly the whole corridor filled to the brim with the substance of the hydra. Pressure mounted against Jaq's armour, and though the armour could withstand far greater stress before crumpling he could hardly move even

under full power. Red tell-tales blinked as he exerted himself.

Rather than overload the suit's resources, he relaxed. The
power axe, clenched in his mailed fist, still hewed away at
the same small area in front of him, but for the life of him
he couldn't push himself into the space it liquefied, nor
could he shift the weapon to left or to right, so firmly was
his arm held by the hydra.

All he could see was tough grey jelly plastered across his
visor. He felt such a writhing impotence. He was out-
guessed. Paralysed. Though nothing as yet had touched his
flesh, he was a titbit trapped in stiffest aspic.

So were they all.

'Cease fire, if you can,' he radioed to his invisible companions. 'We may only hurt ourselves.'

As he strove to release his grip on the control of the
power axe, so the jelly appeared to co-operate. It slackened,
then tightened once again as soon as the axe was inactive.

Presently, Jaq felt the fingers of his gauntlet being forced
apart; and his axe was lifted away. Soon after, he realised
with a chill in his groin that something was opening the
clasps of his suit.

Those cold touches of steel! He realised that a servitor was
stripping him of his armour and removing all detectable
weapons. The robotic thing was working within the substance of the hydra and with its apparent complicity.

Recalling how Meh'Lindi had been violated on that
other occasion, Jaq feared for her sanity once her psychic
hood was removed. Yet he also hoped that she might
retain some weapon, hidden in a hollow tooth perhaps.

When Jaq's helmet lifted clear, the hydra did not flow up
against his face to suffocate him.

'Can you hear me?' he cried.

Only centimetres from his eyes and mouth, the hydra
blurred and soaked up his voice so that he seemed to be
shouting underwater.

Yet soon the glutinous entity was withdrawing far from
his head, allowing him to see it squeezing portion by

portion back into the ventilation system. He still couldn't move. Burly, fearsome servitors held all four of the intruders inflexibly.

The machines were hideous parodies of the human form, their metal casings and flanges moulded so that the robots seemed to be sculptures made of bones welded together, interspersed with flattened, grimacing skulls. Each sported two flails of sinuous steel tentacles and a crab-like claw. The sensors of their faces were indented into a snarling, tusked daemon mask.

Finally, save for inchoate puddles adhering to the floor and the walls, the hydra was all gone.

'What a deal of nuisance we could all have saved ourselves,' remarked Carnelian's voice. 'And now, dear guests, it's party time.'

These disconcerting servitors slid on magnetised feet along the corridor, carrying their prisoners suspended weightlessly. Suits and weapons remained adrift. At least Jaq and the others hadn't been stripped naked. Only Grimm bothered to wriggle and kick.

IN THE VAULTED auditorium to which they were carried, a score and a half of robed figures sat around a horseshoe of data-desks. The robes were of black or crimson velvet – over body armour – and all of those seated at the desks wore identical long masks.

Thirty mock-Emperors regarded the prisoners through tinted lenses; for those masks mimicked the shrivelled features of the Master of Mankind, including some of the tubes and wires which sustained that living corpse.

Only the capering Carnelian showed his true, mischievous face. He was wearing a domino costume of black spots on white on his left side, white spots on black on his right. His high collar was white and fluted. His black half-cloak swirled as he turned to display himself. Magnetic shoes, studded with pearls, were pointy and golden in hue. On his head, a gilded tricorne hat. What a lethal, sly fop the man was.

'In the Emperor's name,' said Jaq. 'You, who mock the Emperor–'

'Be quiet,' growled a voice. 'We *are* of the Emperor. We do His bidding.'

'Hiding here in the warp? Manipulating a creature of the warp?'

One of the pretend Emperors hauled off his mask abruptly. That triforked ginger beard! Those bristling eyebrows!

Shock coursed through Jaq. 'Harq Obispal!'

Yet of course: that shark ship…

The ruthless inquisitor roared with laughter, steel teeth showing amongst his ivories.

'Ostentation can be a mask too, Jaq Draco! A brazen display can distract attention from the true purpose. Though you cannot deny that Stalinvast needed cleansing of its parasites! Ah, those convenient genestealers…'

Obispal's gaze drifted towards Meh'Lindi, and he frowned as if adding the final piece to a puzzle which had been perplexing him, but not liking the pattern that he saw.

Did Obispal's associates realise that the rashly rampaging inquisitor was only present in this auditorium courtesy of Jaq's assassin who had plucked him to safety? Jaq smiled at the impassive Meh'Lindi, blessing her impetuous intervention in that arcade in Vasilariov.

'Hear me, inquisitor ordinary,' he said. 'Obey me. I am of the Malleus.'

Obispal grinned. 'I know full well. What else could you be, snooping on my activities?'

Jaq pressed his advantage, however slim. 'It's as well that I was, otherwise you'd be dead now, torn apart by genestealers, wouldn't you be?'

Several masked figures stirred. One asked, 'Is this true?' Even Carnelian registered surprise.

'It's accurate enough,' allowed Obispal, 'though by that stage my death wouldn't have made a whit of difference to the outcome. I was merely somewhat incautious at one point. One risks one's life for the Emperor always, blessed be His name.' The man's tone was dismissive, and Jaq had to allow him more credit for flexibility than he would have supposed.

'Still,' hissed another mask, 'it would have been a shame to lose so bold a partner in this enterprise of ours; and of His Supremacy's. Recruiting suitable candidates is a delicate business. Which brings us to yourself, Jaq Draco–'

Further around the horseshoe, a voice which struck Jaq as familiar asked him: 'Draco, what is the greatest need in this galaxy?'

Jaq replied immediately: 'The need for control.'

'So let me tell you about our Emperor's hopes for the fullest possible form of control...' The owner of that voice pulled off his mask.

Jaq felt stunned anew. For the man looking at him through one natural eye and a lens in the socket of his other eye, the silver-haired man with a scar bisecting his cheek, to which he had sewn rubies so that the long-healed wound seemed still to gleam with blood – was none other than Baal Firenze.

'Proctor!' Jaq sketched a minor adoration of respect. 'You sent me to Stalinvast–'

'And you have been more quick-witted than even I expected.' Firenze nodded towards Jaq's companions. 'Let's have some total privacy, Zephro.'

Carnelian produced null-sense hoods and proceeded to fit these over Grimm's head, and Moma Parsheen's. Dartingly as a lizard's tongue he kissed Meh'Lindi on the side of the brow before plunging her, too, into silence and blindness.

'As you know, Draco,' resumed the proctor, 'there is an outer order of the Inquisition, and there is an inner order. And then there is the Ordo Malleus – with its Hidden Masters. Within the ranks of those Hidden Masters exists a secret, innermost conclave founded in recent centuries by the Emperor himself, answerable to no one else, and now here in session. This most secret group is the Imperial

Order of the Hydra. Its main tool is, of course, the hydra.
Its long-term purpose is none other than the total control
of all human minds throughout the galaxy.'

And Proctor Firenze proceeded to explain the plan that
motivated this cabal of Hidden Masters gathered there in
the hulk.

WAS IT AN hour later? Jaq still reeled at the grandeur and
abomination of the enterprise.

Some twenty of the cabalists had removed their masks
by now, as if in earnest of good faith. Jaq knew none by
sight – unless they had been surgically altered; nevertheless he could perceive that they were true-human, no
marks of Chaos blemishing their features. He would know
those faces again.

Eight others retained their incognitos. Cloaked in crimson, those were the High Masters of the Hydra. Jaq
detected psychic strength of the utmost degree, yet no taint
of daemonic pollution. This was undoubtedly human
business.

Obispal was a member of this very special Ordo. So too
had Jaq now sworn to become. He had repeated his oaths
dully like a sleeptalker. One of those oaths bound him
never to return to Terra, never to revisit the headquarters of
the Inquisition, nor the even more elusive bastion of the
Ordo Malleus.

In return Jaq had received a new electro-tattoo,
imprinted on to his right cheek by Carnelian. The design
was of a squirming octopus clinging round a living human
head. All of those present who had shed their masks activated their own identical tattoos then willed the image to
vanish again.

So it transpired that the elusive Zephro Carnelian was a
trusted roving agent for the Ordo Hydra. Not an enemy at
all – but an ally in the greatest, most righteous, yet perhaps
also the vilest of plans.

Jaq now had custody of portions of the hydra packed in
an adamantium stasis-trunk fitted with coded locks. When

in future he removed coils of tentacle to seed the guts of the worlds he visited, so – he was assured – the entity would replenish itself, stasis notwithstanding, since the Chaos that underlay the universe connected the hydra together subtly, no matter how scattered its parts.

'I have no further questions,' Jaq finally told the conclave.

'Unhood those useful iotas, then,' Firenze instructed Carnelian.

Meh'Lindi, Grimm, Moma Parsheen: *iotas*, mere jots, tiny ciphers in the vastness of the Imperium and in the huge insidious scheme of the cabalists. Jaq, for his part, wondered whether he too was merely an iota, or had genuinely been promoted to become a moulder of destiny.

Even with rejuvenations it seemed highly unlikely that any of those present could possibly live long enough to experience – to *enjoy* seemed totally the wrong word – the fruits of the hydra enterprise. Unless those eight masked High Masters were sufficiently confident in their associates to try to journey to the next galaxy and back – in some incredible megaship – to take advantage of time-compression! Or to place themselves in stasis for centuries on end? Unless they dared to absent themselves from the slow unfolding of the plan – would not their keen minds continue to be needed?

Therefore the scheme must indeed be altruistic and unselfish, without personal benefit to those who were currently involved. This must indeed be a scheme for salvation in the long term: salvation through utter enslavement.

Carnelian unhooded Jaq's companions, re-admitting noise and light to their senses.

Held motionless in zero gravity by the servitors with no input of information whatever, the three had been undergoing sensory deprivation for the past hour. Grimm dribbled like a happy baby. Meh'Lindi wore a mildly blissful smile which vanished as she came alert again. Moma Parsheen cried out as she sensed environment flooding back, the way that sensation needles through a frozen limb. For the first time in her life, perhaps, the astropath had been psychically blind as well as visually so; utterly isolated.

'It's great that you arrived here, Jaq,' enthused Zephro Carnelian as he folded away the hoods. 'Without wishing to expose myself to obloquy, as you exposed friend Harq before we all became colleagues–'

Obispal guffawed, though there was a sour note to his humour.

'–would you mind confirming exactly how you distinguished yourself by finding us? Purely for the record?'

Surely the Harlequin man must have guessed?

'For the record,' said Jaq, 'it was an astropath trace. A homer in your mind.'

'Ah, ah, of course. Inserted *when*?'

'Don't worry, it'll decay within a few days.'

'*When exactly*?'

Didn't the man know? Hadn't Jaq virtually been led here by Carnelian?

'Why, it was when you transmitted your goading holo into Voronov-Vaux's sanctum, through the spy-flies you stole from me.'

'Ah! The biter, bit. The spy, spied on. That would be just after you decided not to declare *exterminatus* after all... I guess your *exterminatus* decision was really what clinched my respect for your ability to think on a grand scale, Jaq. Be damned if we didn't hope you would simply call in the Space Marines and spread our hydra around some more! Yet no, you think in ultimates. And that is excellent. We need ultimate thinking in the Ordo Hydra, Jaq. So: no harm done and no hard feelings.'

'Except perhaps on the part of the whole population of Stalinvast,' Jaq commented acidly.

Carnelian froze. 'You didn't send the *exterminatus* message, Jaq. As soon as the hydra began withdrawing, you changed your mind.'

Jaq nodded towards the astropath. 'She still sent it. Of her own accord.'

For a few brief moments Carnelian's face might have been that of a polymorphine shape-shifter viewed at speed, passing through absurdly accelerated transformations. For a few instants only, until he laughed.

Carnelian rounded on Moma Parsheen, laughing. And still laughing, he plucked a laspistol from his belt and shot her through one of her blind eyes, boiling her brain.

ELEVEN

'OH NO, WE can't tolerate an astropath who puts homers into people's heads. Not when you consider the calibre of people who are collected here. Oh nil and nunquam and nullity. In a word, no.'

Thus had Carnelian swiftly explained his shooting of the old woman.

REUNITED WITH THEIR space armour and weapons, Jaq and Meh'Lindi and Grimm were escorted through the eerie maze of the hulk by the savage servitors. Grimm towed the Navigator's weightless empty suit along behind him, and Jaq manoeuvred the adamantium trunk. At the hold where all the alien skulls floated, the automatons left the trio.

Out to *Tormentum Malorum* they jetted, only to be greeted with scepticism by the Navigator ensconced inside.

'Come on, open up,' said Grimm. 'You've locked the air-lock.'

'Aha,' came Googol's response over the radio, 'but you may say you are those same three people inside those suits...'

'What's this,' asked Jaq, 'a fit of warp-psychosis? It's us who untied you back in the Emerald Suite. Remember?'

'Aha, but if you are my enemies you'll know about that. Because you would have tied me up.'

'If you don't open up, Vitali,' said Meh'Lindi, 'lovely lady of death will steal away your breath and mock your bones and squeeze your heart and all the rest of it.'

Could a radio wave blush? 'Ah, right, yes,' came Vitali's voice, and the airlock cycled.

NOW THAT THEY were safely back aboard, minus an astropath but plus one locked stasis-trunk, the Harlequin man's excuse for shooting Moma Parsheen failed to satisfy Jaq.

'Was it your impression,' he asked Meh'Lindi, 'that Carnelian was performing a lightning calculation as to whether we might stand any chance of still saving Stalinvast if we jumped back into normal space?'

'Huh, fat chance of saving the planet now,' interrupted Grimm. 'He shot our message service. Was that his idea?'

'It's my impression,' said Meh'Lindi slowly, 'he may have decided there was no hope whatever for Stalinvast. That we'd be too late.' Her tone said that she still loathed the Harlequin man, yet she felt compelled to be accurate.

Jaq agreed. 'I think the news filled him, just for a moment, with grief and rage. I think he cared about the murder of a world.'

'Makes sense,' said the squat, 'if he was hoping to use Stalinvast as a playground for his bally hydra.'

'No, it was a deeper caring than that. He visited... justice, true justice upon Moma Parsheen. For a moment he was a billion people seeking some slight recompense for the waste of their lives.'

So therefore the Ordo Hydra genuinely was a caring organisation. Ruthless and totalitarian, of necessity, yet also in the long run cherishing the human race, although it must needs manacle the minds of men; absolutely, as never before.

Alas for this interpretation, Baal Firenze had reacted with apparent amusement to the revelation that Stalinvast had indeed been flushed down the sink of history. With Stalinvast gone, any remaining evidence of the kindling of the hydra had been obliterated; and Jaq would need to think up an almighty lie to exonerate the command he gave, should official query ever reach him. Which it might not... for twenty years, or more. (In a galaxy of a million worlds!) Jaq would be well advised to steer well clear of Earth until the end of his days and serve the Ordo Hydra loyally. Should he do so – as he had sworn – why, his proctor would of course rubber-stamp the eradication of Stalinvast...

'What went on while we were hooded, lord?' the squat asked. 'And what's in that trunk?'

'What is in the trunk is utterly secret,' Jaq said sternly.

'Just thought it might be something tasty to eat. Pickled grox tongues, for instance. A going-away gift.'

'Maybe it's a bigger, crueller rack, little fellow!' Jaq snapped.

'Sorry, inquisitor. I'm the right size for me already.'

'Then stay that way.'

'Where do we transport it to?' asked Googol.

'Don't concern yourself about it at all, Vitali. I shall lock it away. Erase all memory of it. Where to next? Obviously some world in need of scrutiny.'

As JAQ LAY in his sleep-cell at quarter-light with the trunk sealed in the nearby oubliette, he recalled all that he had learned at the conclave.

That cabal had created the hydra after long research in covert theological laboratories located on the frozen fringe of some barren solar system unclaimed by either the Imperium or by aliens.

Guided by the Emperor's own harsh wisdom and foresight, they had experimented on the very stuff of Chaos and upon slaves permanently immobilised in nutrient vats, and upon prisoners.

The result was a multiform entity against which normal weapons were useless.

However, the hydra's material manifestation was only the tip of the iceberg. When mature, each hydra – all part of the same hydra – would sporulate psychically, infesting human minds planet-wide, while all body traces would melt away. The hydra's psychic spores would remain dormant in human brains for untold generations, passed from parent to child.

'Our aim,' Baal Firenze had explained, 'is to seed the hydra on innumerable human worlds. On the majority. On all. We hope each hydra might escape detection during the period while it grows to maturity – or only be detected by riff-raff, whom no one in power will heed. A vain hope, obviously! Yet let it be detected, let it! *Nihil obstat*, as we say. Eradication programmes by planetary governors or by ordinary inquisitors will seem to succeed yet will simply enlarge the span and final influence of the hydra. Even Malleus men who aren't privy to our secret will only scatter the hydra in their zeal, and then subsequently lack all proof or comprehension of what occurred.'

'Zeal short of *exterminatus*,' Jaq had reminded the proctor.

'Agreed. If nothing remains alive on a world, why then, nothing can be controlled. I warrant there will be few such instances of *exterminatus*. A minuscule percentage.'

Control was the watchword. The hydra would obey the thoughts of its makers. Ultimately the spores of the entity would pervade all of humanity, to which it vectored by design. Eventually the Masters of the Ordo Hydra would activate those psychic spores. These would sprout: tiny hydras in the heads of trillions of people, all linked subtly through the medium of the warp.

Whereupon those masters – the self-proclaimed servants of the Emperor – could control the entire human species galaxy-wide, almost instantaneously.

Jaq had already witnessed, and Meh'Lindi had experienced, how the hydra could be used to invade the pleasure centres of the brain. The pain centres likewise.

'In chosen instances,' Firenze had revealed, 'the total human population of the galaxy will be compelled to function as one mighty mind. Its combined psychic power will be vast enough to scour away all alien life forms and to purge the warp of malign entities. If our Emperor's Astronomican is a lighthouse shining through the warp, this new linked mind will be a flamethrower.'

A SMALL CABAL would control all the minds of men and women for ever more. Able to twist them, direct them, fill them with ecstasy, or torment them. But mainly: to *focus* them collectively, whithersoever the cabal chose.

'This,' the proctor had concluded, 'will be the Emperor's legacy and greatest achievement. No doubt you know he is failing – just as the Imperium is failing, slowly and haphazardly, but failing nonetheless. His Supremacy will leave behind him a cosmic creature which a group of utterly dedicated masters can operate.

'Farewell, then, to daemons when we tap all human psychic potential simultaneously. Farewell to the Powers of the warp.

'Farewell to vicious genestealers and to sly eldar and to vicious pillaging orks. Farewell to the hordes of tyranids like locusts, to all aliens and their mocking, inhuman heresy.

'But most of all, farewell to all the excesses of Chaos – flayed and tamed by the human multi-mind at last!'

A grand and dire vision indeed. And Jaq would spread the hydra far and wide. As he lay musing in his sleep-cell, doubts assailed him.

If he tried to return to Terra in defiance of his oath he strongly suspected that he might never be allowed to reach the homeworld. Surely he would be watched for several years, to ensure his fidelity.

Yet, what *guarantee* did he have that the Emperor was actually the begetter of the hydra project? A project so covert that most Hidden Masters of the Ordo Malleus itself remained ignorant of it! How could the God-Emperor have sanctioned such a plan, if the human race were ever to achieve the destiny he had dreamed of for it? One of eventual freedom and fulfilment? Would the hydra eventually wither away spontaneously? Or had the Emperor... despaired of his dream?

In which case, the core of everything was *rotten*.

The Emperor, popularly supposed to be immortal, only endured by virtue of adamantine, anguished courage and willpower. The seemingly potent forces of his Imperium were stretched as thin as strands of spider-silk in a giant galactic web which was mostly vacant space. Strands of a cobweb are surprisingly strong but they can snap. When too many snap, the whole web collapses into a sticky mess.

Might the object of ultimate attack by the controlled mass-brain of humanity be the Emperor *himself*? The sick spider at the heart of the web? Thus leaving the descendants of the cabal in charge of the Imperium?

How could Jaq know for sure?

Those gruesome servitors which had restrained the trio – and the astropath – reminded Jaq so strongly of images he had viewed of traitor legionnaires, the polluted renegades spawned by the would-be Emperor-slayers of long ago who now lurked in a certain terrible, twisted zone of the galaxy...

His door slid aside.

Meh'Lindi slipped silently into his cell and shut the door. Outlined in the dim light, she was such a menacingly poised silhouette that Jaq's hand closed on the needle-gun under his pillow.

'Pardon me, inquisitor,' she murmured. She moved no closer. No doubt she was aware of the gun.

'Are you somebody else's person?' he asked. 'Did Carnelian change your allegiance? Did he make you his?'

'No... Only yours. And mine own. And the Emperor's.'

'Why are you here?'

'You need solace, Jaq, relief from burdens. I need a different kind of exorcism to free me from what he did to me. While I was hooded I was dreaming of how to accomplish this. To kill him seems forbidden now, does it not? I must regard him as... an ally?'

'True. And you wish to know why. Exactly why.'

'No, I don't need to know why. I'm your instrument. You're the commander of death; I'm death's agent.'

She crept forward and reached out a hand with no digital weaponry on the fingers... though even her naked fingers could kill. She touched him lingeringly.

'Solace, Jaq. For you, for me. Your mind is troubled by impossible contradictions.'

Jaq's heart beat faster. 'Then one must purge those contradictions. Only the Emperor's way is true. We should pray.'

'Pray to be shown *which* true way is the truly true way? If you'll pardon me, I have a better idea. Am I not your mistress in masquerade... trader? The others won't know. And if they do discern, why, Grimm will only grunt, "Huh" while Vitali may compose a forlorn ode. Privately Vitali will feel relieved that his yearning can finally be classed as hopeless – that he need not spur himself recklessly to act in regard to me; and maybe die as a result.

'You're at a cusp of decision, Jaq. But you do not possess... perspective, to perceive which way to leap. I offer a different perspective than prayer.'

She gestured towards the hulk which hung outside *Tormentum Malorum*.

'Those new masters of yours will not expect you to adopt this perspective. They will expect you to bottle up your inner uncertainty, whatever it is about. And so to stifle it. They will expect *purity* to drive you onward. Be impure with me for a while. And seek your light.'

Slowly she began to strip off her clingtight black tunic, and so to become more visible. Soon she was tracing all his tattoos and he her scars.

* * *

As HE LAY beside her later, exalted and still alive, he thought of how he had previously denied himself this ecstasy.

Ah but no! Rather – for years – he had denied himself banality, as if disbelieving in the possibility of such physical transcendence. Truly, an assassin's body was well trained. Maybe she could have surfeited him with pleasure as surely as she could have overwhelmed him with agony. And his ecstasy had soon become her ecstasy, an electrochemical fuel that had ignited in her, burning away all the taint of that earlier false frenzy enforced on her by the Harlequin man.

'Meh'Lindi–'

'It can only happen this once,' she murmured.

'Yes, I realise.' He knew that. 'After climbing the highest peak, who would seek foothills?'

'I know what I see from my peak, Jaq. I see myself again: lady of death. I am purged of corruption.'

'With which Carnelian had infected you... Why did he do that to you? Why did he use pleasure as a weapon?'

From Jaq's own high peak, in his state of exalted altered consciousness, what did he see?

'Perhaps,' he said, 'Carnelian was sending you – and therefore me – two messages in one. Firstly, that if he could do so, he would rather bring joy than pain. Which is why he shot Moma Parsheen, in sheer rejection of her bitter vengeance.'

'And secondly?'

'Secondly, that the human mind can be utterly controlled by the users of the hydra. That message, delivered to you in Kefalov, may not have been a boast but a warning. Meh'Lindi, I need to confide what I learned in that conclave.'

Once Jaq had finished explaining all about the hydra project, she said, 'Zephro Carnelian must be a double agent. He's working for the Ordo Hydra, but also subtly against them. What he did to me... that was to show us

how total a tyranny was being planned, so that I – so that
we – would loathe it. Why do that unless he's secretly
opposed? If we're right, he also loathed the complete
destruction of Stalinvast – even though he co-operated
with Obispal in kindling the hydra, a task that cost millions of lives.'

'So who else does he represent?'

'Are those High Masters human, Jaq?'

Jaq nodded. 'Yet maybe *they* obey hidden masters elsewhere, who may not be quite so human. Truly, the
universe is a skein of lies, deceits, and traps.'

'Carnelian has shown a perverse attraction to you too,
Jaq. Did he deliberately draw himself to your attention
merely to involve you in this new Ordo – or because he
hopes you might lance the boil of a conspiracy without
him needing to show his own hand? While he pretends
to foster it loyally all the while so as to stay in contact
with it?'

'I don't know... Those servitors: they were like some
suits used by traitor legionnaires corrupted by Chaos. You
could almost employ such automatons as emissaries – or
couriers – to the Eye of Terror itself... And where else
could the hydra really have been spawned? Where else? In
some great covert laboratory orbiting the outermost ball
of frozen rock in some uncharted system? Am I supposed
to believe that story?'

'The Eye of Terror, Jaq?' Did Meh'Lindi shudder beside
him? Was even she appalled at the prospect he was
unfolding? He stroked her again, while he still could do
so.

The Eye of Terror... That great dust-nebula hid within it
dozens of hellish solar systems which witnessed no stars,
but only rippling rainbow auroras forever a-dance.

The legions of those who betrayed the Emperor during
the Horus Rebellion had fled to the Eye and thereafter...
had mutated vilely. For the Eye was a zone where truespace and the warp actually overlapped, braiding together
in nightmare distortions.

Where else could an entity composed of blended matter and immaterium really have been conceived and forged but in the Eye?

Could the cabal be a conspiracy against the Emperor and *against all humankind* mounted by the denizens of the Eye, by those twisted bitter enemies of the Imperium?

Not a secret master plan on the part of the Emperor – but a dagger aimed at his heart? And at all human hearts?

'For us to head for the Eye of Terror would be to invite almost certain death,' mused Jaq. 'From the cabal, first of all. Even more so, from the twisted creatures that flourish in the Eye.'

Meh'Lindi gripped his hand. 'No, Jaq, that is not the way to think about this. One does not *invite* death. That is the way of fools and failures who plunge to their own destruction because a part of them has despaired and wishes to die. Thus doom accepts their invitation.

'Think rather that I am the lady of death and that you are the master of death! The Eye of Terror invites death into its own house. It invites *us* – as if calling upon a godly power which is its superior.'

'Aye, to blaspheme against it vigorously and violently, and consume it if it can.' Jaq sighed. 'We could simply flee.'

He was voicing a desire which he feared might only bring him Meh'Lindi's contempt – so soon after she had honoured and anointed him with her body. Yet this needed to be said. Flight was a possible avenue and he must not overlook any of their options.

'We could try to drop out of sight on some far world. We could defect to some alien civilization which might understand the hydra. We could seek exile on an eldar craftworld.'

'Indeed,' she agreed. 'The eldar should be grateful to know about this weapon which would one day be launched against them.'

'Long before the hydra could be activated we would have ended our days amidst aliens – or on some wild frontier world. Why, the galaxy is so vast that in the latter case I could continue to pose – and behave – as an inquisitor; though I would truly be a renegade...'

Even as he spoke, this avenue closed up in his mind's eye like a pupil contracting to a black point. That was why he had voiced this craven option; so as to witness it vanishing.

A different, vaster, sickly eye was staring at him and daring him: the glowing nebulosity where space and unspace wove together.

'No, we must go to the Eye to investigate,' he murmured.

If they survived, why, Jaq must then go to Earth to ask for guidance.

That undertaking would be fraught with enormous peril too. For they could trust nobody. Except themselves.

'Jaq–'

'Hmm?'

'Before one travels among people who are diseased, it's wise to seek an inoculation against their diseases. Before going amongst outlandish strangers, it may be sensible to camouflage oneself. In Carnelian's hands I was vulnerable to the hydra...'

'What are you proposing?'

She told Jaq, and he almost retched.

THE ADAMANTIUM TRUNK yawned open, the glassy coils lying immobile within.

Meh'Lindi had injected herself with the polymorphine. Now she recited sing-song invocations in a language Jaq had never heard before.

She flexed herself, she breathed spasmodically as if to confuse the natural rhythms of her body.

Jaq muttered prayers. '*Imperator, age. Imperator, eia. Servae tuae defensor...*'

Meh'Lindi reached into the trunk and lifted out a small tentacle, which squirmed as it left the stasis-field. Then she sank her teeth into that flesh which was not flesh.

Hastily she bit gobbets loose and swallowed them, bolting down a dreadful and disgusting feast. Those lips, which had so recently roved over Jaq's body, now sucked in the slithery tough stuff of the hydra with the same seeming hunger.

How could she do so without vomiting? The strength of her jaw, the blades of her teeth!

'It's nothing,' she mumbled, catching his expression. 'I was weaned on jungle-slugs. Our mothers squeezed them. Proteins and juices pop into the baby's mouth. The baby sucks until the slug is dry...'

Her foul meal completed, she sat cross-legged and concentrated, brow furrowed. This time, she wasn't metamorphising her own body by will power. In ways Jaq did not understand, she was studying and altering and neutralising the dissolving contents of her stomach, immunising herself to those through the mediation of the polymorphine.

After a long while she belched several times, then said, 'Maybe I'll be more resistant now. Carnelian won't play that trick on me again. Ever.'

Jaq gazed into the trunk. Where the consumed tentacle had rested a mist seemed to be congealing out of nothing as though the hydra was already replenishing itself. The immaterium did not heed all the laws of stasis. The entity remained inert within the trunk yet could still restore what was taken.

'Do you suppose that Carnelian and the cabal can have eaten this same terrible meal?' asked Jaq. 'Do you feel you can control – command – the hydra now, yourself? The way Carnelian does?'

Meh'Lindi brooded, then shook her head.

'I'm not a psyker,' she said. 'Immunity will satisfy me. Maybe if...'

'If I was to eat some too?'

'No, I don't think you should. You have never trained with polymorphine. You have never altered your flesh. It's a hard skill. We have no idea what rituals Carnelian may have used, if indeed he digested a meal of this stuff.'

Jaq felt profoundly glad that he had never studied in the Callidus Temple of Assassins.

'Maybe later I'll learn how,' he said. 'Meanwhile, let's wake the others. We'll leave right away. We'll sail to the Eye. And... thank you, Meh'Lindi.'

'My pleasure. Literally.'

TWELVE

THE EYE WAS five thousand light years distant from the area of truespace corresponding to that hulk adrift in the warp. Fifteen days warp-time, as it turned out.

Meanwhile, perhaps two years would have passed by in the real universe.

Stalinvast would long have been a scorched husk, its jungles rotted utterly by the life-eater, then cremated by firegas, only the plasteel skeletons of its empty cities towering above the barren desolation, dead reefs above a dried-out sea. Many cities would most likely have collapsed into tangled, fused ruins when the firegas exploded planet-wide. There would be not an atom of oxygen left in the now poisonous atmosphere; that too would have burned.

Jaq grieved for Stalinvast and dreamed of that holocaust.

AS *TORMENTUM MALORUM* flew closer to the Eye, the warp grew turbulent, buffeting the ship. Googol navigated with grim concentration, dodging eddies which could pitch them light years off course, maelstroms which could trap them into an endless Moebius circuit until they starved, until even their bones became dust.

At times the beacon of the Astronomican was eclipsed. At other times writhing knots in the fabric of the warp smeared the Emperor's signal across a swathe of unspace so that its actual location became problematic.

Googol's third eye ached. Grimm chanted the names of ancestors by way of a lifeline to the more reliable external cosmos far from the Eye. Meh'Lindi experienced nauseous tides within herself, which she quelled by means of meditation. Jaq felt the first nibblings of concentrated Chaos, Chaos blended with reality, Chaos with an evil purpose. Praying devoutly, he expunged these.

Finally, as they entered the fringes of the Eye, the Astronomican vanished utterly from Googol's awareness. But he had already fixed on the shadows of a dozen of the star systems that lurked within the great nebulosity, the imprint of the mass and energy of those suns upon the shifting, bubbling warp. Fingers dancing over a console, he conjured the pattern of these images holographically.

Jaq matched these traces with a holo-chart from the records of his Ordo, as stored in the ship's brain. Periodically the Inquisition sent screened nullships bristling with sensors racing through the nebula, probeships bearing psyker adepts who could spy on the madness of those who roosted on the cursed worlds within. Even the most loyal, best trained psykers might crumble under the assault of daemonic imagery. Traitor legionnaires could ambush such ships. Or the vessels would succumb to natural hazards. Yet some crumbs of information were retrieved.

'Where to, Jaq?' asked the Navigator. 'To which damned star?'

Jaq unwrapped his Tarot from the mutant skin. He laid down the High Priest card. The wafer of liquid crystal rippled as if static was disrupting it. Small wonder. The Emperor's influence was only negative within the Eye. Jaq wouldn't be surprised if all the cards he dealt were reversed. His face frowned back at him from the High Priest card, riven by stress.

He prayed, he breathed, and dealt.

Behind him... was the Harlequin of Discordia, reversed. Once again the figure which ought to have worn an eldar mask displayed instead the quizzical, impish features of Zephro Carnelian. Inertly so; immobile, frozen.

Accompanying Jaq... was the Daemon, a sinister, almost squid-like entity. Of course. And it too was reversed. Reversal might signify its defeat – unless the proximity of malevolent Chaos had turned the card around.

Impeding Jaq... was a warped renegade of Discordia. Likewise reversed. Which might portend the thwarting of such foes of the Imperium. Or, in the circumstances, might not. Jaq couldn't interpret clearly.

He dealt the last two cards.

And these were magical to such a degree that Jaq once more felt truly guided.

The Galaxy trump sparkled with stars. A starfish of billions of suns turned slowly, arms wrapped around itself, at once milk and diamond. In this grandeur the Eye of Terror was but a tiny flaw. The Galaxy card faced Jaq, affirmatively.

The final card was also positive. It was the Star trump. A naked woman – Meh'Lindi – knelt as she filled a pitcher from a pool in a rocky desert landscape. One intense blue star hung overhead. Arrayed around that first star seven other stars of varying degrees of brightness formed a trapezium pattern.

A pattern which matched Googol's holo; a pattern which framed that one particular blue sun.

This was a true astro-divination.

In spite of the tides of Chaos, the Emperor's spirit – enshrined in these cards – was still with Jaq.

'We steer towards the blue star, Vitali.'

The cards squirmed.

In the Galaxy, black threads spread like instant rot. From the pool where Meh'Lindi knelt, glassy tentacles surged. Spiked plants sprouted. The sky rained severed eyeballs that burst on the thorns. The Harlequin smirked and flourished a laspistol. Behind him, venomous figures capered, part scorpion, part human.

Jaq's own card began to simmer.

Hastily he flipped all the cards over to break the Tarot trance just in case – though this must surely be impossible! – a tiny bolt of energy might burst forth from the Harlequin man's gun and strike Jaq physically.

Averting his eyes he shuffled the pack, randomising it; recased and wrapped it.

'Carnelian is hunting us,' Jaq said. 'The cabal know I'm disobeying them.'

If Jaq's Tarot could so soon seem to turn against him, could the beatific divination have been true? Or were the cards warning him wisely into the bargain?

'Those cards are bugged,' said Grimm. 'Aren't they, huh?'

'I didn't hear Carnelian's voice taunting me on this occasion, little fellow. The cards may simply have been keeping overwatch for me. Whatever I asked them – which they answered! – they also needed to warn me about him. The Emperor's Tarot has a life of its own.'

What kind of powers must the Harlequin man possess, to be able to tap into someone else's Tarot without having even touched it?

'Plainly I can't manage without the cards entirely. How else could we have targeted the blue sun? I can't destroy my own Tarot. It's linked to me.'

'Exactly, boss! How about sticking it in the stasis-trunk? That might slow Carnelian down.'

'I think not!'

'Why not extract the Harlequin card and shoot a hole in it? Could you give our friend a headache?'

Jaq sighed. Grimm might be something of an adept with all sorts of engines, but he had very little insight into theological complexities.

'The Tarot is a unity, a web. You can't simply rip a piece out of the pattern and expect it to hang together as before. How long until we arrive, Vitali?'

'Maybe twenty minutes of warp time. Then days of ordinary flight, of course. We'll be deep inside the Eye. Could be debris everywhere. Our deflectors'll be working overtime.'

The ship juddered as a warp surge caught it, tossing it like a leaf.

'I must concentrate–'

VEILS OF SICKLY pigment draped the void in all directions, lurid, gangrenous and mesmerising, as if an insane artist had been set loose here to paint, on a cosmic canvas, the kaleidoscope of his mad, shapeless nightmares.

Scarlet, chartreuse, cyanotic were the gas clouds. Here was bile and jaundice and hectic gore, as the suns within the Eye excited the billows of gas and dust in a zone of space vexed and fevered by the pressure of the warp.

Only a handful of the very closest and brightest stars glowed faintly through rifts in the veils; and then only like distant lighthouses seen through dense fog. The blue sun ahead wore a livid halo as if space itself was diseased. Which it was.

Now that *Tormentum Malorum* was back in truespace, Meh'Lindi had taken over piloting. Vitali Googol recuperated in his sleep-cell from the stresses of the warp. Grimm was tinkering with the artificial gravity, causing moments of leaden heaviness, others of vertigo. Now that the warpscope had nothing to display, other screens and some uncovered portals let Meh'Lindi and Jaq view the delirious spectacle outside and probe for planets.

Tormentum Malorum proceeded under full camouflage and psychic screening.

A sensor beeped; a display unit switched to farsight.

'Traitor legion raider,' said Jaq. 'Has to be.'

The other ship was shaped like a crab. An armoured canopy of dingy brown above and below, dappled with daemonic emblems. Two jutting, articulated claws that could probably tear through adamantium. Jointed, armoured legs, hairy with aerials and sensors, moved to and fro in unison so that the raider seemed to scuttle through space in search of prey.

Checking the scale estimate, Jaq realised to his horror that the other ship was huge. *Tormentum Malorum* was a shrimp compared to the traitor vessel. Those 'legs' were probably entire fighting craft in themselves. Were those making ready to detach themselves from the parent? Jaq imagined the crustacean vessel grappling with *Tormentum*, seizing and crushing their own shell, its horny mouth sucking tight to the opening it tore, and spewing merciless abominations through.

Meh'Lindi switched off all superfluous on-board systems including gravity.

'What's the big idea?' shouted Grimm from another crypt, offended.

'Whisper-time,' she called back.

Eyes on stalks telescoped up from the crab-like ship: observation blisters. Jaq invoked an aura of protection. He willed their own ship not to be sensed. Pouring his own psychic power into the artificial shields until he sweated, he thought: *invisibility*.

The crab-ship was still heading outward, away.

It turned over, so that its underbelly was facing in the direction of travel.

'It's getting ready to jump,' Meh'Lindi whispered.

In a rainbow implosion, the crab disappeared.

Off to another star within the Eye; or out of the Eye entirely, marauding.

Jaq relaxed; he hungered.

He ate marinated sweetmice stuffed with Spican truffles.

THE PLANET THAT hung below them several days later might have been swaddled in poisonous chlorine, except that the ship's sensors diagnosed a breathable atmosphere.

Here was where immaterium was leaking through gaps between Chaos and the real universe, polluting the visible spectrum with phantom hues of ill-magic. In part, mists of mutability were responsible, pouring through the sieve between the realm of wraith and this solid world below. Also in part, those on board *Tormentum Malorum* were viewing a psychic miasma hiding whatever vile sights lay underneath – red tell-tales on the instrument panel glowed, warning of daemonic signatures.

Here, if anywhere, the hydra might have been conceived, crafted by cunning psychobiotechnicians.

'I don't suppose we'll meet many pureblood people down there,' said Jaq. 'Long exposure to such an environment would change any living creature.'

Maybe the cabal needed to use those bone-sculpture automatons as go-betweens not merely to present an acceptably hideous face to the local inhabitants – but because such beings at least might not mutate before their mission was accomplished?

Jaq recollected that he had not *seen* the faces of the High Masters of the Hydra; though on the other hand he had sensed no foul taint.

'Just as long as there's some decent fighting to attend to,' said Grimm, to hearten himself. The world below did not exactly look inviting. If the mask itself was so plague-stricken, what dire countenance did that mask hide?

What price, Jaq asked himself, had the cabal paid to obtain the hydra? Suppose for a moment that the members of the cabal were honourable yet sorely misguided. Would Chaos collaborate in the eventual purging of Chaos?

Ah yes, it might. The scheme could appeal to the renegades who so bitterly hated the Emperor if it involved his replacement. Weren't the descendants of the cabal also likely to quarrel and jockey for leadership in the aftermath? One whole sector of the galaxy – controlled by one cabalist – might direct a mind-blast at a neighbouring sector. The psychic convulsion would be titanic. The rampant insanity. Human civilisation could collapse once more into anarchy, torn by psychic civil war. The majority of surviving human beings would by then harbour a parasite from the warp in their heads, a little doorway for daemonism.

If the Emperor had initiated the hydra plan, surely he must have foreseen just such a possibility?

Unless, Jaq reflected with horror, the Emperor himself was mad. Supremely dedicated in one aspect, yet in another aspect... demented. Perhaps one aspect of the Emperor did not know what the other aspect was thinking and plotting.

Though Jaq recoiled from this heretical thought, it would not leave him.

What if the High Masters of the cabal likewise knew that the Emperor was going slowly insane – and must at all costs be deposed, replaced? Their awareness of this must be the most terrible secret in the universe, one that they might not even dare to confide in their fellow conspirators. Hence the lie that the Emperor himself had originated the plan.

If it was a lie.

If the Emperor was even still truly alive.

Once again Jaq asked himself whether the denizens of the Eye could possibly have been duped into providing a tool for the destruction of the very powers that sustained and twisted them. Or at least duped into allowing the hydra to be conjured forth here in the Eye of Terror.

That would be a master-stroke indeed.

'No orbital monitors,' said Googol, consulting scanners. 'No satellites, no battle platforms.'

Even through the miasma, other instruments detected centres of energy use. Perhaps half a dozen such, scattered across the world.

Just as when, long ago, he had lain abed in the orphanage on Xerxes Quintus sensing the sparks of mental phosphorescence, only now in full mastery and able to guard – so he hoped – against any backlash, Jaq opened himself up to the world below, and let... filth... flood through him, fishing for the signature he sought, any awareness of the existence of the hydra.

'Open the trunk, Meh'Lindi.' He had told her the lock combination. 'Bring me some of the entity to hold–'

She did so, returning with a small coil.

Jaq was swimming upstream through a vast vaulted sewer filled with the excrement of deranged minds, searching for the shadow of an amorphous shape... Avoid those creatures that fed in this faecal torrent! Do not attract their attention!

The sewer branched six separate ways, each as large and as full as the combined cloaca downstream. Beware of the polyp that bobbed towards him!

Swim *that* way swiftly. Hint of hydra? *Maybe. Almost for sure.*

Jaq withdrew. He handed the coil back to Meh'Lindi, who hastened to restore that troublesome substance to stasis before more was propagated.

When she returned, he tapped the viewscreen gridded with reference lines.

'Here's where we'll land. Near this power source, though not too near. And we don't wish to stay too long. I don't believe any inquisitor has raided a world of the Eye before.'

'As you say, Jaq, they mightn't exactly welcome wholesome-looking types down there, might they?'

'They might not indeed.'

'Huh, so shall I pretend that you're my prisoners?' said Grimm. 'Shall I lead you about on a chain? I suppose you're thinking that I'll do nicely as a mascot of deviant abhumanity.'

'No,' said Meh'Lindi, 'you're comely too.'

'Comely? Comely?' The short abhuman flushed and blushed.

'You're a perfect squat, agreeable in appearance.'

'Comely? Huh! Why not ravishingly handsome, in that case?' Grimm twirled his moustache defiantly.

'Thou art as a wondrous warthog,' began Googol.

'Shut up, Three Eyes.'

'Shall I alter myself into the genestealer shape?' volunteered Meh'Lindi. 'I shall seem tainted by Chaos then, shan't I? What better protective coloration could we wish for?'

Jaq could only rejoice at her offer. He nodded in grateful admiration.

'Do it, Meh'Lindi. Do it.'

THIRTEEN

LIGHTNING FORKED ACROSS a jaundiced sky as if discharging the tensions between reality and irreality. Some clouds suppurated, dripping sticky ichor rather than rain. Clumps of clouds resembled clusters of rotting, aerial tumours. Some of the scene was lit biliously by a green-seeming sun filtering through that apparently chlorinous overcast. The sun mildewed the gritty landscape from which fretted spikes and spires of stone arose. The camouflage-screened *Tormentum Malorum* appeared to be but one more natural feature.

Illusions whirled as if attempting to solidify themselves, the way that milk turns to butter. Globular plants twisted hairy flowers that were all the hues of rotting flesh in the direction of those dancing wraiths, hungrily.

THEY WERE CHALLENGED to combat an hour later, in a fiendishly playful fashion.

A bull of a man clad in plate-mail led a dozen capering monstrosities out from behind a stalagmite-like tower of rock.

'Ho-ho, ho-ho,' bellowed the bull-thing. 'What have we here to divert us, my lovelies?'

Formidable horns curved from the sides of the leader's head, jutting forward streaked with dried gore. His armour was wrought in the contours of bones. Metallic bones were bent into hoops around his thighs. Bones welded to bones made runic designs. Leering alien skulls capped his knees. Giant toe and finger bones encased his boots and gauntlets. An obscene codpiece of artificial bone bulged, encrusted with bloodstones suggestive of ulcers. He also wore a fine satin cape that cut a dash in the breeze, and a golden necklace with an erotic amulet. To Jaq's senses, the bull-man radiated an eerie, brutal sensuality. His gear seemed to say that even bones could copulate, that even metal could debauch itself... though not in any soft style.

Behind the leader trotted an upright tortoise of a man, whose squamous head poked out of a barrel-like shell spangled with iridescent stars and crescents as if he was a walking galaxy or a mad magician. Silk ribbons fluttered like streams of burning gas. Did he ever crawl out of his shell on to some couch at night, tender-bodied, squashy, all of his pleasure-nerves exposed to the ministrations of some large, wet tongue? Jaq shook his head to clear that image away.

Another warrior wore a brass waistcoat and leggings glued with gold braid as if furry caterpillars crawled upon his armour; in place of his left arm he sported a sheaf of tentacles. On his head, an exuberantly ringleted periwig.

Yet another, who was visibly hermaphroditic, in plascrystal armour, thrust forth a great lobster claw studded with medallions. One thin tall small-breasted fighter, braced with a clanking baroque exoskeleton, bore the head of a fly, upon which perched a cockaded plumed hat. A brassbound ovipositor jutted from her loins. Her neighbour was a striding, slavering, two-legged goat in rut, with a starched organdie ruff fanning around his neck, lace ruffled at his elbows, and a velvet cloak.

Only one massive man appeared to be true human. He
wore a nightmare parody of noble Space Marine armour,
engraved with a hundred daemon faces, though disdaining
a helmet. Great flanged pipes soared sidelong from behind
his head as if copying the bull-man's horns in reverse. That
head was of statuesque marble nobility, the hair bleached
white and permed into waves. At the tip of his aquiline
nose he wore an emerald ring that suggested to Jaq a drip
of mucus. One cheek was tattooed with sword and sheath
poised like lingam and yoni.

Alongside this Traitor Marine there danced a mutant
woman who was at once beautiful and hideous. Her body,
clad in a chain-mail leotard trimmed with rosettes and
puffs of gauze, was blanched and petite, her hair blonde
and bounteous. Yet her jade-green eyes were swollen ovals
set askew in an otherwise sensual face. Her feet were
ostrich-claws, ornamented with topaz rings, her hands
were chitinous, painted pincers. A razor-edge tail lashed
behind her plump buttocks. How like a daemonette of
Chaos she seemed! Googol groaned at the sight of her, and
took an involuntary step forward. Grimm gritted his teeth.

This band were armed with damascened boltguns and
power swords, the shafts of which were inlaid with
mother-of-pearl. They spread out in a fanciful skirmish
line and paused to scrutinize the three figures attired in
orthodox power armour – two full-sized, one dwarfish –
their open visors framing natural faces.

Before disembarking, Grimm had sprayed their own
great-shouldered armour a jaundiced hue to blend with the
desert and to mask the counter-daemonic runes and devout
red icons. Feeling a sense of disgust and deep unease, Jaq
had daubed on some warped renegade emblems such as
the Eye of Horus – sloppily so that they might have less efficacy, but could persuade at a casual glance. Jaq's weapons
rack cradled a force rod, psycannon and a clingfire thrower
tubed to a clip-on tank; in a steel sleeve-holster nestled an
ormolu-inlaid laspistol. Grimm and Googol favoured boltguns, laspistols, shuriken catapults.

The band eyed three ambiguous, well-armed intruders... accompanied by a version of a genestealer. Oh yes, she was their safe-conduct, their guarantor, if anyone could be.

'Slaanesh, Slaanesh,' bleated the goat, and fluffed his ruff. The fly and the tortoise took up the chant. The fly doffed her hat sarcastically.

'Glory to the Legion of the Lust!' shouted that caricature of a Marine. Was he saying 'the Lust' or 'the Lost'? Or both? The man grinned mockingly.

Ice slithered down Jaq's spine. Slaanesh, lord of perverse pleasure and of joy in pain, might indeed preside over a planet where an entity could be forged that would tamper with the pain and pleasure centres in the brain.

This motley crew that barred the way – these chic abominations – seemed inclined to play some absurd if vicious game. The question was, could they be fooled? At Jaq's side, Meh'Lindi hunched as though about to rush into their midst with the lightning speed of a stealer.

She clacked her claws together; her savage equine head jutted forth. With a gesture, he checked her.

'As you can see by the shape of my companion here,' Jaq called out, 'we have spat on the so-called Emperor's face.' He clapped Meh'Lindi proprietorially on the shoulder. 'This is my familiar lover, my changed one who shows me bliss and agony.'

The bull-man gazed at Meh'Lindi. Did he truly perceive her as someone possessed? He licked his lips and turned to his band.

'We embrace *renegades*, do we not, my carnal companions?' He snorted mightily. 'Though of course first we must test their sense of ecstasy, hmm?'

Their thenth of ecthathy... The Imperial Gothic of these degenerates was decadently accented with lisps.

The fly giggled. 'Oh yes, an initiation is doubtless in order.' *Inithiathon ith doubtleth in order.*

Which, thought Jaq, it was doubtless important to avoid if possible. Adopting an air of lordly disdain, he gestured around.

'This is a sordid, dreary refuge. I seek more than a rocky desert watered with pus. I seek the home of the hydra. I'm an emissary from the High Lords of the Hydra.' Jaq plucked a strand of the entity from the containment pouch in his suit and threw it, writhing, upon the ground.

'Haaa,' the bull replied with a grin, 'those lovely cheating lords...'

Cheating? In what way, cheating? Had the cabal cheated the traitors on this world – or were the cabal cheating on the Imperium?

The bull-man called out, 'You must visit the delightful torment dungeons in our city, Renegade, for full appreciation of what this world has to offer.'

Was that an invitation, or a terrible threat? The thought processes of this champion of Chaos eluded Jaq, being in themselves... chaotic.

At that moment Jaq felt a powerful urge to divest himself of his armour and grapple with Meh'Lindi. If he should but demonstrate his boast before this audience of monsters, why, they would let him pass. They would tell him everything he yearned to know.

The malign insinuation blasphemed against all that he had felt was precious in their lovemaking on the ship. He was under psychic attack of a lascivious and perfidious kind.

So was Meh'Lindi. She hissed and clutched a claw to her midriff. Stealers did not possess reproductive organs other than their tongue that kissed eggs into victims. Yet now a pouch was forming below Meh'Lindi's belly, as if to receive Jaq. Her mind – the mind that controlled her false body form – was being manipulated. Not by the scrap of hydra that flopped on the gritty ground. She was immune to that. But by...

And the aim? Why, to divest Jaq of his power armour, to seduce him out of its sanctuary. The dozen mustn't exactly trust their own weapons and strength against power armour. Jaq snatched out his force rod and fired at the goat, who staggered back, his sly psychic attack neutralised.

'I shan't be cheated so easily,' Jaq shouted in defiance.

'Evidently not,' replied the bull. 'Graal'preen here misinterpreted me. As I said, we must test your ecstasy before we embrace you. This means that *your* loving champion must accost *our* paramour.'

The lovely and ghastly female shimmied forth, tail slicing the air, pincers clicking.

'Are they well matched? Perhaps not well enough. Our nephew – and niece – in debauchery, Cammarbrach, will assist her.'

The hermaphrodite with the giant claw and the power sword clutched in his/her true hand stepped forward, and bowed derisively.

'And, I think, Testood too. Though without his gun. We do not wish to be unfair.'

So the tortoise tossed down his boltgun and advanced, still armed with a power sword.

'Ah, but wait,' added the bull. 'We will draw a battle circle and enforce it with a little spell of containment. With which, lord psyker,' and he eyed Jaq venomously, lowering his horns, 'you will not interfere. Slishy, do it!'

The mutant woman danced at speed, dragging her sharp tail through the dirt. She cut a wide circle, leaving only one little gap unsealed.

Jaq calculated. Surely he and Grimm and Googol, being better armoured, stood a good chance of cutting down all dozen of these warped renegades?

Yet what would he learn then? Of course, they might succeed in taking the leader prisoner...

What use would Jaq's excruciator be against a disciple of Slaanesh who taught his minions how to revel in agony?

Meh'Lindi chittered. Grimm interpreted.

'Use subterfuge, boss. She's prepared to fight.'

Subterfuge was the better strategy. So therefore Jaq must seem to accept the challenge. Meh'Lindi must fight against three opponents, two armed with power swords. She wasn't a complete genestealer with four arms. Wouldn't her stealer crouch impede an assassin's acrobatic skills?

Meh'Lindi didn't wait for instructions but paced into the circle to join the other three. Slishy sealed the line with her tail. The air shimmered as if an energy dome enclosed the arena.

'I can't bear to watch,' muttered Googol.

'Go to it!' shouted Grimm.

Jaq reminded himself to remain wary of any psychic thrusts; he mustn't let the fight occupy his entire attention.

Rearing as high as she could, Meh'Lindi darted at the tortoise, who looked to be the most cumbersome of those who faced her. He swung his sword high. She threw herself flat. Rolling under the swing, she gripped his feet with her claws and tugged, sending him crashing backwards to the ground, head already retracted within his shell.

Instead of pressing her advantage by mounting her adversary, she immediately rolled in a different direction. Thus she avoided the down-sweep of Cammarbrach's power sword – which sawed into Testood's shell instead, opening a rift, before the wielder reversed its course.

During that moment while the hermaphrodite and the tortoise man were tangled, Meh'Lindi leapt at the pseudo-daemonette. Claws grappled with pincers. The tail whipped round, slashing Meh'Lindi's horny skin. The mutant woman pivoted backwards in Meh'Lindi's grip bringing up both sharp-taloned ostrich feet in an effort to eviscerate her opponent. Talons raked across Meh'Lindi's toughened carapace. Already Meh'Lindi was tossing Slishy away, one pincer crippled. Meh'Lindi even caught an ankle in her claw, crushing quickly, releasing her hold while Slishy shrilled with what seemed to be elation.

Meh'Lindi wasn't seeking to kill any of her opponents outright. The extra moments involved in such a manoeuvre could have hindered her long enough for one of the others to surprise her.

Instead, she darted from one to the next, delivering a blow, a bite, a pinch of her claw... until the three who confronted her were tattered and tired.

Now Meh'Lindi paused a little longer with each. Batting Testood's sword arm aside, she ripped at his riven shell, wrenching it further apart. She snipped off Slishy's injured pincer. Wary of Cammarbrach's lobster claw, she tore armour from his/her sword arm – and returned to lacerate flesh and muscle; the sword fell.

Slishy died first, warbling deliriously.

In a moment of confusion, Testood slashed Cammarbrach; the lobster claw sagged, spasming.

Moments later Testood was disarmed. Meh'Lindi punched through the gap in his shell, crushing organs. The tortoise man collapsed. Cammarbrach fled, though only as far as the edge of the circle. Shrieking, he/she batted against the invisible barrier of force – until Meh'Lindi reached the hermaphrodite, whose neck she crunched with a claw.

'Ha!' cried Grimm.

'So we embrace you,' roared the bull-man. He pointed. 'That jelly thing is some powerful talisman.'

'You don't know what the hydra is, do you?' Jaq accused. 'Or who the High Masters are?'

'Maybe I *do*, cousin renegade. Truth is mutable in the Eye of Terror. All is mutable. You too will soon be mutable – if you're to win favour.'

'Cancel the force field.'

'The enchanted circle?'

'Psychic barrier! Whatever. Lower it.'

'You have destroyed our luscious deadly heart-throb. You must donate your champion to our group in exchange.'

'Boss.' Grimm was nudging Jaq's midriff.

From the east, scuttling from the shelter of one rocky column to the next, came Chaos spawn: dozens of spiderkin, hideous hairy unhumans with eight arachnid legs.

'Bastard's been playing us for time, boss.'

'I regret so.'

'What do those things do, you reckon?'

'Spin webs around us? Sting us?' Jaq levelled his force rod and discharged it at the circle inscribed in the grit.

Meh'Lindi charged free and ducked out of the line of fire as Jaq shouted, 'Destroy the polluted!'

After which, he could no longer keep up any pretence of being a renegade. He and Grimm and Googol opened fire simultaneously at the devotees of Slaanesh.

Jaq's laspistol sewed silver lines across air and armour and parts of warped limbs that were exposed. Grimm's boltgun bucked and clattered, its little shells exploding percussively on contact or else winging away vainly to fall elsewhere – until, to his annoyance, it jammed. He too plucked free a laspistol to cross-stitch the scene. Googol had levelled a shuriken catapult resembling a species of miniature starship with its flat round magazine apeing an elevated control deck and its twin pod-tipped fins abeam of the muzzle suggesting thrusters. Their magnetic vortex hurled a swishing hail of star-discs with monomolecular cutting edges.

Most targets fell quickly. However, the big Chaos Marine charged, firing bolts. An explosive concussion against Grimm's armour knocked the abhuman over like a skittle. A similar hit winded Jaq, blurring his vision. Blinking, he slammed his visor shut and fired a stream of superheated chemicals at the bull-man who was charging thunderously too. All was happening within moments. The bull raced past, screaming rapturously, haloed with clingfire, trailing an odour of boiling gravy.

The Traitor Marine was singling out Googol. That statuesque bare head seemed impervious to weaponry, protected by some great hex. Googol's star-discs flicked to left and right as though deflected by a fierce magnetic or anti-gravitic field. Shurikens, that could slice bone like butter, only scratched the man's armour. Though the false Marine's boltgun had also seized up, he had pulled a power sword from a scabbard in his armour. That warrior was almost upon Googol when the Navigator dropped his catapult and reached inside his own open helmet. Googol tore the bandana from his brow and stared death from his warp eye.

At last that mighty blasphemy of a Space Marine sagged, drooled and fell, almost crushing Googol.

Jaq wrenched the ribbed, flanged, exorcistically garnished psycannon from his weapons rack and sprayed at the onrush of spiderkin. Those were summoned creatures. In the normal universe outside of the Eye summoned creatures were unstable, vulnerable to a psycannon beam. But here inside the Eye?

One burst followed another.

Googol writhed free. 'Don't look me in the eye,' he warned. Finding his bandana as first priority, he wadded the material across his brow inside the helmet. By now Grimm was on his feet again, lasering at the spiderkin, severing legs, though there were many legs to laser. As the rush arrived, Meh'Lindi leapt high to stomp down on the Chaos spawn with her genestealer feet. She crumpled bodies with her claws. Spiderkin keened. Their spinnerets gushed milky adhesive threads, which she dodged. Jaq reverted to laser. Googol joined in.

Presently, thwarted and leaderless, the remaining spiderkin scuttled away, scaling spires.

'We won,' said Googol.

'We lost,' Jaq corrected him. 'We learned nothing.'

They continued circumspectly through the desert of spires, Meh'Lindi ranging ahead as a scout.

FOURTEEП

LUMINOUS VEILS DRIPPED from the glowing soup of the night sky. The buildings of the city ahead were gross idols to corrupted pleasure.

Some of those buildings were modelled to represent lascivious deities: many breasted, many organed avatars of twisted lust. In the weird veil-light the hunchbacked shadows of dark gods seemed to brood everywhere. Spouts of flaming gas leapt up, adding further spasmodic illumination.

Other great buildings were giant mutated solo genitalia. Horned phallic towers arose, wrinkled, ribbed, blistered with window-pustules. Cancerous breast-domes swelled, fondled by scaly finger-buttresses. Tongue-bridges linked these buildings, sliding back and forth. Scrotum-pods swayed. Orifice-entries pulsed open and shut, glistening. Some buildings were in congress with each other: headless, limbless torsos lying side by side, joined abominably.

Through his magniscope Jaq spied nipples that were heavy-duty laser nacelles, and lingam shafts that were projectile tubes.

The inhabitants were mere ants by comparison with this architectonic orgy. Eager, scurrying ants. Jaq's ear-bead picked up wailing music, drumbeats, screams, chants, and the throb of machinery. The city pulsed and palpitated flexibly. Somehow plasteel and immaterium were alloyed together. Thus buildings moved, butted one another, penetrated one another, crawled upon one another. Towers bowed and stiffened. The deity buildings caressed and clawed at one another. And the ant-like inhabitants swarmed within and around and over, sometimes being crushed, sometimes sucked into vents, or spewed out.

Jaq turned away sickened, muttering exorcisms. Meh'Lindi's claw closed on his gauntlet and squeezed a couple of times consolingly.

'Are we to go into the body of that city?' whispered Googol. 'The *body*, aye, the body!'

'Huh, living in that lot it must be some relief to get into the desert!' said Grimm. 'You reckon the hydra was made there, boss?'

'Maybe... They do seem to possess a technology of immaterium in the service of foulness. Ah: party heading out this way, I'd say.'

'In search of their lost bedmates?'

Jaq's own band lay on a shelf of rock overlooking a road which wended away from the lascivious, living, cruel city. An anti-gravity palanquin – a cushioned platform sheltered by an awning – bore a gargantuan individual upon it. Four enormously long-snouted quadrupeds, striped blue and red as if wearing livery, pulled this palanquin along, hovering a metre above the road.

Probably the buoyant land-raft could have proceeded under its own power except that the monstrous passenger preferred this ceremonial charade. Or maybe the passenger's fingers were too fat to manipulate the control levers accurately – if she could even reach them.

Rows of tattooed breasts circuited her enormous trunk and belly; through each nipple, a brass ring. Coiling in and out amongst all those glistening, oily bosoms, squeezing its way between, was a long thin purple snake, its origin, seemingly, the woman's navel. A birthcord grown to hosepipe length, it bound her around like a rope, creasing and squeezing so that flesh flowed forth. The snake's flat venomous head wavered hypnotically alongside her cheek, caressing it.

The fat woman's face was bovine, with big oozy nostrils, large liquid eyes, floppy lips, and a jaw that seemed to chew cud, ruminating placidly. Her snake – her other self – did not seem so placid.

A dozen bare-headed Traitor Marines escorted her, encased in mock-bone armour. They carried plasma and projectile weapons.

In the vanguard danced a dozen sisters of Slishy, lashing their tails, swirling their pincers.

The procession advanced almost to where Jaq's party lurked, then halted. The Slishy look-alikes pirouetted to the rear, to join the legionnaires. The creatures that pulled the palanquin crouched, stabbing their snouts underground through the very fabric of the road. The enormous, mutated woman faced out into the desert of spires, her snake swaying beside her.

'Boole!' the woman mooed mightily into the veil-lit night.

'Cover your ears, Meh'Lindi!' ordered Jaq. 'Visors down. Switch off audio. She will be deafening.'

'B-O-O-L-E! BOO-OOO-OOO-LEEEEE!'

Even with microphones deadened, the great noise seemed that of a starcraft at take-off. Her voice jarred and vibrated their very bones inside their suits. A stone spire shattered and fell. Meh'Lindi writhed, clutching her unprotected head. That voice was directional like a searchlight beam. Legionnaires and Slishy-sisters behind the palanquin merely rocked to and fro in the backwash of echoes.

'WHERE ARE YOU, BOOLE? I WISH TO BE HUNG UP BY A HUNDRED RINGS! THEN BY FIFTY LESS! THEN BY TWENTY LESS!'

Letting his psychic sense loose, Jaq was invaded by a vision of the massive, multibreasted, altered woman hanging suspended on many strong slim chains clipped to her many nipple-rings. Of her being joggled up and down on variable numbers of rings, moaning in distorted delight, while the bull-man served or slapped or kneaded her, or pricked her with his horns.

At such times, Jaq perceived, the woman's snake participated too, entering her by one orifice or another, completing the circuit.

The giant woman gathered herself again, her head turning in a different direction.

'BOOOOOOOOOLEEEE! BOOOOOOOOLEEEEE!'

Earth shook; another pinnacle snapped apart. Jaq lay stunned.

A muted roar of anguish answered the woman's call from out of the radiant, iridescent night.

The bull-man came pounding into sight. He was eyeless, faceless, burned to the bone. The flesh had crisped to crackling on his arms and chest. His very horns were black and twisted.

Her voice had called him back. Could she raise the dead with that shout? Or had he been stumbling blinded, half-cooked, in the desert, yet kept alive by daemonic protection? Through *her* protection, if she was possessed by Slaanesh.

She must – thought Jaq – be the mistress of this whole evil, animate city. If anyone knew the truth about the hydra, she should.

When Boole – the bull-man – reached the palanquin he collapsed and lay still. The woman's snake whiplashed free from amongst her bosoms. Unfastening itself at such speed that the friction must burn or split her unctuous skin, it arced out to taste the fallen body with a flickering twin tongue.

The woman quaked and howled.

'AIIEEEEEEEEEEE! BOOOOOOOLEEEEE!'

The blue and red animals unplugged their heads from the ground and lurched widdershins, foaming at the mouth. The palanquin rocked and rotated. The woman's head swung from side to side. Her voice caught legionnaires and pseudo-daemonettes. Some ran around behind the gravity-sled to try to stabilise it. Others collapsed, gaping, eyes, bulging.

'AIIEEEEEEE! OHAAAAAAAA!'

The voice was reaching back to the very city. Buildings responded by wobbling and shaking. Some, like gargantuan snails, sought slow refuge behind others. A few shuffled slowly in the direction of the voice. Tongue-bridges tore. Breast-balconies bled white juice. The antlike inhabitants tumbled. Lasers started firing at imaginary targets amongst the cascading lurid veils.

Jaq banged Googol and Grimm on the shoulders while the voice was pointing away from them. He gesticulated with his gauntlet.

Their laser beams and bolts sliced and hammered accurately at the woman's escorts. Some of these returned fire, but the palanquin continued to swing around, dragged by the rabid-seeming beasts. The defenders dodged. Jaq targeted and killed, before crouching, gritting his teeth against the great noise. As soon as the stunning thunder-front passed by, Jaq popped up and shot the proboscis-beasts one by one. Their dead weight dragged the palanquin to a halt.

How to silence the monstrous woman, so that she could be captured? Puncture her windpipe, carving through the slab of fat that was her neck? That wouldn't help her to answer questions. He might even decapitate her unintentionally.

The snake part of her! Jaq thought of the soul-threads descending from living beings into the abyss of uncreation.

Could the snake be a materialization of something akin? A tendril of Slaanesh rooted into her navel, nourishing her umbilically with power?

The snake continued to arc out as though afflicted by rigor mortis – the mortis in question being that of Boole.

Muttering an exorcism, Jaq aimed psycannon with one hand and laser with the other, both at the serpent's neck.

When the snake's head hit the ground, it exploded in the manner of electricity earthing. Span by span from the front, the snake's long body detonated backwards like a firecracker, golden fire gushing out until the pyrotechnic display arrived at the woman's navel. Then whatever had been rooted in her burst forth in a spray of blood and excremental juices. Her bosoms closed the wound swiftly, compressing it shut. The thunder had stopped.

Meh'Lindi had scrambled to her knees, and was shaking her long snout from side to side as if she was a swimmer trying to dislodge water from her ears. Whether Meh'Lindi was deafened and stupefied or not, they must all act now. Her training must take over. An assassin should fight on, even if a leg and two arms were broken. Jaq threw up his visor, signalled Grimm and Googol to do likewise.

'Boss, buildings are heading this way.'

It was true.

'But not very *fast*. We must hijack the gravity sled, haul it into the wilderness–'

The four descended at speed to where the wounded lady squatted vastly on her floating litter, surrounded by dead and incapacitated legionnaires and Slishy-kin. Her injury seemed minor compared with her bulk. The woman's mouth opened and closed but she only lowed quietly in protest. Or maybe loudly; compared with earlier, her lamentations and vituperations didn't register as amounting to a din.

Slishy-kin were already rotting, dissolving. As Grimm delivered the coup de grâce to a lingering legionnaire who might use his last erg of energy to snap off a shot in the back, Googol cut the corpses of the proboscis-animals loose and gathered the traces to fashion a harness... into which Meh'Lindi began to slip herself willingly.

'No, no,' Jaq told her. 'I'm wearing power armour. You're not.' He attached himself instead.

'Boss: ugly customers boiling out of the city.'

Yes indeed. But two kilometres away. Beginning to haul, Jaq powered up the slope towards the maze of spires. As he overcame the inertia of the giantess on her raft, so he ran ever faster, and cast a psychic haze of confusion behind himself and his companions to hide them like a cloud of mental dust.

THEY WERE DEEP inside the desert, perhaps half way to the ship. Rock spires flashed by; Jaq had to calculate well ahead when to deviate the sled. Pursuit seemed nonexistent.

Grimm panted up alongside Jaq – even though the armour amplified their actions they were still doing the work of sprinting. 'Boss, boss, I've been figuring. We can only get her on board *Tormentum* – if we trim her down. Don't have a good enough medikit with us for that – without her expiring, do we?'

Grimm was right. 'Vitali, slow the sled!'

Googol applied himself to the rear of the speeding palanquin, digging in his heels to kill its momentum. The squat was a little too short to assist in this task, but Meh'Lindi soon caught up and pitched in. Presently the vehicle was hovering at rest. Jaq strengthened the aura of protection around the little group.

The woman glowered at them malignly as Meh'Lindi hoisted Grimm to peer over the lip of the litter. The little man evaded a sluggish, dropsical foot almost as large as himself and stabbed at a lever. The palanquin began to sink. The woman's nipple-rings clinked against each other as all her breasts heaved. A pig-size arm swung slackly at Googol, knocking the armoured Navigator over. Deprived of her serpent, though, she was definitely less than she had been. Swearing, Googol picked himself up as the litter settled. Grimm deactivated it entirely, and the mountainous woman slumped backwards shapelessly, suggesting that the sled had been providing other uplift too, a supportive corset of antigravity.

'We'll do what we have to do here,' Jaq unpacked his excruciator, a bundle of seemingly frail rods.

He telescoped out the spidery yet supremely strong device and slapped it down over the giantess. With much wrestling they attached its hoops to her extremities – more for the sake of holding those extremities in place and thus avoiding being swatted, he thought to himself. Where was the point in racking a person who enjoyed being dangled and stretched from rings? Many rings, then fewer rings!

Fumbling off a gauntlet, Jaq produced an ampoule of veritas to press against her skin. Bearing in mind her mass, he used a second and a third dose. The recommended Inquisition procedure was to induce extreme pain first of all. This, he reasoned, might be counter-productive, aside from the fact that the prospect nauseated him somewhat.

'Name?' he demanded.

The woman spat at Jaq, at least two handfuls worth of reeking drool, and he sprang aside.

'Jus' clearing my throat,' she explained. 'Seems as how I've lost my old voice.' ...*lotht my old voith.*

'What do you know about an entity called the hydra?'

'My name's Queem Malagnia. An' my beaut Boole just die. Never pierce me again with his horns after rousting against the Grimpacks.' ...*againtht the Grimpackth.*

'He was monkeying around with a daemonette,' Grimm said wickedly.

'Very little,' stated Queem Malagnia.

Was that said in answer to Jaq's last question, or was it a comment upon Grimm's remark? Had the fat woman been reduced to the condition of an imbecile by the amputation? Or was she prevaricating slyly?

'What do you know?' Jaq repeated sternly.

'I know something's missin' from me!'

'The serpent that possessed you is what's missing. Now let's get down to business. Tell me all you know about the hydra, or I shall kill you.'

'You wouldn't know nothin' then, would you? No, that ain't so. You'd know whatever you knew beforehand?' Her jaw convulsed. She could no longer hold back the truth – yet unfortunately he had given her licence to tell *all* that she knew. 'Why, hydra is a name,' she said slowly. 'Am not exac'ly a scholar but ah hazard it's spelled with a haitch and a why and a dee–'

'Stop. Was the hydra first made in your living city?'

'Aha! *First* made, now there's a question. What does *first* mean? Originally, primarily? Whatever made immaterium in the first place, if it's stuff that's essentially unmade? Ah take it we're talking about summat made of immaterium?'

Would pleasure perhaps hurt her? How could he define pleasure for such a person? In a well-equipped dungeon over a period of several days, oh yes. Yet on the spur of the moment? Jaq glanced askance at his companions.

Little Grimm stepped forward. He jiggled some of Queem Malagnia's brass rings, those that he could reach. Each ring was incised with miniature scenes of depravity. From a tool kit he produced a small pair of shears and held them up in Queem's line of sight. Since Grimm's earlier taunt had been aimed intelligently at unsettling the woman, Jaq let him proceed.

'Listen, you freak,' said the squat, 'I'm gonna steal all your stupid rings for my souvenir collection.'

He snipped and withdrew one ring from a nipple, gently, not tugging.

Queem gasped. It was as though Grimm had pulled a plug. The breast deflated, disappearing. The teat became a mere blemish, which quickly faded.

'Warp-stuff is bulking out her body!' the squat exclaimed. 'She's like a hydra herself. Each ring is a seal. Here goes number two.'

He snipped and slid the severed ring free. Another breast collapsed.

Queem whimpered.

Jaq doubted Grimm's mechanistic explanation. The small man had little instinct for the workings of arcane thaumaturgy.

Grimm stood up on tiptoe and smirked into Queem's great face. 'Huh, we'll soon have you trimmed down to size! You'll fit on board our ship.'

'Leave my lovely rings alone,' begged Queem. 'I'll tell you anything.'

'I don't wish to hear *anything*,' snarled Jaq. 'I wish to hear quite specifically... Grimm, cut off ten rings.'

Snip-snip.

'Nooooooo!'

Snip.

'Noooo–'

Snip.

'Please stop it–'

Snip.

'What's a hydra, anyway?'

'Do you *know* what it is?' barked Jaq.

'It's an entity,' she said viciously and that was all she said.

Blood erupted from her neck. She gagged. Her head lolled back, half severed.

'Don't anyone move!' cried a familiar, teasing voice.

FIFTEEN

FROM A HUNDRED metres away, partly sheltered by a spire of rock, Zephro Carnelian was covering them with a heavy boltgun. He must almost instantly have discarded the laspistol he had used so accurately on Queem Malagnia, so as to grapple with the more devastating weapon. Its brass-bound chrome glittered, reflecting the abnormal, sickly luminosities of night. In the midst of spying, had the Harlequin man actually taken some time out to polish the dust of the chase from that boltgun and burnish it stylishly?

Carnelian was wearing grotesque bone-armour with spurs and spikes, his impertinent face peering out of a flanged, horned helmet. One of the robots from the hulk flanked him, cradling a plasma gun.

'I just can't abide to witness suffering!' he called.

'I wasn't racking her, you fool,' Jaq shouted back. 'I wasn't intending to. How else do you pin down a megapig? Now you've killed her like you killed Moma Parsheen.' Pretend still to be an ally.

189

'How do you know what evil that woman consummated while she hung in her rings, Draco?'

'So you've been inside her boudoir! That settles one doubt in my mind.'

'Stop moving apart, you four.' Carnelian fired warning bolts to right and to left, causing the ground to erupt. 'I too can have visions, Sir Inquisitor, Sir Traitor. *You* are a blasphemer of solemn oaths, a despoiler of duty.'

'And you seem singularly at home in the Eye of Terror, Harlequin man.'

'Ah, but I'm at home everywhere, aren't I? And nowhere too...'

'The hydra was first forged here, not in some orbital lab.'

'Is that what you suppose? Did *she* say so?'

'You know she didn't have time. You stopped her.'

'I wouldn't believe much that a servant of Slaanesh says. Wouldn't she lie, to trouble your soul and confuse you, Jaq?'

'She was under the influence of veritas.'

'Veritas, indeed?'

Why didn't Carnelian and his servitor simply open fire? Gobbets of plasma and heavy explosive bolts could do severe damage to even the best armour; and never mind about the contents. Meh'Lindi, who was unprotected but for her chitin, would instantly be blown apart. Yet the Harlequin man continued to toy with Jaq.

'What is truth?' cried Carnelian. '*In vinculo veritas*, wouldn't you say? Truth emerges within the dungeon, in fetters. Yet if truth is chained, how can it be true? Is not the whole human galaxy bound with chains? Is not our Emperor manacled into his throne? Who will ever free him? Only death.'

'Idle paradoxes, Carnelian! Or are you threatening to dispose of the Master of Mankind?'

'Tush, what paranoia. Wouldn't the hydra set everyone free by binding them tight?'

'I ask you: whose hands will steer the hydra? Who are those masked Masters really?'

'Really? "Really" is a truth question. I thought we had just disposed of the truth. There's no truth at present, Jaq, not in the whole of the galaxy. You know very well, as a secret inquisitor, that such is the case. The truth about genestealers? Truth about Chaos? Such truths must be suppressed. Truth is weakness, truth is infirmity. Truth must be tamed as psykers are tamed. Truth must be soulbound and blinded. Our Emperor has banished truth, exiled it into the warp, as t'were. Yet there *will* be truth. Oh yes!'

'When the hydra possesses everyone in the whole damn galaxy? If everyone thinks the same, I guess that must be the truth.'

Carnelian cackled hectically. 'Truth is a veritable jest, Jaq. The lips that tell the truth must also laugh. Laugh with me, Jaq, laugh!'

Carnelian fired another explosive bolt, well clear of Jaq's party, though dirt spattered them.

'Dance and laugh! Our Emperor has banished laughter. From us, from himself. Yes, he has exiled joy from himself so as to save us. He has outcast truth, for the sake of order. Because truth, like laughter, is disorderly, disturbing, even chaotic; and there can be no hilarity in the dungeon of lies.'

What did Carnelian mean? The Emperor if anyone should know the truth – about human destiny, about history; he who had reigned for ten thousand years! If the Emperor did not know the truth – was unable to know the truth – why then, the galaxy was hollow, futile, doomed. But maybe the Emperor no longer knew what the truth was; no longer knew why his Space Marines and his inquisitors imposed his rule with iron dedication.

As Carnelian smirked at Jaq under the lurid sky of this corner of Chaos, so Jaq's resolve to travel to Earth with his – admittedly ambiguous – evidence strengthened. If he could but escape from Carnelian's clutches!

Another bolt exploded, showering grit.

'Shall we try to take him, boss?' muttered Grimm.

How could they? Compared with Carnelian they were out in the open. The combat servitor held a heavy plasma gun. Meh'Lindi would probably be incinerated... though an assassin's duty was to die, if need be.

'Jaq: let me give you a snatch from a very ancient poem to riddle out during your last remaining moments. Which moments may refer to the immediate future right now, or alternatively to when you are a very doddery embittered old man looking back on your life before the light finally dims forever for you... In this snatch of verse a God is speaking. Perhaps he is like our own God-Emperor surveying his galaxy. Ahem.'

Carnelian cleared his throat, and recited:

'Boundless the deep, says God, because I am who fill
Infinitude, nor vacuous the space.
Though I uncircumscribed my self retire,
And put not forth my goodness, which is free
To act or not...

'Pretty words, eh? How they roll off the tongue.'

How they mystified Jaq. How the meaning escaped him, just as Queem Malagnia's confession had eluded him so frustratingly.

'Ooops!' shrieked Carnelian. He fired one bolt that clipped Grimm's shoulder. It ricocheted onward unexploded, since it hadn't penetrated. Even so, Grimm was punched sideways.

Jaq had no choice but to return fire; Googol too. In another moment, Grimm. Carnelian had already disappeared behind the spire, as had his robot.

Bolts hammered away and plasma gushed from the rear of the stone column – away in the opposite direction. Legionnaires in baroque bone-armour hove into view, darting from column to column, firing back as they came. Pincer-waving daemonettes and scuttling Chaos spawn accompanied them.

'Run for the ship!' ordered Jaq, summoning auras of protection and distraction.

They sprinted, abandoning the palanquin with its gross corpse and Jaq's excruciator, unused. He was glad he had lost it.

As *TORMENTUM MALORUM* rose on a tail of plasma out of the festering ionosphere, a couple of near-space fighters, hawk-ships, attacked but Googol outdistanced these and continued boosting outward in overdrive. The starship sang with the strain on its engines.

'Your tinkering seems to have been of some use,' Googol finally conceded to Grimm.

'Huh, tuned 'em good, didn't I?'

'For the moment ! You didn't recite a single litany. How can you expect an engine to perform properly if you scorn its spirit?'

'Its spirit,' said Grimm, 'is known as fuel.'

'Just don't let it hear you say so.'

'Huh, catch me talking to an engine.'

'Vitali's right,' said Jaq. 'Spirit pervades all things.'

'Huh, so I suppose you understand all that stuff our Harlequin man was spouting, about pervading infinitude?'

'The Emperor pervades. He's everywhere. Everywhere within the compass of the Astronomican, at least.'

Grimm shrugged. 'I'm a mite bothered why Carnelian let us go. With his fancy marksmanship he only clipped me. He was herding us back towards our ship, boss. Basically. He held those legionnaires off–'

'After attracting them by firing off a few bolts.'

'Why shoot at them if they're his allies?'

'Maybe,' suggested Vitali, 'with their first lady kidnapped and her escort wiped out the renegades were in a bad mood and would shoot anyone who wasn't from Sin City?'

'You're dense,' said Grimm. 'Maybe Carnelian killed that Queem woman to make us think the hydra came from that place, even if it didn't.'

'It must have originated here in the Eye,' Jaq said flatly. 'And on Queem's world too.'

'Hers no more,' said Googol. 'Good riddance. She wasn't exactly my prototype of fatal beauty.'

'Carnelian seems to have agreed with you,' observed the squat.

The thought of Carnelian herding them – towards Earth now? – irked Jaq extremely.

'I'm not quite so dense,' said Googol, 'when it comes to interpreting verse. The God-Emperor in that poem seemed to be saying that he had separated off part of his power. That part is elsewhere, independent of him, free to go its own way or fail to go its own way. Is that the good part? In which case the remaining part would be evil.'

'The Emperor cannot be evil,' said Jaq. 'He is the greatest man ever. Though he can, and must, be stern; without a smile.'

'A fact which Carnelian seemed to regret.'

'So that he could have the laugh on us,' jeered Grimm.

Truly I'm scurrying through a maze, thought Jaq; and maybe this maze has no true exit at all.

'Speaking of prototypes,' Grimm teased Googol, 'here comes yours.'

Meh'Lindi had returned to her true flesh, and now returned to the control crypt.

'So that was Chaos,' was her comment.

'No,' Jaq corrected her, 'that was merely one world out of hundreds where Chaos intrudes.'

'Do you know, I felt almost at home there in my grotesque body? Something appealed to my altered senses.'

Jaq was instantly alert. 'A taint of Chaos?'

'Something in the air. No, in the hidden atmosphere. I didn't feel the same way when I changed in Vasilariov. That was... a job. This was more like a vile seductive destiny.'

'Could changing your body be habit-forming?' the squat asked with concern.

'On a Chaos world, I think so. You would be trapped, becoming a monster and not being able to change back again. Chaos is the polymorphine of the mad and the bad, of sick minds, of brains that crave without control. You become the content of your own nightmare, which starts as a delirious and enticing dream. Then the nightmare shapes your flesh. The nightmare possesses you. You still believe you're the dreamer. But you aren't. You are what-is-dreamt. I wonder–'

'What?' asked Jaq. Meh'Lindi seemed on the verge of some revelation – maybe akin to the false enlightenment of a drug fugue, when a crushed beetle seems pregnant with cosmic importance. 'What, Meh'Lindi?'

'I wonder whether a truly remarkable person could escape from the sway of Chaos by her own power. Or by his own power. Such a person would then be immune to Chaos, just as I'm immune to the hydra – or hope I am.'

'Would such a person be Zephro Carnelian?' Googol asked quietly from his Navigator's couch. 'At home everywhere, according to his boast! Able to romp across a Chaos world without contamination.'

'I hate him,' she answered vaguely. 'Yet... I've been touched by him deep within.'

More deeply than by me? Jealousy pricked at Jaq.

'I smell the reek of *cults*,' he announced severely. 'Of crusades and saviours. The human mind is very prone to cults. Stealer cults, cults of Chaos, cabals... But there's only one redeemer. He is the Emperor. Cling to that one strong chain.' (*Though how strong was it in reality? How strong did it remain?*) 'Let that chain bind you. Welcome its protective bondage.'

'In that case,' asked Grimm, 'oughtn't we to welcome the bondage of the hydra? If it'll really scour the galaxy clean of daemons and mutants and wicked aliens?'

Jaq glared at him. 'And of abhumans too, little one? Why not of anyone who diverts from the human norm? Until there is only that norm everywhere, in a galaxy of monomind.'

That was the positive face of the hydra plan; the flip side being... a galaxy boiling with Chaos spawn.

'I wasn't the norm, I recall.' Contradictions warred in Jaq's soul. He cradled his brow in his hands. He muttered prayers – to what, to a failing Master of Mankind?

'I was only asking, boss,' Grimm said humbly as if Jaq's anguish communicated itself.

'The whole galaxy *asks*.' And what answered the plea? A devious cabal of potential slave-masters? A trickster Harlequin man? Or the crumbling rock against which the tides of Chaos burst?

'Where shall we head for?' the Navigator wanted to know.

Aye, another iota was asking for guidance. And of course the hydra promised to bestow total guidance. If only Jaq could believe the cabal... but he couldn't.

'We're aiming for sacred Terra, Vitali. Where else? We shall sneak in announced. That should challenge your piloting skills.'

'I wasn't, um, especially requesting to be challenged. Not in that sort of way, at any rate! Not that I don't welcome opportunities... But Vitali Googol versus the whole of the solar system's defence network, um, right, very well...'

'This flight could become legendary,' hinted Grimm. 'You might compose a praise-song about your piloting.'

Meh'Lindi smiled bleakly. 'Alternatively, a suicide ode.'

'First,' said Jaq, 'we must jettison that trunk of hydra. Set it on a lazy course into a blazing sun. The blue one hereabouts should serve the purpose as well as any.'

'That's your only proof, boss. The hydra's your evidence.'

'Do you think I would dream of smuggling that into the heart of the Imperium? Imagine the hydra let loose in the bowels of our birthworld, in the headquarters of humanity. Impossible!'

Nevertheless, he reflected, some of the substance of the hydra would travel all the way to Earth notwithstanding. Some was subtly hidden within Meh'Lindi's own body, incorporated, neutralised.

He imagined Meh'Lindi confined in a dungeon of his Ordo. He imagined her stretched out and opened like a toad in a daemonological laboratory of the Malleus, being investigated, probed to destruction, first of her mind, then of her flesh.

His mind rejected this vision, though not before her troubled gaze had met his.

SIXTEEN

THE EYE OF Terror lay far out near the fringe of the galaxy, to the galactic north-west, in a region as lonely as Jaq sometimes felt himself to be these days. His spirits were hardly raised when Grimm almost deserted ship mid-way to Terra...

The squat had insisted that the distance was simply too great to attempt in one warp-jump with the fuel remaining in the tanks of the *Tormentum*.

He was undoubtedly right. Vitali Googol should have been the one to point this out. Indeed the Navigator insisted that he would have done so just as soon as their ship had left the system of the blue sun, just as soon as *Tormentum* was running, storm-tossed, through the warp once more.

Did Googol in his heart wish to obstruct their flight to Earth by limiting their options as to a refuelling stop – so that they might be obliged to call at some major base where awkward questions could be asked, or agents of the cabal could strike at them more easily?

Worse still, was Googol's attitude becoming cavalier? Did he not care whether they were marooned or not? The Navigator protested, in a hurt tone, at Jaq's semi-accusation.

From tortured snatches of verse that Jaq overheard subsequently, it seemed that the memory of that beringed giantess was preying on their poet's mind, eroding his romantic soul like acid, for reasons which Jaq only half comprehended and thought it wiser not to pry into. Had Queem Malagnia represented some sort of anti-ideal to Googol, some appalling pattern of sexuality which haunted him even as he tried to reject and purge it, failing to?

What romantic formula could he possibly fit Queem into? If he did not do so, how could he forget her? How could he come to terms with forsaking the dark lusts of that corporeal, living city – in the way that he had come to terms with never attaining Meh'Lindi?

This depressed Jaq.

They aimed for a lone red dwarf star named Bendercoot, a thousand light years inward towards Segmentum Sola. Records listed Bendercoot as parent to only four small rocky worlds, all uninhabited. The outermost hosted a minor orbital dockyard for Imperial Navy and trader vessels. The gravity well wasn't deep: a mere two days to travel inward from the safe jump-zone, two days to travel outward again.

It was to be hoped that this dockyard hadn't been destroyed by alien attack or abandoned; records could be centuries out of date. Failing Bendercoot, the travellers had at least three other obvious options – ports on minor routes they could call at. Jaq hoped that Googol was navigating faithfully, and cursed himself for his doubts.

However, the millennium-old dockyard was still circling Bendercoot IV. An Imperial cruiser was moored upon it: a cluster of fretted, fluted towers linked by flying buttresses studded with death's heads. Also, a pocked, patched, bulbous old freighter.

Grimm, who had spent further long hours fine-tuning, then polishing, *Tormentum's* engines, went 'ashore' inside the orbiting dock to convey a satchel of rare metals for payment and to 'sniff the air,' so he said.

Came the hour for their departure, Grimm was still missing.

'Shall I go and seek him out?' asked Meh'Lindi.

Jaq stared from the porthole across a scalloped plain of metal bristling with gantries and defensive weapons blisters. Bright-lit towers cast groove-like shadows. This was a minor dockyard, yet doubtless it housed many kilometres of internal corridors and halls. The fuel and oxygen tubes had already snaked away.

'*Sapphire Eagle*, clear for departure,' crackled a radio voice. 'Human purity be yours.'

'Be yours too,' replied Jaq. 'We'll hold for half an hour.' To Meh'Lindi he said, 'If he's in any trouble, that could snare us.'

'He left the engines in good trim,' said Googol. 'I'll miss the little tyke.'

'Do you believe he has skipped ship, Vitali?'

'Maybe he doesn't feel much like diving down the throat of a tiger... I don't know much about the protocols of you inquisitors but you're probably posted as a renegade by now.'

The journey to the Eye and then the return to Terra, though measured in weeks of warp time, would have cost Jaq years of real time. Once it was certain that Jaq was heading towards the Eye with Carnelian in pursuit, an astropath could have signalled Earth instantly, using Malleus codes. Perhaps the Harlequin man even had his own tame astropath aboard *Veils of Light*. He had made sure that he murdered Jaq's star-speaker, Moma Parsheen.

Bael Firenze was powerful. Obispal, on the other hand... he could be netted and forced to confirm Jaq's story. Obispal might be anywhere in the galaxy.

They waited.

For fifteen minutes.

Twenty.

Twenty-five.

'Prepare to leave, Vitali.'

Jaq had valued the squat. Jaq had spoken in defence of abhumans... Now the squat was betraying him. Although this was only a trivial betrayal compared with the cosmic treachery planned by the cabal, yet it still stung.

Jaq himself might need to betray Meh'Lindi by handing her over to the Malleus laboratories. If Meh'Lindi suspected this, would she still remain loyal, girded by her assassin's oaths?

At the twenty-eighth minute Grimm bustled back aboard.

'Sorry, boss,' he said. 'Thanks for waiting. I met some brothers. We got to drinking. Hey-ho, hey-ho.'

'And off with them you thought you'd go?' asked Jaq sadly.

Grimm didn't exactly deny this, which at least was honest of him. 'I feel the tug of kin, boss. I'm the roaming kind, but still...'

'You thought you'd see whether our ship left without you, thus deciding the matter.'

'Launching now,' warned Googol. *Tormentum* began to pulse slowing away from the dock.

'Huh, so you *were* going to abandon me!' Grimm managed to inject a note of indignant reproach, at which Jaq couldn't help but smile wanly.

'Course, I also thought to myself: *Earth*. Likely never see Earth otherwise. See Earth and die, don't they say?'

How true. How many shiploads of young psykers arrived on Earth, only to die. By some people the Master of Mankind was dubbed the Carrion Eater. Would he likewise consume Jaq?

'Sorry, boss. Really!'

'You did come back, Grimm; that's the main thing.'

Squat, Navigator, assassin: which could Jaq be one hundred per cent sure of? He prayed not to fall victim to the paranoia of which Carnelian had accused him – or else his story, whenever he managed to tell it, might seem wholly unbelievable.

Was not paranoia a touchstone of sanity in this universe of enemies and deceit?

Trust no one, not even yourself, he thought, for you, too, may stray from the pure path without even realising it.

Jaq fasted.

TERRA.

All comm-channels burbled with vox traffic hours, minutes or seconds old. Astral frequencies would be quite as crowded with telepathic messages of even greater urgency, though such messages wouldn't be time-lapsed by the speed limit of electromagnetic radiation. Long-distance radar registered the blips of hundreds of vessels heading in-system or climbing the last shallow incline out of the deep gravity-well of the Sun.

To scan even the approaches to the home system from beyond the outermost challenge-line would seem ample confirmation that the hub of the Imperium could never falter. Yet Jaq hardly needed to remind himself how warp storms had formerly isolated the home system from the stars for several thousand years. The first flowering of human civilisation throughout the galaxy had wilted, rotting into the cesspool of the Age of Strife. That earlier heroic age was eclipsed so utterly that it was now whelmed in obscurity.

He hardly needed to remind himself that during the thirty-first millennium the possessed rebel warmaster Horus had laid waste to Luna and invaded Earth, breaking through to the very inner palace. The putsch was defeated, oh yes, but at what dire cost. Thereafter the wounded Emperor could only survive from grim millennium to grim millennium immobile in his prosthetic golden throne.

What Horus had almost accomplished by main force and using fighting machines of the Adeptus Mechanicus, Jaq hoped to finesse by guile – assisted by a lugubrious

Navigator, a squat whose reliability was now in question, and an assassin whose thought processes increasingly puzzled him.

Jaq stabbed a finger at one particular blip on the radar screen. 'Display that one, Vitali.'

Googol fiddled with the magniscope and brought a flying, dark castle into sharp focus. He gasped. 'A Black Ship, inward bound, Jaq.'

'Match its course. We'll board it. Inquisition inspection.'

'Won't that be among the most vigilant of vessels?'

'It'll have been on tour for a year or so. If I'm on a black list of criminals I doubt that any resident inquisitor will know.'

Jaq spoke with a show of confidence. He was a Malleus man. Therefore let the Black Ship be carrying an ordinary inquisitor; this could work to Jaq's advantage.

Inquisitors frequently travelled on Black Ships while the vessels traversed the galaxy, harvesting fresh young psykers. An inquisitor was extremely useful to the officers of a Black Ship who needed to test their human cargo and root out any malignant weeds en route. As Jaq knew only too well; for he had been similarly rooted out, not as a weed but as a precious flower, transplanted, advanced to greater things. He remembered Olvia. Many such as Olvia would be crowding the dismal dormitories of the Black Ship, their prayers crescendoing as the ship dipped ever closer to Earth, their spirits focusing mournfully upon the impending sacrifice of themselves. The oppressive psychic miasma inside such a vessel would provide a useful protective fog for Jaq.

'What about *Tormentum*?'

'Program her to head away beyond the jump zone under ordinary drive towards the comet halo, then just to drift. We'll know roughly where she is, if we can ever rendezvous with her again.'

Googol nodded. Few ships strayed out beyond the jump zone. Ships were either in-system vessels, remaining within the confines of Sol space, or else they were interstellar – in which case they would dive into the warp as soon as they could. *Tormentum* could remain undetected, yet reachable aboard a conventional craft, offering an option for the unpredictable, dark future.

How *much* Jaq's companions knew by now! They knew of the Ordo Malleus, of the cabal, of the hydra, of the Eye and of creatures of Chaos. More, much more, than ordinary mortals ought to know. If Jaq's mission succeeded, his accomplices in it ought really to be mindscrubbed... Ought to be, as Marines were mindscrubbed after participating in a daemonic *exterminatus*; reduced to the condition of babies so as to safeguard their innocence and sanity. Or else honourably executed.

'Meh'Lindi, I'd like to speak to you alone,' said Jaq.

He walked ahead of her through the ebon corridor past twinkling niches to his own sleep-cell, which he cloaked in privacy.

Memories of that other occasion when they had been alone together teased him turbulently, even though he knew that there could be no repetition of that exultant night. Nevertheless he yearned to know her true feelings.

'Yes, inquisitor?'

'You do realise, Meh'Lindi, that you're the only repository of hydra hereabouts?'

'Just as I knew,' she replied, 'that you would need to travel to Earth and would feel obliged to jettison that adamantine trunk.'

'Was *that* why you ate some of the hydra? Not to protect yourself from it – so much as to preserve some trace?'

'An assassin is an instrument,' she said expressionlessly. 'A wise instrument; yet still an instrument in the service of greater goals.'

'You would give yourself to be tormented? Dissected?' There: he had said it. He had confessed his guilty fear to his one-time mistress.

'Pain can be blocked,' she reminded him, 'as it is when I alter my body.'

He knew that this was less than the whole truth. The pain of physical injuries could be blocked. Yet inside the brain was the centre of raw, absolute pain itself. It could be reached by cerebral probes. Did she know how to isolate *that* from her consciousness? Aye, and what of the terror of having one's very identity taken apart entirely? Must that not be agonising in the deepest possible way?

'If I could give you a gift, Meh'Lindi, what would it be?'

She considered for a while. 'Perhaps... oblivion.'

Now he understood her even less.

Unless... unless she realised – as Grimm and Googol undoubtedly did not suspect – that it was the sacred duty of the Ordo Malleus to erase the very knowledge of monstrous Chaos from human minds, lest this knowledge seduce the weak. Such knowledge must be obliterated.

Was Meh'Lindi forgiving him in advance for the possible fate of his companions, supposing that he *succeeded*?

That indeed was loyalty.

Jaq staunched the flash of anguished pride he felt. Loyalty to anyone who was not the Emperor was a dangerous commodity, was it not? As the hosts of Horus had proved.

Still, he promised himself then and there that he would do his utmost to save Meh'Lindi and Googol and Grimm. Even if this made him, in some small way, a traitor. Even if, in so doing, he denied Meh'Lindi the gift of utter amnesia she requested.

On the point of departure, she paused.

'I have much to forget,' she told him. 'Inside this body of mine lurks plastiflesh and flexicartilage in which is written the permanent memory of a certain evil shape.'

'Do you mean you feel as though there's a kind of *rune* of evil written inside you? Do you feel that you're somehow cursed? Rather than blessed by your wondrous ability?'

'An ability to become one thing and one thing only! When I use polymorphine now I can't adopt the appearances of other human beings. I will trigger the genestealer pattern within me. Thus I deny my chameleon possibilities. I ask you: is that *Callidus*? Is that *cunning*?

'So do you suspect you're false to the traditions of your shrine? Yet your shrine asked this of you.'

She nodded. 'It was done to me with my consent.' Perhaps she felt that her shrine had cheated her.

He hesitated before asking, 'Were you pressured into consenting?'

She laughed bitterly. 'The universe always applies pressures, does it not? Crushing pressures.' That was no real answer, nor had he really expected one. Would an assassin betray the secrets of her shrine?

'Yet on Queem's world,' he reminded her, 'you felt illuminated... about Chaos, and the possible nature of the Harlequin man.'

Meh'Lindi pursed her lips; those lips that had roved over his body once, those same lips that had stretched into a terrible snout.

'Darkly illuminated,' she corrected him. 'Darkly.'

And even so, he would not wish to extinguish her light.

SEVEПTEEП

'FRUITFUL TRAVELS, JOURNEYMAN?' Jaq asked a young bearded inquisitor who could almost have been his earlier self.

Rafe Zilanov wore some alien foetus pendants dangling from his ear lobes. The man seemed alert, though a little inexperienced. Whatever his special talents – however well honed those were to diagnose any daemonic contamination among the passengers – the moaning psychic static aboard the Black Ship provided just the level of astral interference that Jaq had hoped for.

'Fruitful? A net of eleven hundred psykers for the Emperor. I think that's fruitful. We were only obliged to eliminate half of one per cent. Five per cent seem worthy of advancement.'

And ninety-five per cent worthy of feeding to the cadaverous Master of Mankind to power his Astronomican. How long, how long, could the noble agony of the human galaxy continue? Maybe the cabal had the right idea, to replace this cannibalistic system with the ultimate totalitarian control.

Oh no, they did not. And oh no, they were almost certainly not what they seemed.

Jaq grunted.

'Is something wrong?' asked the skew-eyed, brawny captain.

The lines on Captain Holofernest's ruddy face told of many years exposed to the psychic migraine of those he must transport. Here, thought Jaq, was an unsung hero of the Imperium. Not a Marine, not a Terminator Knight, but a hero even so. An ignorant hero, blessedly ignorant, his uniform hung with amulets. A hero to be browbeaten.

Tapestries of space battles cloaked the walls of the captain's cabin – permanent reminders of a more active destiny that might have been his?

Jaq noted faint ring-marks from liquor glasses on the captain's desk. Private drunkenness, while his Navigator steered through the warp, was Holofernest's solace, his consolation, anaesthesia – and his weak spot.

Jaq had activated his tattoos for Zilanov's benefit, so that the journeyman understood that Jaq was his superior in ways that the young man did not wholly comprehend, yet knew enough not to query.

Still, Zilanov reserved his opinion; as Jaq too would have done. The journeyman scrutinised Jaq's motley companions curiously. He appeared to have identified Meh'Lindi as an assassin.

'Wrong, captain?' drawled Jaq, as nonchalantly as he could. 'Oh, something is wrong. I'm investigating a certain matter. It relates to ships such as yours. Specifically, what happens when they deliver their cargo to Earth orbit.'

'Our passengers get sorted out a second time,' growled Holofernest. 'To double-check our own good work; and very wise too. Then shuttles convey the majority to the Forbidden Fortress for long Astronomican training followed by brief duty. What of it?'

'Whereabouts is that Forbidden Fortress, captain?'

'Hah! That information is forbidden to such as me. Very wise too.'

'Where do you suppose it is?'

'I shouldn't dream of speculating, inquisitor.'

'Very wise.'

The stronghold of the Adeptus Astronomica was inside the mountain range known as the Himalayas. One whole mountain was sculpted into the upper half of a sphere of rock that housed the Astronomican.

'You speak of *long* training and *brief* duty. Why do you add those details? Do I detect grievances? A streak of softness in your soul?'

Holofernest glanced at Rafe Zilanov for reassurance.

'Loose tongues!' snarled Jaq. 'Those are best torn out. I'm sure you'll be more discreet in future in your implied criticisms of the Imperium – unless of course *liquor* loosens your lips. But no matter. What concerns me is illicit slavery – namely the creaming off of a tiny percentage of comely psykers.'

Zilanov knit his brow, and the captain gaped. 'Who by?' And visibly wished he had not asked. 'Not that I'm inquisitive. Not that I–'

Jaq favoured Holofernest with the thinnest of smiles. 'I almost hesitate to say it. By perverted officials relatively high in the Imperial court.'

Illicit slavery, thought Jaq, as opposed to legitimate *dedication* to the Emperor... Would those illicit slaves of whom he spoke live longer in private hands? He rather doubted it. Their brief existence might be positively vile in the hands of connoisseurs of degradation. Admittedly no such connoisseurs *existed*, to the best of his knowledge, except in his own imagination. It was a good idea to believe one's own lies, then others might believe them too.

'I need hardly emphasise the peril of harbouring untrained psykers even in the outer palace,' he went on. 'Even if such persons are kept prisoner behind psychic screens, any one of these might still become a conduit for a daemon; especially since they will call out in their pain and misery for any form of assistance. If a daemon possesses just one slave, and that slave escapes inside the palace – consider the possible consequences!'

'Our passenger manifests are always accurate,' protested Holofernest.

'I don't doubt it. Yet what of the tiny percentage of passengers that every Black Ship needs to eliminate? Do you store their corpses to be counted and tallied too?'

'You must know that we scuttle such corpses into the warp.'

'What if that tiny percentage did not in actuality become corpses, but are held alive in stasis in some nook or cranny of a ship as cavernous as this?'

'Not on board mine, I assure you!' The captain glanced towards his desk where his liquor glass habitually would rest. He was yearning for it now.

'I make no personal accusations,' said Jaq. 'You have now received privileged information; that is all.'

'What do you want us to do?' asked Zilanov. The young inquisitor almost believed. Why should he not? The story was plausible enough to send a shiver down the spine of any Emperor's man. Why should a senior inquisitor be lying?

Jaq said, 'I need to be smuggled into the number three south-eastern port of the Imperial palace in exactly the way we suspect these illicit slaves are being smuggled, namely in stasis food chests. Myself, and my companions.'

'You'll be utterly vulnerable,' Zilanov pointed out.

'Until the stasis deactivates at a pre-set time, that's true. Do you suggest we should evade danger, when by risking ourselves we can lay a hand on the perpetrators of this crime?'

Zilanov believed completely now. No traitor would make themselves so utterly helpless or risk delivering themselves paralysed into the possible hands of enemies.

'This is an undercover operation of alpha-prime importance,' said Jaq. 'You are sworn to total secrecy. Now I'll explain the routing codes you must use for the caskets...'

* * *

AND STASIS CEASED.

Jaq cracked open the lid of the container in which he had lain cramped in an enforcedly foetal position.

He had felt no sensation whatever. He had expected to know nothing, either.

Instead, his consciousness had been suspended in a single quantum of thought; and that thought had been anxiety. Maybe the workings of his consciousness had progressed ever so slightly during the timeless interval of his encapsulation, as his psychic sense of protection attempted to lift the siege of anxiety. Yet essentially he had been suspended frozen at that point of dread – his whole being composed of apprehension and nothing else. No memories, no active thoughts, no sluggish dreams; only an impersonal distillation of anxiety occurring within the same endless ever-instant.

Now that he was Jaq again, he shook with accumulated fear. What if he had entered stasis already in a state of terror or of pain?

Ultimately, he hoped that his psychic talent might have soothed and opiated him, altering the nature of that ever-instant.

What if not? What if he had possessed no enchantments? He suspected that he had discovered a new and terrible torture or punishment. For at the height of torment a prisoner might be dropped into a stasis casket to experience that climactic moment for a year, for a century.

Jaq squinted up at massive rusty pipes beaded with condensation. Ah, those mottlings were not rust. Generations of pious runes had faded and been overpainted and had faded again. The mottlings were moving past a couple of metres overhead. He heard clanking, creaking, distant tintinnabulations of metal ringing on metal. His casket was obviously on a conveyor belt.

Just as it should be. Mastering the fear which had washed over him in the release from stasis, he stood up. The four caskets were indeed travelling slowly along a segmented steel belt through a dismal, seemingly endless downhill tunnel. Dull orange light ached from glow-globes. The air was frigid. No one, nor any servitor, was in sight.

Clambering to the nearest neighbouring casket, Jaq lifted the lid. Meh'Lindi sat up, a snake rearing to strike. She did not sting. She kissed Jaq fleetingly.

'Thank you for that taste of oblivion, master.'

'Master?' he echoed.

'We're pretending to be slaves, aren't we?'

'We can forget about that now. Any ill effects?'

'We assassins know how to blank our minds if need be, to induce hibernation. I became a blank, aware only of beloved nullity, the state before universe and Chaos came to be, when God existed, God the Nothing.'

She was, he suspected, harking back to some strange half-remembered cult of her long-lost home world. The true God, the ever-dying Emperor, eater of souls, beacon of suffering striving humanity, was almost within reach now, perhaps only four hundred kilometres distant through the palace.

Meh'Lindi in turn raised the lid of Grimm's casket, and the abhuman exclaimed, 'Huh. Huh.' As if uttering his own restored heartbeat.

Jaq opened the final stasis-box.

'Void,' whispered Vitali, 'endless void. The third eye did not cease to see. It ranged an empty infinitude. Did you know that there are degrees of nothingness? Shades of unlight?'

"Nuff of that guff,' said Grimm gruffly, popping up alongside Jaq. 'Quite like the old home caverns, this place, 'cept I don't see any stone. Don't seem much of a palace, though. Where is everyone? Sure we've taken the right route, boss?'

'Oh yes. This is an ancient deep supply tunnel, a tiny tendril far away from the heart. Even so, we've been rather lucky that no members of the Adeptus Terra are labouring down here right now.'

'Huh, now he tells us.'

* * *

IT MIGHT HAVE been winter in the outside world. Though truly there was little of the outside world in existence on Terra. All of Earth's continents – save for the south polar icelands, deep under which the Inquisition lurked – were clad, often kilometres high, in the labyrinthine sprawl of one edifice of state or another. Palace, ecclesiarchy, huge bureaucracies, virtually worlds unto themselves.

Generations could live out lifetimes within a single Imperial sub-department, almost oblivious to the stars above except as notations on data-slates or in ledgers, never seeing a wan sun peer through a poisoned sky.

Presently the air began to warm and to catch foully in their throats. The belt was bearing them onward and downward towards intimations of noise and activity, towards distant stabs of light. Evidently their tunnel would soon debouch into somewhere vaster.

After heaving the stasis boxes off the belt, they took from them strap-on oxygen bottles and breathing membranes. Those membranes also served to shield their eyes from an increasingly gassy and acrid atmosphere. Whispers of oxygen refreshed their lungs now.

Behind them in the orange obscurity other cargo was looming. Collapsing the stasis boxes, they hid those in a dusty side chamber. They walked on, alongside the trundling belt.

IN A VAST pillared hall of plasteel, cyborgs and amputees bonded into machines ground to and fro on caterpillar tracks or clanked about on tarnished metal legs. The floor was awash with oily chemical spillage fitfully iridescent in the glance of shifting lights.

Some of the mechanised workers serviced cable-sinewed thudding engines. Others tore open crates from the belt with powered pincers, inspected bills of lading, and transferred the incoming cargo to a branching array of mighty, rusting pneumomagnetic tubes which despatched items in distant directions with a fierce hiss and thunderclap of compressed air and a sizzle of electromagnetic surge.

Smashed empty crates disappeared into the maw of a fur-
nace, a throat of fire which ruddied the sloshing wash of
liquids around it. The hall echoed with rumble, hiss, clap
and roar.

Even as the four intruders watched from a ledge of concealment, one of the tubes ruptured, spraying ochreous
flakes. A welder-servitor trundled to repair the sprung
plates.

Perhaps this kind of accident was a regular occurrence.
Perhaps that automaton did nothing else but reweld tubes.
Had those not burst from time to time, its monotonous
life would have been empty. Jaq and companions were in
a very minor oesophagus of an ancient, neglected, far
fringe of the palace – or more properly, underpalace.

Did the cargo from the stars which arrived by this route
ever reliably reach its intended destination? Perhaps it
did. Just so, did much of the Imperium itself function,
rupturing, then being rewelded. Yet at the same time,
mighty energies were being deployed. And there was vigilance too.

On impulse Jaq removed his Tarot significator card, of
the black-robed High Priest with the hammer. Surely
Carnelian was far far away, hundreds, thousands of light
years away, and couldn't intrude again...

Jaq's image was shading his eyes with the hand that
clutched the hammer in the manner of someone peering
from brightness into an obscure distance. The card
twitched. It throbbed. Abruptly it pulled like a dowsing
rod as though, should Jaq release the card, it would
promptly fly away under its own impulse.

'Boss–' Grimm reached as if to catch the card, should it
spring free, but jerked his fingers back. 'Are you doing that
yourself?'

Am I? wondered Jaq. Is my hidden mind, in which all
engrams of memory are recorded, prompting me to recall
the safest route through the topographic nightmare of the
palace? Or does some power unseen preside over this, our
journey?

Whose power? That of the God-Emperor himself?

The card yanked urgently. 'This card will be our guide,' he said. 'We must hurry from this place.'

None too soon. Scarcely had they skulked through the vast hall from shadow to shadow, from pillar to pillar, sliding along in the slosh of foul liquid, avoiding the spotlights and scrutiny of the trundling servitors, than – staring back through his magniscope – Jaq spied a tall figure far away scrutinising the area around the conveyor. Boots, leather breeches, long black cloak... The ominous tall helmet was a three-tiered brazen skull tipped with crenellations from which antennae sprouted. The figure stirred the poisonous soup that hid the plates of the floor with the butt of a laser-spear.

'Who's that guy?' asked Grimm.

'Custodian,' murmured Jaq. 'Palace guardsman. Maybe we triggered a sensor beam.'

Just then a giant warty rat, its matted coat faintly phosphorescent, scuttled from the tunnel mouth. The custodian levelled his spear and lasered the creature.

Jaq spoke a conjuration of stealth. '*O furtim invisibiles!*'

The Tarot card tugged gently towards one of several archways.

THEY DESCENDED THROUGH several strata of plasteel where whole rivers flowed, of dirty oil and chemicals, where torrents of effluent vented into lakes abrew with luminous algae. They dodged mobile machines, patchworked with stains, that might have contained human beings or at least the torsos and heads of cyberworkers. They slept in the cab of a derelict mammoth bulldozer half-sunk in glittering sludge.

AND NOW THEY climbed, by circular stairways hidden within the cores of columns, up into a twilit mall where scribes scrivened by electrocandle outside their family cells.

This mall stretched for a kilometre. Several hundred hooded scribes in black fustian laboured at penning data

from implants in their brows into massive ledgers bound
in skin, perhaps the skin of their fathers and grandfathers,
lovingly flayed after death, cured and dedicated to the
work that had occupied those bygone lives.

Other scribes were copying the fading penmanship of
ancient, crack-backed dusty volumes into newer tomes.
Tottering, spiderwebbed towers of codices rose from floor
to ceiling, ladders propped against some. Many scribes
whispered as they worked. A toothless crone of a curator in
brown habit perched like some shrivelled mummy in a
high chair. An antique alien manuscript lay open on the
high desk before her, but she was more occupied in super-
vising her scribes through the magnilenses of a lorgnette.
She pointed a rod that caused her target to twitch and
sweat. Couriers came and went, some bringing data-chips,
some carrying ledgers away.

'Who goes?' she cackled as Jaq and party approached.

'The word is powerful,' replied Jaq.

'Pass by. Pass by.'

WEARING STOLEN GREY robes of Administratum auditors –
and Grimm the buckskin of a kitchen servant – they strode
through a busy basilica housing arcane machinery. Sacred
klaxons wailed. Tech-priests fiddled with vernier gauges.
Sandalwood incense rose, sweetening a haze of acrid
fumes.

Later they crossed a cathedral-laboratory. Icons marked
with symbols of the elements dangled from internal flying
buttresses. Sodium vapour flambeaux behind high false-
clerestory-windows of stained glass painted patches of
amber ichor, sap, and haemoglobin across the tessellated
floor. Athenor furnaces glowed and alembics bubbled,
purifying and repurifying rare drugs extracted from the
organs of alien animals being vivisected by surgeon-
butchers behind armour glass.

Trumpets screamed and brayed, drowning howls.
Evidently such organs must be extracted live without use
of soporifics for full efficacy. Orange and golden blood ran

through tubes, pumped by scrofulous bondsmen chained to bellows. Lift platforms rose into view, carrying new specimens; and sank, bearing carcasses and offal.

A laser-armed tech-priest dressed in a cream robe accosted them. 'Your business? Your rank?'

'We're accountants for the synthdiet administration,' said Jaq, casting an aura of persuasion. 'I'm Prefectus Secundus of the Dispendium, the office of Cost and Loss.'

'I have never heard of that.' Yet this fact need not rouse the priest's suspicions. If anything, the contrary! The estimate that ten billion people were involved in the administration of the palace perhaps erred on the miserly side.

Jaq nodded at Googol and Meh'Lindi. 'These are my Prefectus Tertius and Sub-Prefectus. The squat is a servitor. We suspect protein is going to waste in these experiments.'

'You call these *experiments*?' cried the priest indignantly. 'Some molecules of immortality for the Emperor's own use are extracted here.'

'Leaving much good meat,' groused Grimm.

'That's *alien* meat, you inhuman turnspit! It's indigestible.'

'Could be rendered into diet.'

'Rubbish, impertinent scullion. How dare a servitor address me thus?'

'Excuse us, I'm sure!'

'Wise adeptus,' interrupted a beige-clad novice.

The priest excused Jaq's party, wearing only a slightly puzzled frown. This might have deepened had he been able to concentrate on remembering that auditors had supposedly been about to commence an investigation – yet had vanished out of sight instead.

Their exit from that cathedral through a heavily guarded checkpoint was easier than entry would have been by that same route.

Yet beyond, a seemingly endless, grumbling queue of applicants twenty deep crept like some hugely elongated snail along a gloomy arcaded boulevard towards some

distant office of the Administratum, seeking... what? A
permit? An application form? An interview?

The most foresightful applicants hauled minicarts on
which fellow applicants, who would return the favour,
curled up snoozing. Hawkers of sweetmeats and glucose
sticks and vendors of stale water toured the queue.
Hunched sanitizers in khaki coveralls drove mobile lava-
toria to and fro.

An Arbites patrol team was maintaining surveillance
from parked land-cars, while a bus of shocktroopers
lurked in reserve in case of riot. Jaq spied their plumed hel-
mets through the blue armoured glass.

A team of armed monitors was working its way along the
queue, using portable psychodiagnostic kits. Occasionally
an applicant was arrested. One broke free and was shot.

'Out of the frying pan into the fire,' said Grimm. 'We'll
never squeeze our way past that lot.'

The queue was growing restive now. The Arbites were
readying their suppression shields.

Jaq's Tarot card tugged.

EIGHTEEN

IF VIEWED FROM low orbit through the foul atmosphere, the continent-spanning palace was a concatenation of copulating, jewel-studded tortoise shells erupting into ornate monoliths, pyramids, and ziggurats kilometres high, pocked by landing pads, prickling with masts of antennae and weapons batteries. Whole cities were mere chambers in this palace, some grimly splendid, others despicable and deadly, and all crusted with the accretion of the ages.

Common sense – and the High Priest card – insisted that Jaq and company eschew the option of renting a vehicle and taking to one of the multi-decked roads that bored through the palace. At precinct boundaries scrutiny teams would surely demand to scan electronic tattoos.

Thus instead they must detour on foot through a sprawling, rearing tenement-conurb of densely populated shafts and conduits, of crumbling many-times-braced and scaffolded urban cliffs that crowded closer than canyon walls under a grey steel roof held up saggingly by a suspensor field.

Even the scaffolding was colonised with tin shacks, torn
tents, tattered plastic bedrolls. Here, the basic protoplas-
mic rump of humanity festered and simmered, in this
breeding ground of those whose greatest dream was that
their brats might become the lowest of adepts, hereditary
slave-workers. Starvelings haunted the walkways like
wraiths, seeking for recent corpses. Tattooed gangs
roamed, armed with home-made blades. The susurrus of
people was a sea of sound, often sinisterly hushed.

They stole rags to cloak themselves, they evicted beggars
from ventilator ducts in which to shelter, on guard. They
filched food from the starving.

Meh'Lindi killed; Jaq killed; and Grimm too.

For a while they seemed to be more distant than ever
from their goal, as if backtracking. As day followed day
they even reminisced nostalgically about the cathedral-
laboratory and about the mall of scribes. Always Judges
seemed to be in the offing, exercising random vigilance;
much less often, the proud elite palace Custodians.

'Becoming quite the little nomad family, aren't we?'
puffed Grimm on one occasion, after they had fled and
hid.

Jaq stared at him. Oh yes, they were more than mere
companions now. Disloyalty might have hovered – and
the greatest, needful betrayal might yet await – nevertheless they pursued this last, seemingly interminable stage of
their enterprise as family, of a kind.

Of a kind.

A SPOTLIT ZEALOT of a confessor was screaming through a
megaphone at an arena packed with humanity, under a
coruscated domed ceiling. The glittering shimmer above
twinkled hypnotically, now forming the Emperor's face,
and now potent runes, as if this was a planetarium of devo-
tion and self-incrimination. The shifting lights and the
booming words combined to work a spell such that the
audience surged within itself, thrusting elements of itself
forward, expelling individuals as a sickly body sheds cells.

These body-cells were heretics, or people who imagined they were heretics, or whose neighbours believed – at least in that setting – that they were corrupted.

Purity squads hauled such individuals away for execution, or perhaps for excruciation and redemption.

Jaq and comapnions stood near a young couple who had, so they gathered, set out with two Imperial credits to squander on a visit to a column-top cafe where real coffee from a starworld was served and which overlooked a vista of floodlit factories and shrines. The young woman had turned aside into the arena, enchanted by the vibrant words. Presently she began shoving against her young man, whispering bitterly to him, until in despair he squeezed forward to denounce himself.

Meh'Lindi had to hustle Grimm away. Even Jaq felt the urge to betray himself.

Jaq had never liked zealots. That night, after killing a guard, they broke into the residence of the preacher who had purged so many hundreds of hysterics (as well as, yes, accursed heretics). Meh'Lindi nerve-blocked and heart-stopped the hapless man and his family. Jaq and party bathed away the stink of days, feasted soberly, prayed, slept deeply. They thieved new clothes before pressing onward circuitously, evading the vigilance that was ever more evident, as omnipresent as the Emperor's spirit – yet also seemingly purblind, foxed by the intricate, degenerate immensity of that which must be overseen.

ONE DOES NOT tell exactly by what route – and by what chicanery – an enemy might slip from the outer palace into the inner palace. Oh no.

Some secrets must remain secret. Almost, they must remain secret from those people who themselves know them.

The journey of Jaq Draco and his companions from the number three south-eastern port to the Column of Glory took as long as their flight from the Eye of Terror had cost them in warp-time, and more.

At one time they masqueraded as ciphers, servitors who had memorized messages of which they had no under-standing, and who trotted along in a hypnotic trance.

At another time they disguised themselves as historitors whose whole career was to revise subversive records, and to forge more reverend versions. Thus Jaq and companions counterfeited themselves.

They adopted the camouflage of a returning explorator team, which, in a sense, they were.

Always lying, pretending, stealing – robes, insignia, regalia – and sometimes compelled to kill, acting as though they were some covert traitor terror squad pledged to deep penetration of the ultimate sanctum. Meh'Lindi, as a Callidus assassin, was invaluable.

They passed increasingly amidst priests, battlemasters, astropaths, scholastics, and the retinues and brood and servants of these.

Once, as an extreme ploy, Jaq pretended to be an inquisi-tor; and afterwards was shocked to remember that he was indeed one in reality.

Could they have tried – having come so far – to surren-der to an officer of the Adeptus Custodes, thus to crave audience with a commander of those exalted warriors who guarded the throne room itself? Could they have revealed themselves?

The reach of the cabal might easily extend as far as an officer of those final defenders of the Throne.

Besides, their journey of penetration had by now attained a bizarre dynamic all of its own, an almost self-sustaining momentum.

Fatigue became an anaesthetic. Ever-present anxiety must needs be deposited in some increasingly constipated bowel of the soul, where it mutated paradoxically into a stimulant.

Jaq felt as if he was forcing his way down into the depths of an ocean, where pressure measured itself in tonnes. Yet he and his companions trod a shining path, in a state of mind which alternated between dream and nightmare,

and which had certainly ceased to be ordinary consciousness.

This path was luminous to themselves, yet obscure to
strangers – as though their track was detached by a hair's
breadth from reality; as though they were stepping along
some twisting corridor, embedded within the palace, that
nevertheless ran parallel to the true world of the palace.

Jaq's Tarot card led him like a compass; and behind the
High Priest with the hammer there now hovered in the
liquid crystal of the card the shadow of a figure, enthroned,
that was coming ever more closely to resemble the
Emperor, as though that other card of the arcana was
fusing with Jaq's own significator card.

'We're in a trance,' Jaq murmured to Meh'Lindi once,
while they rested. 'A trance of guidance. A voice seems to
say to me: *Come.*' He refrained from mentioning that
other echoing voices – shadows of voices – seemed to
disagree.

'We're pursuing the ultimate ideal assassin's path,' she
agreed. 'The path of cunning invisibility. This is the peak of
achievement of any assassin of my shrine. Its goal must be
our deaths, I think. For the paragon of assassins would be
she who, after a long and terrible quest of sly subterfuge,
tracked down none other than herself, and slew herself
impeccably.'

'Huh!' said Grimm, and spat.

Googol, for his part, hunched in a daze.

One does not describe the precise route they took, oh
no! That would be wicked treason. It may be, it may just
be, that the selfsame pathway they followed towards the
Emperor's presence, that identical pattern, only existed for
Jaq and his comrades during that particular slice of time,
unrepeatable ever again.

Comrades. Four members of a strangely braided family...
who had once been total strangers, and might yet become
so again. Jaq the father who made true love only once.
Googol the wayward junior brother. Meh'Lindi the feral
mother who carried within her not a child but the

implanted lineaments of a monster shape. Grimm the child-scaled abhuman.

HERE NOW AT last was savage grandeur. Here was the Column of Glory itself.

Under a vaulted dome so lofty that clouds had formed to obscure its frescoed arcs, a slim tower of multi-hued metals rose half a kilometre high. The suits of White Scars and Imperial Fist Space Marines, who had died defending this palace nine thousand years earlier, studded that column. Within those shattered suits their bones still hung. Their skulls still grinned from open faceplates.

Crowds of young psykers, robed as acolytes, prayed there under the watchful gaze of their instructors. Soon those psykers would be led onward to be soul-bound, agonised and blinded, and consecrated for service.

Squads of helmeted Emperor's Companions stood to attention vigilantly, armed with bolters and plasma guns, black cloaks aswirl around ancient, ornately carved power armour. Dissonant music – gongs, harps – boomed and twanged and rippled, matching the pulse of ancient, adored machinery. Incense reeked.

Jaq was currently wearing the robes of a secretary to a cardinal, Meh'Lindi was a battle-sister of the Adepta Sororitas, Googol was a cardinal's majordomo, while Grimm was a robed tech-priest.

Two immense Titans, embodiments of the Machine-God, flanked the great archway that led onward, serving as columns, one blood-red, one purple. High over the archway, in obsidian, the wide winged double-headed eagle of the Imperium was mounted. The bowed carapaces of these giant fighting robots sustained golden mosaic roofing in which, as Jaq knew, were buried the heavy macro-cannons and multi-launchers of the Titans, just as their great cleated feet were locked underfloor. Purity seals and devout banners dangled everywhere they looked.

By each side of the archway sagged a power fist which could seize and crush to liquid any unpermitted interloper. The other jointed arm of each Titan terminated in a massive, poised defence laser.

Inside the jutting armoured head of each Titan, rotas of warrior adepts of the Collegia Titanica had roosted on honour-guard during thousands of years. During thousands of years those two Titans had stood as columns, immobile, statuesque, awing all who approached. Yet in ultimate emergency their plasma generators could presumably power up rapidly from standby mode. Energy could flow through hydroplastics coupled to actuators. The electrically-motivated fibre bundles that served as muscles could tear their heaviest weapons free from the roof, bringing tonnes crashing down as a blockade. The god-machines could wrench their feet free. They could open fire devastatingly. During overhauls throughout the millennia the appropriate maintenance litanies would have been chanted faithfully.

Even on standby, Jaq suspected that those power fists might flex and pluck a body from the floor if the devotees in those vast metallic heads saw fit...

'How did we get here?' whispered Googol, aghast with wonder.

'*Per via obscura et luminosa,*' replied Jaq. 'By the shining, hidden path–'

Time twisted.

Time shifted.

Time was, and was not.

An eerie silver power flowed through Jaq, as though he had invoked it by those words. The power used his mind as its conductor. He sensed how the time stream itself was being negated and annulled.

Some psykers of the highest level could distort time thus. Not Jaq, hitherto.

Never Jaq.

Yet now...

Was he *possessed*?

By no daemon, certainly. But by the shining path itself. To his senses that path now appeared to be the track of a

phosphorescent arrow through twisted geometries. The
arrow had accumulated a charge at its point until that
point could transfix the fabric of time itself, pinning
time temporarily like a moth with a needle through its
spine...

'Run, now!' cried Jaq.

Did he and his abnormal family flit like hummingbirds
which seem to flicker directly from one point in space to
another, passing in and out of existence? Afterwards Jaq
believed they must have darted thus – across the static,
time-stopped Chamber of Glory, past the frozen
Companions, and through the Titan Archway between the
motionless menacing colossi.

And still the lustrous arrow impaled the tissue of time.

THROBBING PIPES RIBBED the walls of the vast throne room
beyond. The muscles of the room were thick power cables
feeding stegosaurian engines. The air was spiked with crisp
ozone and bitter myrrh, and ointmented with balmy,
somewhat greasy fragrances. The holiest battle banners,
icons and golden fetishes flanked the arena of dedication
where psykers were soul-bound.

Squads of Emperor's Companions who guarded that
vast hall, a mob of tech-priests ministering to the machinery, a gaudy Cardinal Palatinate and his entourage, a
red-robed High Lord of Terra and his staff – not to mention great clusters of astropaths, chirurgeons, scholastics,
battlemasters: *all were motionless.*

The immense, soaring, tube-ridged throne resembled
some fossilised, metastasised sloth crafted by some mad
master of the Adeptus Titanicus. And it seemed to Jaq,
though he did not know whether what he saw was true, or
mere delusion instilled by that same psyker-dream, that
this enormous, sacred prosthetic device, more precious by
far than any gold, framed the wizened, mummified face of
the God-Emperor.

Who looked not; though he saw through eyes of the
mind, saw far beyond his throne room and his palace and

the solar system. Who breathed not; yet he lived more fiercely than any mortal, enduring a psychically super-charged life-in-death.

'WE ARE CURIOUS,' came a mighty, anguished thought which itself transcended time.

'WE HAVE FOLLOWED YOUR INTRUSION INTO OUR SANCTUARY, OUR ANTRUM AND ADYTUM.'

'My lord.' Jaq sank to his knees. 'I beg to report to you before I am destroyed. I may have uncovered a major con-spiracy—'

'THEN WE WILL STRIP YOUR SOUL BARE. RELAX, MORTAL MAN, OR YOU WILL SURELY DIE IN SUCH PAIN AS WE ALWAYS ENDURE.'

Jaq breathed deeply, slowly, stilling the panic that flut-tered under his ribs like a trapped bird. He surrendered himself.

A hurricane roared through his mind.

If the story that he had thought to relate were a tangled forest — and if each event in that story were a tree — then within moments all the leaves were stripped away from all of the trees, denuding them to bare wintry twigs, to a raw basic life without the foliage of memories.

He was drained of his story; that was sucked from him in a trice, all of those leaves whirling into the mind-maw of the Master.

Jaq gagged. Jaq drooled.

He was an imbecile, less than an imbecile.

He was less than a new-born baby.

He neither knew where he was, nor who he was — nor what it even meant to be a someone.

The inquisitor sprawled. All that was known to his body was distress, the gurglings of the guts, breath and light.

Light from afar.

ABRUPTLY, ALL MEMORY flooded back. On that instant, each leaf sprouted anew to recloak the forest of his life.

'WE HAVE PUT BACK WHAT WE TOOK AND TASTED, INQUISITOR.'

Trembling, Jaq regained his kneeling posture and wiped his lips and chin. The previous moments were a hideous limbo, unknowable, immeasurable. He was Jaq Draco again.

'WE ARE MANY, INQUISITOR.' The voice boomed in his mind almost gently – if gently was how an avalanche would sweep away a doomed village, if gently was how a scalpel might strip a life to the bare aching bones.

'HOW ELSE COULD WE ADMINISTER OUR IMPERIUM–'

'AS WELL AS WINNOW THE WARP–'

'HOW ELSE?'

The Emperor's mind-voice, if that truly was what it was, had dissociated into several voices, as if his great undying soul co-existed in fragments that barely hung together.

'SO DOES THE HYDRA THREATEN US?'

'IMPERILLING OUR GREAT AND AWFUL PLAN TO STEER HUMANITY?'

'DID WE OURSELVES DEVISE THE HYDRA?'

'PERHAPS IN A PART OF US, SINCE THIS HYDRA PROMISES A PATH?'

'SURELY A MALEVOLENT PATH; FOR HOW COULD HUMANITY EVER FREE ITSELF?'

'THEN WE MUST BE MALEVOLENT TOO. FOR WE HAVE EXPELLED OUR SENTIMENTALITY LONG AGO. HOW ELSE COULD WE HAVE ENDURED? HOW ELSE COULD WE HAVE IMPOSED OUR RULE?'

'YET BY VIRTUE OF THAT WE ARE PURE AND UNCONTAMINATED BY WEAKNESS. WE ARE GRIM SALVATION.'

Beside Jaq, the squat twitched as if he had heard himself named. At that moment did the voice resonate within the abhuman? Jaq felt that he was listening to a mighty mind-machine argue with itself in a way that no Imperial courtier had perhaps ever heard, and that no High Lord of Terra even suspected could occur. Were Meh'Lindi and Googol aware of the voices in the way that Jaq was? Or was he imagining it all, caught up in some warp-spawned delusion, yet another twist in this labyrinthine conspiracy? He sensed the fabric of time attempting to tear free, and guessed that not much longer of this strange stasis remained.

'NOTHING THAT SAFEGUARDS HUMANITY CAN BE EVIL, NOT EVEN THE MOST STRENUOUS INHUMANITY. IF THE HUMAN RACE FAILS, IT HAS FAILED FOREVER.'

Maybe Jaq was too young by hundreds, by thousands of years, and his intellect too puny to comprehend the multiplex mind of the master who was forever on overview, whose thoughts battered in his mind. Or maybe the master's mind had become chaotic. Not warped by the Ruinous Powers it surveyed, oh no, but divided amongst itself as its heroic grasp on existence ever so slowly weakened...

'WHEN WE CONFRONTED THE CORRUPTED, HOMICIDAL HORUS WHO ONCE USED TO SHINE LIKE THE BRIGHTEST STAR, WHO USED TO BE OUR BELOVED FAVOURITE – WHEN THE FATE OF THE GALAXY HUNG BY A THREAD – WERE WE NOT COMPELLED TO EXPEL ALL COMPASSION? ALL LOVE? ALL JOY? THOSE WENT AWAY. HOW ELSE COULD WE HAVE ARMOURED OURSELVES? EXISTENCE IS TORMENT, A TORMENT THAT MUST NOURISH US. EVIDENTLY WE MUST STRIVE TO BE THE FIERCE REDEEMER OF MAN, YET WHAT WILL REDEEM US?'

'Great lord of all,' whimpered Jaq, 'did you know of the hydra before now?'

'NO, AND WE SHALL SURELY ACT IN DUE TIME–'

'YET SURELY WE KNEW. HOW COULD WE NOT KNOW?'

'ONCE WE HAVE ANALYSED THE INFORMATION WITHIN THIS SUB-MIND OF OURS.'

'HEAR THIS, JAQ DRACO: ONLY TINY PORTIONS OF US CAN HEED YOU, OTHERWISE WE NEGLECT OUR IMPERIUM, OF WHICH OUR SCRUTINY MUST NOT FALTER FOR AN INSTANT. FOR TIME DOES NOT HALT

EVERYWHERE WITHIN THE REALM OF MAN. INDEED
TIME ONLY HALTS FOR YOU.'

'WE ARE AN EVER-WATCHFUL LORD, ARE WE NOT?
DID YOU HOPE TO GAIN OUR UNDIVIDED ATTEN-
TION?'

'HOW ELSE SHOULD WE SOUL-BIND PSYKERS AND
OVERVIEW THE WARP AND BEAM THE ASTRONOMI-
CAN BEACON AND SURVIVE AND RECEIVE
INFORMATION AND GRANT AUDIENCES ALL AT
ONCE, UNLESS WE ARE MANY?'

'AND YET STILL WE MISS SO MUCH, SO VERY MUCH?
SUCH AS THAT WHICH GUIDED YOU HERE.'

'OUR SPIRIT GUIDED YOU.'

'NO: ANOTHER SPIRIT, A REFLECTION OF OUR
GOODNESS WHICH WE THRUST FROM US.'

'WE ARE THE ONLY SOURCE OF GOODNESS, SEVERE
AND DRASTIC. THERE IS NO OTHER SOURCE OF HOPE
THAN US. WE ARE AGONISINGLY ALONE.'

Contradictions! These warred in Jaq's mind just as they
seemed to coexist in the Emperor's own multimind.

Was another power for salvation present in the galaxy,
unknown to the suffering Emperor – concealed from him,
though somehow partaking of his essence? How could
that be?

And what of the hydra? Did the Emperor truly know of
it or not – even now? Might he refuse to acknowledge what
Jaq had reported to him?

The Emperor's voices faded from Jaq's mind as time tried
to stretch back into shape.

Grimm tugged at Jaq's sleeve.

'It's over, lord. Don't you understand?' Yes, Grimm must
have heard something – other than what Jaq heard; some
simple order. 'We gotta go, boss. We got to get out.'

'How can a minnow understand a whale?' Jaq cried. 'Or
an ant, an elephant? Have we succeeded, Grimm? Have
we?' Jaq's own voice rose to a scream in that holiest of
chambers, yet somehow it was hardly audible. His words
echoed like a flock of screeching, ultrasonic bats.

'Dunno, boss. We gotta go.'
'Out, out, out,' chanted Meh'Lindi. 'Away-way-way.'
And then...

epilogue

So HAVE YOU finished scanning the *Liber Secretorum*?' asked the black-robed master librarian.

'Yes indeed.'

The man with the hooked chin and piercing green eyes sucked his cheeks in thoughtfully. He too was robed and badged as a Malleus man, his face almost hidden by his hood. The two men were shut inside a dimly lit room that was fashioned like a skull. Save for twin electrocandles illuminating icons of the Emperor in the two niches that corresponded to sockets, only the scanner glowed greenly.

'Where and when was this recorded?'

'Lord, it was delivered under inexplicable circumstances to the then-master of our Ordo more than a century ago. That was soon after Jaq Draco was declared a renegade for his *exterminatus* of Stalinvast, and disappeared. As to where this was recorded... perhaps on Terra?'

'The assassin? The Navigator? The squat? What of them?'

'A Meh'Lindi certainly existed, as the present Director of Callidus Assassins can confirm. But that is all the Director

will acknowledge; and that she vanished from view, presumed dead. The Officio Assassinorum will admit
nothing regarding the experimental surgery. Maybe that
proved to be a fiasco, of which they wish to obliterate all
memory. Or maybe it has an extreme security classifica-
tion. Thus supposedly nothing in their records links her
to Jaq Draco.

'The Navis Nobilitate cannot, or will not, authenticate
the existence of a Navigator by the name of Vitali Googol.
They have too much independence, in my view! Maybe
Googol was the person's poetical sobriquet. Maybe Draco
invented the name, if indeed he did not invent everything,
other than the *exterminatus* which certainly occurred. As
regards the visit to the throne-room of His Terribilitas, no
member of the Custodes reported anything. It is utterly
inconceivable that such an event ever took place.'

'The squat?'

'Grimm is a common name amongst his ill-fated kind,
and this squat was of no importance to the Imperium.'

'What of Captain Holofernest and Inquisitor Zilanov?'

'Why, Inquisitor Zilanov executed that captain for dere-
liction of duty.'

'For drunkenness?'

The librarian nodded. 'There was... trouble on board
that Black Ship. A rebellion among the passengers, some
of whom were possessed. Zilanov died too. Draco could
possibly have known of this before the *Liber* came to our
attention, and therefore before it was composed. If Draco
composed this at all! Why did Draco avoid the first person in his story, unless he was lying? *Did he even compose
it?*'

'Our Ordo denies that any such project exists under our
own aegis?'

'All Hidden Masters at the time denied belonging to such
a cabal. Baal Firenze, who declared Draco a renegade, volunteered for the ministrations of deeptruth, metaveritas.
Nothing relevant was learned. Proctor Firenze became as a
baby thereafter.'

'He was re-educated?'

'Oh yes, Hidden Master. He redeveloped a personality, anew. He was rejuvenated, trained all over again as a dedicated inquisitor.'

'Harq Obispal?'

'Aliens ambushed and killed him shortly after the events which the *Liber* purports to describe.'

'How convenient.'

'His murderers were believed to be eldar.'

'Ah? Indeed? That's known for sure?'

'No, not for sure.'

'Our Ordo has never discovered any trace of this hydra on any world?'

'None. We track down any distorted whisper, yet we gain no hard evidence at all. Naturally, if Draco's account is correct we could hardly expect to find *material* traces...'

'So the *Liber* may actually have been a weapon aimed at Baal Firenze by some unknown enemy – to discredit him, to sabotage his career and his very identity.'

'Aye, or to sow distrust amongst the Hidden Masters of our Ordo, and thus to undermine us all.'

'Or to... or to sow doubts about the Emperor himself, blessed be His name.'

'That too. Truly, all is whelmed in darkness and the Emperor is the only light. Of course, Draco's narrative isn't *only* of negative value. We do now use the stasis coffin as an adjunct to interrogation, where time isn't of the essence...'

A note of doubt crept into the librarian's voice. 'You are newly a Hidden Master, and naturally you must research the secrets of our Ordo now. Would you let me admire your tattoo just once again?'

The green-eyed man said, 'Why, certainly.'

When the visitor to the Librarium Obscurum drew back his sleeve, the librarian only had an instant to note the digital needle gun fitted to the Hidden Master's slim finger... before the librarian's face stung, and toxins convulsed his whole frame.

The librarian's body flopped on the floor, muscles pulling every which way. His bowels had emptied stinkingly. Blood poured from the old man's nose and mouth.

The visitor started to giggle hectically. He needed to bite on his sleeve to silence himself. His teeth ravaged the cloth as if a hound had caught a hare, or in the way that someone who was experiencing inner agony might seek to distract himself from a sensation or spectacle that he found abominable. The librarian was already dead; it was only a corpse that twitched.

The visitor left the first page of the *Liber Secretorum* displayed upon the dimly glowing screen. And beside it he tucked a Tarot card – of an inquisitor whose featureless face was a tiny, psychoactive mirror to whoever would next look at it.

Wrinkling up his jutting nose, he slipped away out of the skull room.

THE INQUISITION WAR had begun.

Though in another sense it had begun years earlier when Jaq Draco first uttered the words, *Believe me. I intend to tell the truth...*

ABOUT THE AUTHOR

Ian Watson received screen credit for the Screen
Story of Steven Spielberg's movie A.I. Artificial
Intelligence, on which Ian worked previously with
Stanley Kubrick. Playboy published
his reminiscences.
Ian started writing science fiction as a way of staying
sane while teaching in Tokyo years ago, after living
in East Africa, and his first SF novel, *The Embedding*,
won the French Prix Apollo in translation. His
books have appeared in 13 languages so far.
In 2001 Ian mutated into a poet when DNA
Publications issued his first book of poetry, *The
Lexicographer's Love Song*; and Golden Gryphon Press
also published his 9th story collection,
The Great Escape. Currently Ian is co-editing
an anthology to help save the Asian Elephant
from extinction.

**Now available
from the Black Library**

STORM OF IRON

**A Warhammer 40,000 novel
by Graham McNeill**

**Here is a preview of
the carnage to come...**

FROM *STORM OF IRON*
By Graham McNeill

NEARLY A THOUSAND men died in the first seconds of the Iron
Warriors' initial bombardment of Jericho Falls spaceport.
The battle barge *Stonebreaker* fired three salvoes of magma
bombs into the desolate rocky slopes surrounding the
spaceport, blasting vast chunks of rock hundreds of metres
into the air and flattening almost all the torpedo silos in the
mountains with unerring accuracy.

Alarm sirens screamed and the spaceport's weapon batteries rumbled into firing positions as their gunners
desperately sought to acquire targets before being annihi-
lated. A few hastily blessed torpedoes roared upwards
through the orange sky on pillars of fiery smoke and powerful beams of laser energy stabbed through the perpetually
cloudless heavens.

More bombs fell, this time within the perimeter of Jericho
Falls, demolishing buildings, gouging great craters and hurl-
ing enormous clouds of umber ash into the atmosphere.
Flames from burning structures lit the smoke from within
and bodies lay aflame in the wreckage of the shattered
spaceport. Smashed aircraft littered the ground and more
exploded as the heat from the fires cooked off their weapons
and fuel tanks.

Bombs slammed into the rockcrete, scything lethal fragments everywhere. Others smashed into the runways,

cratering them and melting the honeycombed adamantium with the heat of a star.

The Marauders and Lightnings out in the open took the worst of the barrage, pulverised by the force of the explosions.

The noise and confusion were unbelievable; the sky was red with flames and black with smoke. Heavy las-fire blasted upwards. A number of shells impacted on the main hangar's roof. Its armoured structure had absorbed the damage so far, though vast cracks now zigzagged across the reinforced walls and roof.

The main runway was engulfed in flames, burning pools of jet fuel spewing thick black smoke that turned day into night.

Hell had come to Hydra Cordatus.

THE FIRST WAVE of drop-pods fired from the *Stonebreaker* landed in clouds of fire and smoke as their boosters slowed them after their screaming journey through the atmosphere. As each pod hit the ground, the release bolt on its base slammed home and the sides unfolded to reveal their interiors.

Each pod in this wave was Deathwind class, equipped with an auto-firing heavy gun platform. As they opened, the weapons began to pour their lethal fire in a spinning, circular arc. Fresh explosions erupted across the ready line as the bolts found their marks in the exposed attack craft and pilots. The volleys from the battle barge in orbit ceased as more streaking lines of fire followed the first wave. Gun turrets mounted on armoured bunkers engaged the weapon pods, methodically targeting them one at a time and destroying them with well-aimed gunfire. But the Deathwinds had done their job, keeping the gunners occupied as the second wave of drop-pods slashed downwards, unmolested, through the atmosphere towards the base.

KROEGER GRIPPED HIS chainsword tight and repeated the Iron Warriors' Litany of Hate for the ninth time since his Dreadclaw drop-pod had fired from the belly of the *Stonebreaker*. The pod shook with the fury of its fiery journey through the atmosphere and, as their passage became smoother, he knew that the curses and offerings to the Powers of Chaos had appeased their monstrous hunger. He grinned beneath his helmet as he watched the bone-rimmed altimeter unravel, counting the seconds to their landing.

They would now be within the lethal range of the spaceport's guns, but if the half-breed, Honsou, had successfully completed his mission, then there should be little or no incoming fire to meet them. His lip curled in contempt as he thought of that mongrel leading one of the Warsmith's grand companies. It was unseemly for a half-breed to attain such responsibility, and Kroeger despised Honsou with every fibre of his being.

He cast his gaze over the armoured warriors who sat around the steel-panelled walls of the drop-pod's interior. Their dented power armour was the colour of dark iron, heavy and baroque, none less than ten thousand years old. Each man's weapon had been anointed with the blood of a score of captives, and the stench of death filled the pod's interior. The men strained at the harnesses that held them in place, eyes fixed on the iris hatch on the pod's floor, every thought slaved to the slaughter of their foes.

Kroeger had picked these killers personally; they were the most blood-soaked berserkers of his grand company of the Iron Warriors, those who had trodden the path of Khorne for longer than most.

The Blood God's hunger for death and skulls had become the driving imperative for these warriors, and it was doubtful that they would ever break from the cycle of murder and killing that had swallowed them. Kroeger himself had revelled many times in the fierce joy of slaughter that so pleased Khorne, but had not yet fully surrendered to the frenzy of the Blood God.

Once a warrior lost himself in that red mist, he was unlikely to survive and Kroeger had agendas yet to follow, paths yet to tread. For Khorne was no sanguineous epicure. He cared not from whence the blood came and as the worshippers of the Blood God often discovered, their own vital fluid was as welcome as that of the enemy's.

The drop-pod's retros fired, filling the cramped vessel with a howling shriek like a banshee's wail. Kroeger took the hateful screaming as a good omen.

He raised his sword in the salute of the warrior and roared, 'Let blood be your watchword, death your companion and hate your strength.'

Barely a handful of the warriors acknowledged him, most too immersed in thoughts of the blood they would shed to even register that he had spoken. It was immaterial; the hated Imperial followers of the corpse-god would die screaming as he ripped their souls from their torn flesh. His blood sang at the prospect of killing yet more of their ancient foes and he prayed to the Majesty of the Warp that the honour of the first kill would be his.

He felt the bone-jarring impact of the Dreadclaw drop-pod through the thick ceramite plates of his power armour as it slammed into the ground. Scarcely had the bottom hatch irised open than he dropped through it, bending his knees and rolling aside as the next warrior followed him down.

Thick, grey smoke from the retros obscured his vision, and the flames burning across the spaceport rendered the heat augurs in his helmet useless.

He drew his pistol, offering his thanks to the power of Chaos for giving him such a chance to bring death to his enemies.

ADEPT CYCERIN WAS close to panic. He had had no response to his pleas for aid from the citadel, though they must surely be aware of their plight. The thought that there were enemies with the power to circumvent their surveyors and approach their fastness, unseen and unknown, had all but unmanned him. He cursed the weak, organic part of him that felt such bowel-loosening terror and wished again for the emotional detachment of his superiors.

The data-slate on the wall indicated a breach in the outer wall and garbled contact reports howling across the vox circuits told of giants in armour of burnished iron slaughtering all those who stood before them. He could not co-ordinate a defence without better reports and the chaos of battle was...

Chaos.

The very word sent a hot jolt of fear down Cycerin's spine and suddenly he knew how their enemies had managed to elude their auguries. Accursed, warp-spawned sorcery must have confounded the spirits of the machines and rendered them blind to the monstrous evil that approached Hydra Cordatus. As soon as this first thought had struck, a second followed.

There could only be one reason the followers of the Ruinous Powers would come to this place and the thought made him shake with fear. Confused icons flashed on the holomap of the base, representing friendly forces deploying from barracks and attempting to engage the invaders. Cycerin could see that it would not be enough; there had simply been too much devastation in the opening moments of the attack.

But he consoled himself that he and his staff were safe enough in the Hope. Protected high within its armoured structure, there was no way an enemy could penetrate its security. No way at all.

HONSOU HACKED HIS sword through a weeping soldier's torso, separating his upper and lower halves with a single blow. Their attack through the breach in the wall had caught the mustering Imperial soldiers completely by surprise. Most were already dead, crushed by masonry blasted from the wall by his heavy weapon teams.

An enemy officer attempted to rally his men from the hatch of his command Chimera, screaming at them to stand firm. Honsou shot him in the face and vaulted a rebar-laced chunk of rockcrete, swinging his mighty sword amongst the horrified soldiers.

Gunfire raked the ground beside him, explosions of ash kicked up in red spurts by the Chimera's hull-mounted heavy bolter. Honsou rolled aside as the turret began traversing in his direction.

'Take that vehicle out!' he yelled.

Positioned on the walls, two iron giants carrying long barrelled cannons on their shoulders swung their heavy weapons to bear. Twin streaks of incandescent energy blasted into the vehicle. Seconds later, it vanished in an orange fireball, raining yet more debris down upon the battlefield. Honsou picked himself up as another Chimera attempted to back away from the breach, firing its weapons as it retreated. His gunners on the wall methodically swept their weapons around and destroyed it with contemptuous ease.

The base was in flames, but Honsou's practiced eye could see that the vital runways and landing platforms had escaped most of the violence of the bombardment. As his men gathered at the foot of the wall, he aligned himself with the map projected on the inside face of his visor. Through the smoke and billowing flames, he could see the faint outline of a tall tower with a flattened circular top. This must be the control tower and it was his next target. Wreckage and bodies littered the battlefield: drop-pods, aircraft and burning vehicles, their crews either dead or battling for their lives.

The sky was streaked with lines of fire as more Iron Warriors descended to the planet. His fellow company commanders, Kroeger and Forrix, would even now be bringing death to this world. He could not be seen to be doing less in the eyes of the Warsmith.

'We have them now, brothers, and there is death yet to be done. Follow me and I will give you victory!'

Honsou raised his sword and set off at a sprint towards the control tower, knowing that its capture would earn him great reward. He wove a zigzag course towards the tower, pools of burning fuel and wrecked machines forcing him into frustrating detours. After three months of creeping through the mountains, it was a cathartic release of his fury to be amidst such brutality. The air was thick with death, and though he was no sorcerer, even he could feel the actinic tang of slaughter that they had brought to Hydra Cordatus.

Here and there, they met pockets of resistance, but the sight of his thirty blood-soaked warriors charging towards them broke the courage of all but the most stalwart.

Honsou's blade was dripping with gore as he and his men finally reached the tower.

Grudgingly he was forced to admit that its construction and defences were formidable. Soldiers in prepared positions surrounded it in well-constructed, angled redoubts, laying down a hail of bright las-bolts. Behind four linked and high-walled berms, Honsou could see the aerials of tanks, but what pattern they were he could not yet tell. Armoured bunkers at each of the compass points sprayed the area in front of the tower with deadly bullets, turning the open ground into a killing zone.

Honsou and his men moved into concealed positions behind the twisted wreckage of a Marauder bomber, as the thunderous crack of a tank's main gun activated the dampers on his armour's auto-senses. Clouds of dust and rubble rained down and Honsou could hear the cries of those wounded by the blast. They had to move fast or the citadel's defenders would be able to counterattack before the Iron Warriors were able to consolidate their position here.

He peered through a ragged hole torn in the side of the aircraft, wrenching the pilot's bloody corpse out of the way and pondered the situation. The corner bunkers were the key: take them and they could roll up the Imperial line with ease. The gunfire sawing from the bunkers was murderous; anyone who attempted to charge through it would pay the price for such stupidity. He grinned wryly as he saw several of Kroeger's men, berserkers by the look of them, lying torn open, their blood leeching into the dusty ground. He wondered if perhaps Kroeger himself might be numbered amongst the dead, but knew that, despite his recklessness, Kroeger was no fool and would not risk his own neck if he did not have to.

Even as he formed the thought, he caught sight of his nemesis some two hundred metres away, firing his pistol ineffectually at the Imperial defenders. Kroeger's attack on the tower had failed and Honsou knew that this was his chance.

He crawled along to his heavy weapon gunners and hammered his fist on the shoulder guards of the warriors with the lascannons, slung across their shoulders as easily as a human soldier might carry a walking cane.

The gunners turned, acknowledging their leader with curt nods.

Another rain of debris fell around them as a tank shell exploded nearby. Honsou pointed towards the tower, shouting, 'When I give the order, aim for the salient angle of the near bunker, and keep firing until you break it open.'

The gunners nodded and Honsou moved further down the line. He knew he was condemning those men to death, but didn't care. Another of his heavy gunners carried a hissing weapon with a wide, flaring barrel etched with elaborate traceries of flame. The gunner's armour was dented and scorched in places, but the weapon was pristine, as though freshly pressed from a weapon forge.

'When the lascannons blow open the bunker, I want you to put enough melta fire into that bunker to make the rock run like liquid.'

Without waiting for a response, Honsou rolled over towards the lascannons and jabbed his fist towards the bunker, voxing the order to stand to throughout his squads. He scrambled to the edge of the wrecked Marauder, watching as the two warriors carrying the lascannons moved into firing positions and aimed their weapons. Bolt after bolt of powerful las-blasts slammed into the protruding salient angle of the bunker, blasting away huge chunks of armaplas and rockcrete. Realising the danger, Imperial gunners switched their fire to the two heavy gunners, tearing up the ground in a storm of las-blasts and bolter fire.

The two Iron Warriors paid no attention to the incoming fire, sending shot after shot of unimaginably powerful energy into their target. Honsou watched as the angled corner of the bunker cracked wide open, the rockcrete burning orange in the heat. For a moment it appeared that the gunners might survive the hail of shots directed at them.

But the thunder of Imperial battle cannons settled the matter, obliterating both gunners in an explosive storm of ordnance. Before the echoes had died, the Iron Warrior with the multi-melta rose from his concealment and

charged forwards to fire. The gun's discharge built to a deafening screech before erupting from the barrels in a searing
hiss. The warrior's aim was true and the air within the
bunker ignited with atomic fury, spurts of vaporised flesh
and superheated oxygen blasting from the weapon slits.

A huge hole had been blown in the tower's line of defence.
Honsou rose up from his cover and screamed, 'Death to the
False Emperor!'

He leapt over the Marauder's fuselage and sprinted
towards the molten hell of the wrecked bunker, its walls
now flowing like wax across the ground. His men followed
him unquestioningly. To his left, he could see Kroeger gath-
ering his men for the charge, obviously realising that
Honsou would beat him to the tower.

Honsou leapt onto the remains of the bunker, his iron-
shod boot sinking into the molten rock. The heat scorched
his leg armour, but it held firm as he pushed off and
dropped into the heart of the defence.

He caught a glimpse of the carnage his men had inflicted
and rejoiced to see that his labours had borne such bloody
fruit. Scorched and blackened limbs lay strewn about, all
that remained of those stationed too close to the bunker;
the backwash of the melta impact had burnt flesh and bone
to cinders in an instant. An open mouthed head lay
perched bizarrely atop a pile of rubble as if placed there by
some macabre prankster. Honsou punched it aside as he
passed.

Imperial soldiers were frantically reorganising their battle
line as the Iron Warriors poured in through the gap in their
defences. Honsou could see a tank – a Leman Russ
Demolisher – reversing from its revetment and bringing its
ponderous turret to bear on the attackers. Honsou dropped
as the sponson-mounted weapons sprayed shells overhead,
the ricochets tearing up the blasted rubble around him.
Another white-hot blast of melta fire flashed and the
Demolisher's turret was engulfed in the inferno of the
impact. Steam and smoke obscured the tank for brief seconds, but, unbelievably, it continued onwards through the
boiling cloud.

Time slowed as Honsou watched the barrel of its main gun depress and knew that any second it would blast him to atoms. Then, with a terrific explosion, the turret lifted clean off, the tank detonating spectacularly from within as the shell exploded inside the main gun. Deadly shrapnel whickered through the Imperial ranks, scything men down by the dozen and ripping them to bloody rags. Honsou roared in release as he realised the heat of the melta blast must have warped the barrel enough to cause the weapon to misfire and the shell to detonate prematurely.

He rose to one knee and opened up with his bolt pistol, raking his fire over those fortunate enough to survive the destruction of the Demolisher, killing everything he saw in his battle rage.

Kroeger's blood-maddened berserkers clambered across the shattered walls of the redoubt, ignoring wounds that would have felled a normal human a dozen times over. Not for them the elegance of precisely orchestrated attacks using sound principles of military engineering. Bodies were hurled aside, ripped apart with their bare hands when there was no weapon to wield.

Honsou spotted Kroeger amongst his men, wading through a press of bodies, hacking left and right with his chainsword. He raised his own sword in acknowledgement towards his fellow commander, but Kroeger ignored him, as Honsou knew he would. He smiled beneath his helm and sprinted through the blazing wreck of the Demolisher towards the tower.

Read the conclusion of this epic story of war and betrayal in

STORM OF IRON

Now available from the Black Library

More Warhammer 40,000 from the Black Library

THE GAUNT'S GHOSTS SERIES
by Dan Abnett

IN THE NIGHTMARE future of Warhammer 40,000, mankind is beset by relentless foes. Commissar Ibram Gaunt and his regiment the Tanith First-and-Only must fight as much against the inhuman enemies of mankind as survive the bitter internal rivalries of the Imperial Guard.

FIRST & ONLY

GAUNT AND HIS men find themselves at the forefront of a fight to win back control of a vital Imperial forge world.

GHOSTMAKER

NICKNAMED THE GHOSTS, Commissar Gaunt's regiment of stealth troops move from world from world, playing a vital part in the crusade to liberate the Sabbat Worlds from Chaos.

NECROPOLIS

ON THE SHATTERED world of Verghast, Gaunt and his Ghosts find themselves embroiled within a deadly civil war as a mighty hive-city is besieged by an unrelenting foe.

HONOUR GUARD

GAUNT AND HIS men are sent on a desperate race against time to safeguard some of the Imperium's most holy relics.

THE GUNS OF TANITH

THE GHOSTS MUST recapture Phantine, a world rich in promethium but so ruined by pollution that the only way to attack is via a dangerous – and untried – aerial assault.

More Warhammer 40,000 from the Black Library

THE EISENHORN TRILOGY
by Dan Abnett

IN THE 41ST MILLENNIUM, *the Inquisition hunts the shadows for humanity's most terrible foes – rogue psykers, xenos and daemons. Few Inquisitors can match the notoriety of Gregor Eisenhorn, whose struggle against the forces of evil stretches across the centuries.*

XENOS

THE ELIMINATION OF the dangerous recidivist Murdon Eyclone is just the beginning of a new case for Gregor Eisenhorn. A trail of clues leads the Inquisitor and his retinue to the very edge of human-controlled space in the hunt for a lethal alien artefact – the dread Necroteuch.

MALLEUS

A GREAT IMPERIAL triumph to celebrate the success of the Ophidian Campaign ends in disaster when thirty-three rogue psykers escape and wreak havoc. Eisenhorn's hunt for the sinister power behind this atrocity becomes a desperate race against time as he himself is declared hereticus by the Ordo Malleus.

HERETICUS

WHEN A BATTLE with an ancient foe turns deadly, Inquisitor Eisenhorn is forced to take terrible measures to save the lives of himself and his companions. But how much can any man deal with Chaos before turning into the very thing he is sworn to destroy?

More Warhammer 40,000 from the Black Library

THE SPACE WOLF NOVELS
by William King

From the death-world of Fenris come the Space Wolves, the most savage of the Emperor's Space Marines. Follow the adventures of Ragnar, from his recruitment and training as he matures into a ferocious and deadly fighter, scourge of the enemies of humanity.

SPACE WOLF

On the planet Fenris, young Ragnar is chosen to be inducted into the noble yet savage Space Wolves chapter. But with his ancient primal instincts unleashed by the implanting of the sacred canis helix, Ragnar must learn to control the beast within and fight for the greater good of the wolf pack.

RAGNAR'S CLAW

As young Blood Claws, Ragnar and his companions go on their first off-world mission – from the jungle hell of Galt to the pulluted hive-cities of hive world Venam, they must travel across the galaxy to face the very heart of evil.

GREY HUNTER

When one of their Chapter's most holy artefacts is siezed by the forces of Chaos, Space Wolf Ragnar and his comrades are plunged into a desperate battle to retrieve it before a most terrible and ancient foe is set free.

More Warhammer 40,000 from the Black Library

THE LAST CHANCERS
by Gavin Thorpe

ACROSS A HUNDRED blasted war-zones upon a dozen bloody worlds, the convict soldiers of the 13th Penal Legion fight a desperate battle for redemption in the eyes of the immortal Emperor. In this nightmare eternity of war, Lieutenant Kage and the Last Chancers must fight not just to win the next battle, but for their very survival!

13th LEGION

THE 13TH PENAL Legion, led by the redoubtable Colonel Schaeffer, are plunged into battle after battle, each more dangerous than the last. Is it fate or design that leads the survivors to their final mission, to infiltrate the impregnable rebel stronghold Coritanorum?

KILL TEAM

COLONEL SCHAEFFER HAS a new mission for Kage – assemble and train a team to assassinate an alien commander whose militaristic actions are threatening the fragile alliance between the Imperium and the Tau Empire. But who will prove Kage's most dangerous enemy – the Tau, or the very men under his command?